R...
OF T...

Paula Marshall

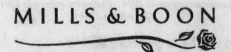

MILLS & BOON

MILLS & BOON LIMITED
ETON HOUSE, 18–24 PARADISE ROAD
RICHMOND, SURREY, TW9 1SR

MILLS & BOON, the Rose Device and LEGACY OF LOVE are trademarks of the publisher.

*First published in Great Britain 1994
by Mills & Boon Limited*

© Paula Marshall 1994

*Australian copyright 1994   Philippine copyright 1994
This edition 1994*

ISBN 0 263 78728 1

*Set in 10 on 12 pt Linotron Times
04-9409-84968*

*Typeset in Great Britain by Centracet, Cambridge
Printed in Great Britain by
BPC Paperbacks Ltd*

CHAPTER ONE

'The heart has its reasons which reason does not know of.'

Pascal

'NO ONE, I repeat, no one,' declaimed Louisa, Lady Bampton tragically, 'could possibly believe that even my late brother-in-law could be quite so abominably careless! Oh, I know,' she continued, making great play with a fine lace handkerchief, 'that he was eccentric. How else can you describe a man who was a bishop as well as an earl, and didn't believe in God. . .?'

Her eyes rolled at this point, and the handkerchief was used to hide her stricken face. 'Who spent his time in Italy digging up pieces of a town buried for nearly two thousand years, married a girl — my poor young sister, who was less than half his age — fathered a daughter whom he made his secretary when she was fourteen. . .'

She stopped, overcome, then repeated mournfully, 'His secretary, and then is inconsiderate enough to die when she is only eighteen, having appointed as her guardian Lyndale — James Lyndale, of all people.'

'Be fair,' said her brother, Gervase Markham. 'There's no doubt that Silchester meant to leave her to the care of Lyndale's father, his old friend, who was steady enough, God knows. Doubtless he was so engaged in his excavations at Herculaneum that he

5

never knew that his friend had died and that his son had inherited. Doubtless he was unaware that Lyndale is as eccentric as himself, a loose screw turned recluse.'

'Then how can Lyndale take over her care,' Lady Bampton was plaintive, 'if he is the wrong man? I am sure that he will not wish to. The idea is nonsensical.'

Gervase Markham was patient. He explained again to his sister how the accident had happened. 'The will specifies James Chavasse, Earl of Lyndale — it does not specify which Earl. As Silchester's executor, I asked the lawyers if there was anything to be done to prevent Lyndale from taking over the wardship, but there is nothing, they say. The will stands. Lyndale is most assuredly James Chavasse. Our niece is his ward, I fear.'

'One more example of our brother-in-law's folly, then,' mourned Lady Bampton. 'Oh, what a tohu bohu! And the child has left Italy for England, you say? Pray when is she expected?'

Gervase gave a nervous cough. 'She is not expected, Louisa. She is already here. She was delivered into my care late yesterday evening. I am come to ask you to take charge of her, and her woman, until we send her to Haven's End.'

'Haven's End,' sighed Lady Bampton, distracted. 'What an inappropriate name for Lyndale's home! Poor motherless little thing. There can be no haven for her there. What have you done with her, Gervase? Why did you not bring her in immediately?'

'She is in the morning-room with her woman, being served chocolate by Brunton,' replied Gervase. 'I had meant to speak to you before she arrived in England. I did not expect her for another week, but the winds were favourable. I wish you to say nothing to her about this mix-up. It would be wrong for us to pre-judge the manner in which Lyndale may treat her. We must go carefully, Louisa. Nor must we express disapproval of her father, however distressed we may be by his carelessness. I gather that they were very close.'

'Being given chocolate by the butler,' said Lady Bampton fretfully. She had a habit of seizing on the unimportant and the inessential. 'And close to her father! How could she be? He was over seventy, after all. Poor child! Poor child! To think that she had to turn for comfort to him. She needs a woman's love. After all, she never knew her mother. She will be lost, quite lost, finding herself among strangers.'

Gervase Markham's expression was a curious one. 'Well, yes,' he said a little awkwardly. 'So one might expect.' He coughed. 'Perhaps I ought to warn you. . .'

'Warn me!' Lady Bampton's eyebrows rose. 'Of what, Gervase? She is presentable, I suppose?'

'Presentable, yes.' Gervase stopped. 'I think I ought to bring her in to meet you.'

'By all means. I am only sorry the poor little thing will have to be sent on to Lyndale—he has accepted the wardship, I suppose?'

'Yes.' Gervase turned at the door. 'You may imagine how my heart sinks when I think to what we are consigning her. His answer was as follows. "If I must, I must." That was all.'

Lady Bampton's outrage was such that she was engaged by it until Gervase's return. She did not know with whom she was the more annoyed, her dead brother-in-law or James Lyndale, and since both of them were beyond her reach she could only sit and fume until the door opened and Gervase arrived, escorting two women.

'My dear,' he said gently, for Gervase was always gentle. 'Allow me to introduce you to your aunt, Louisa, Lady Bampton, your late mother's older sister. Louisa, this is our niece, Lady Cressida Mortimer and her companion, Miss Sykes, who was engaged to escort her from Italy.'

Lady Bampton stared at both of them. The companion was unexceptional, a tall wisp of a woman in her mid-forties, discreetly dressed. But her niece was something else. 'Cressida?' she achieved. Somehow she could think of nothing else to say, Cressida was so unlike any young lady of quality whom she had previously known.

Cressida shook her head vigorously. Everything about her was vigorous. She was just under the middle height for a woman, with an ivory complexion and thick dark chestnut hair with deep waves in it. It was loosely screwed on to the top of her head in an unfashionable Greek knot. Her eyes were grey, her profile was as pure as that of a piece of classical statuary and her mouth was warm and generous. If she was not plain, neither was she beautiful. The word 'pretty' was hardly applicable.

Her clothes were deplorable: a rather battered paletot coat in dark blue, beneath which she wore an old-fashioned high-waisted wool dress of the same colour. 'Shabby' was the only word Lady Louisa could think of. Her stare turned into a glare.

But worst of all was Cressida's manner. 'Oh, no, Aunt Bampton,' she said, advancing on her, hand outstretched to shake Lady Bampton's, as though she were a frank boy and not a lady of quality, her pretty voice pleasantly firm. 'Not Cressida. Cressy it is, must and shall be! Robert would have me called by no other name. Poor Mama chose it before she died, but he never liked formality. Oh, no, I could not bear to be Cressida.'

'Robert?' Lady Bampton's voice gew faint before this hoyden, who was staring about her in the most unashamed fashion, taking in everything in Louisa's dainty salon, from the pretty water-colours on the wall to the pale blue wallpaper, and the elegant curtains draped before the long windows. It was likely that she had never seen such a civilised room before. To her horror, Lady Bampton found herself shaking hands — she pulled the offending member away as quickly as she could, and said shakily, 'Pray who is Robert?'

Cressy gave her aunt the sweetest smile; it quite transformed her face. It was patent, she thought, that Lady Bampton was not quite all there, or was having a bad day. Only time would tell.

'My father,' she replied patiently, turning to Gervase as she spoke. 'I know it may sound odd, Uncle Gervase, but Robert — Father, I suppose I ought to call him, but no, that would be strange — Robert wanted no formality between us. He said that we were all children of the Eternal Spirit and equal in His eyes.'

Gervase could not quite suppress a grin at Lady Bampton's expression on hearing this.

'I thought your father didn't believe in God — or so he informed me before he took your mother off to Italy.' Lady Bampton's voice was fainter than ever.

'Oh, yes, my father was not a believer in God — and nor am I for that matter — but he does. . .did. . .believe in the Eternal Spirit which rules the Universe, which has no form or shape — the term "eyes", you see, was purely a figurative one; it does not mean that the Spirit has real eyes,' she explained kindly.

'Oh, indeed.' Lady Bampton's voice was almost extinguished, and Gervase could not look at her lest he laugh. Whatever else, it was plain that Lady Cressida Mortimer, despite her youth, was no poor child to be patronised.

Cressy, who had not yet registered that Louisa had considered her a hapless orphan to be cosseted, now turned briskly to Mr Markham and said to him in judicious and commanding tones, for it was plain that she was used to being obeyed and listened to, 'By the by, Uncle Gervase, I suppose it is not too early for me to do something about this wretched wardship? I finally gouged from the lawyers — they seemed to consider me a pea-brained child who could not understand plain English — that Robert made this will when I was eighteen *months* old. Knowing him, I cannot believe that he thought that at eighteen *years* I needed a guardian, or indeed, any kind of parent or adviser at all. I have been managing his affairs for him for the past three years. Besides, I wish to return to Italy to carry on his work — as soon as that can be arranged.'

'Italy! Carry on his work! I can hardly believe this.' The lace handkerchief came into play in earnest. Lady Bampton had seldom spent such a distressful morning.

'Herculaneum, to be precise.' Really what a fuss about nothing, was Cressy's judgment on Lady Bampton's and Mr Markham's response to her quite reasonable wish. 'Robert and I had just uncovered a most interesting small site. A temple, we thought. Some of the figurines we rescued were quite fine. I really should not have left, but Mr Hargrove, your man of business, and Miss Sykes, were most insistent that I was required in England to sort out the legal nonsense. All the more reason I should return as soon as possible. I am sure that Lord Lyndale does not want me, and I am equally sure that I don't want *him*. He is an elderly man, I collect?'

Both her hearers assumed this to mean that she was referring to James Lyndale's thirty-seven years, elderly-seeming to a girl of eighteen. They were unaware that no one had seen fit to tell Lady Cressy of her father's error.

'My dear child,' said Gervase Markham gently. 'I am sure that Mr Hargrove and Miss Sykes explained to you that it was not proper for you to live in Italy, on your own, once your father had died.'

Cressy closed her eyes. Were there no reasonable souls living in England? 'I was not on my own,' she said, a little annoyed. 'There was the Countess Caterina Franceschini, Robert's mistress, to look after me, and her family, which is even older and nobler than ours. It goes back to the days of ancient Rome, as I am sure you are aware. There were all our servants, and the British Minister at Naples, a great friend of mine. The war has been over for three years; 1818 is much safer than 1815, I think you will agree, although Robert and I had no difficulties in living in Naples even during the French occupation. General Murat was quite our friend. He was *so* interested in Robert's work.'

'I do not believe this,' repeated Lady Bampton. 'To be a friend of the French usurper, to be looked after by your father's mistress — you should not know such persons! Pray sit down, child. Take off that dreadful coat you are wearing, and allow Gervase to send for some Madeira. I know that I could do with some, and it might settle you. After that, I must explain to you what a young lady of your age may or may not do in Society. I need hardly say that jaunting off to Italy to live alone among foreigners is something which is definitely not done. And then we must buy you some respectable clothing before you go to Wiltshire.'

'Oh, really, Aunt,' said Cressy, looking quite puzzled as she inspected her clothes. What could be wrong with them? They might be plain, but they were most serviceable. 'I'm sure I don't wish to go to the trouble and expense of buying new clothes when those I have are perfectly adequate for any reasonable activities I might follow. I suppose it is too much to expect that there are any good sites to excavate near Lord Lyndale's home? I suppose that he will inform me if there are when I reach there.'

Gervase thought that his sister-in-law was about to burst. 'Trouble and cost?' she exclaimed faintly. 'I'm sure that you must be aware of the magnitude of the fortune which your father has left you. You are the last of the Mortimers and it is quite improper for you to be going about dressed like a superior servant. Miss Sykes!' she said, her voice suddenly strengthening. 'Pray inform your charge that as an Earl's daughter, and the owner of one of the largest estates in the whole of Great Britain, she has a duty to dress in a fit manner.'

Miss Sykes bowed her head, and replied in a submissive voice, 'So I have tried to inform her, Lady Bampton, but I fear that in the company in which she has been living, such matters are seen in a different light. I think Lady Cressy will begin to realise that. . . changes must be made, when she enters Society.'

'She will not be entering Society yet,' said Louisa exasperatedly. 'She will be going to Lyndale's place at the other end of nowhere, and if I know Lyndale will doubtless stay there.'

Cressy listened to this with an expression of acute interest on her face. 'Well, if so,' she announced, more briskly than ever, 'in that case, we may as well save ourselves the pother of buying new clothes. They certainly won't be needed at the other end of nowhere!'

Gervase Markham thought it might be kinder to intervene before his sister actually broke into hysterics.

'My dear Cressy,' he said in his kind voice. 'I really think that you ought to pay heed to your aunt. You will be going to a nobleman's mansion, and you must be fit to take part in his social life. Even in the country you will be expected to set a certain standard, particularly as, as your aunt rightly says, you are an exceedingly wealthy young lady, the heiress to a great estate.'

'Robert,' announced Cressy, firmly and truthfully, 'never allowed such considerations to prevent him from doing what he pleased. Now that I have inherited, I expect to continue in the same manner as he did.'

'Oh, oh, oh,' Lady Bampton began to wail into her handkerchief and to rock herself gently. Normally quite self-willed even if a little flighty, such an encounter as this was proving to be too much for her. She could only be grateful that Cressy had not been left in *her* care.

'Miss Sykes,' she finally said, 'I understand from my brother that at least until you reach Haven's End you will be acting as Lady Cressida's duenna. It is your bounden duty to instruct her in the manner in which a young lady of good family is expected to behave. She has obviously been brought up by her father to conduct herself as a wild young man might. This will not do! Cressida, listen to me — no, do not turn away. It is my duty to ensure that you conduct yourself as you ought, and Miss Sykes's duty to carry out my wishes in the matter. It is your duty to do as your elders and betters instruct you.'

Cressy's immediate and frank response to her aunt's distress was to run to her and throw her arms about her. 'Oh, pray, dearest Aunt, do not distress yourself. There is really no need for you to worry about me at all. Think how much simpler it would be for all concerned if I went straight back to Herculaneum and carried on Robert's work. I know that it is what he would have wanted me to do. He was most particular about that just before he died.'

Her uncle thought that it was time that he intervened again. 'My dear,' he said. 'You are no longer under your father's care. Lady Bampton spoke of duty. It is mine, and hers, to see that you are delivered safely to your legal guardian. It is he who will decide your future life until you marry. I am afraid that returning to Italy is quite out of the question. Perhaps, when you are older, and if your future husband is agreeable, you may visit Herculaneum again.'

Cressy's expression was mutinous, but she knew when she was cornered. Nothing had gone right since Robert had died. And while Miss Sykes was kind, like Lady Bampton she wished her to do all kinds of things which were not in the least agreeable to Cressy. But for the moment she must bow to the inevitable, and then begin to think up ways and means of going back to the place where she had been so happy.

'Very well, then,' she replied submissively, crossing her fingers as she spoke. Then, unknowingly echoing what James Lyndale had written to her lawyers, said to herself, 'If I must, I must.'

After that she allowed herself to be led away by Miss Sykes, to be prepared for visits to milliners, dressmakers, bootmakers and suppliers of hosiery, so that she might not look too outré when she was finally delivered to her elderly guardian.

'No,' said James Chavasse, fourth Earl of Lyndale, to his sister, Verena Davenport, who was paying him a courtesy visit. She and her husband Fred lived at nearby Comyns in Wiltshire, and Fred had cried off. He was recovering from an early attack of the gout, and preferred to sit happily in his comfortable drawing-room rather than drive over to Haven's End.

'No, Verena, I do not welcome being the guardian of a flighty girl, left to me by a careless old fool who mistook me for my father. What should I be doing with an eighteen year-old miss?' And then, as his sister began to laugh, exclaimed, 'No, do not answer me. I know that I left myself open to your raillery, but at least do me the favour of admitting that my taste was never for virgin innocents. What happened to me in my extreme youth ended that for me forever.'

'No, indeed,' agreed Verena, with a knowing grin, her head on one side, admiring the figure her brother presented. 'I must acquit you of *that*. Birds of Paradise, experienced barques of frailty, but never bread-and-butter misses. You were always a high-flyer, James.'

And then, mischievously, '*Were*, James? Is were still correct? Do you still affect the monk?'

'Good God, Verena,' he returned. 'We should not be discussing such things.' He walked restlessly to the window and looked out at the early spring landscape, the first leaves just showing a tender green. 'I suppose the best thing I can do is marry her off. That way she will be someone else's responsibility, not mine.'

'You are still determined to be a hermit?' his sister asked, her face suddenly serious.

James became quite still. Verena remembered him doing the same thing in their childhood when he felt challenged. What a handsome creature he was! Tall, with good shoulders and a splendid physique, but perhaps the most remarkable thing about him were his amber eyes and the thin hawk-like face beneath his springing black hair which fell naturally into the deep waves other men's valets created for them. There was such an air of hauteur about him, of knowing his own mind, that most people were wary of him.

James could feel his sister's gaze hard on him, and the most furious resentment ran through him. He was his own man, no one else's, and however much he loved Verena he would not allow her to dictate to him.

At last — 'And if I am?' — and his voice was dangerous. His back was now turned completely to her, and Verena spoke to it.

'I thought, James, that you might be returning to Society, might be taking your rightful place.'

'Oh, and what rightful place is that?' He knew that his voice was harsh and cutting, and could almost feel Verena wince at his sudden rejection of her.

'James, all the world knows what a good soldier you were until you were invalided out during the Peninsular campaign, and then you became a promising politician, one of George Canning's young men. There's no reason why you shouldn't take up that career again, and every reason why you should. I understand why you threw everything up when you did, but reflect, it has been nearly five years now. Oh, I know how humiliated you felt. Few men are left at the altar, it is a fate usually reserved for women, but most people have forgotten the old scandal, and I don't think that many felt other than pity for you at the time.'

'Pity!' His voice was scalding. 'It was pity I ran from. And then, less than six months later, William died, and Father almost immediately after, and I inherited; I was no longer a poverty-stricken younger son. I saw her, at Bath, soon after, accidentally, and do you know what she said. . .?'

He paused, looking out of the window, and his sister, seeing that he was not about to resume, asked quietly, 'Yes, what did she say?'

'What a fool she had been. That if she had only had the foresight to accept me instead of running off with Gaunt, she would have been Lady Lyndale. Old Gaunt proved a harsh master, it seems. She offered me her fair body, adding in the same breath, what a pity it was that William had not died six months earlier.'

'You refused her, I suppose. I know how much you loved her.'

'What an inquisition, Verena. Must you know every full stop, every comma of my folly? No, I didn't. . .and that was the worst thing of all. When I saw her again and talked to her, I couldn't believe that I had loved such an empty-headed fool. Taking her to bed simply confirmed that judgement. . .'

He stopped, then began again, wearily. 'We shouldn't be talking of this. What finished me was the knowledge that I had loved such a creature so desperately. It called into question everything that I thought I had known of myself, and all of that on top of what had happened to me when I was a boy. I vowed after I lost Margaret so tragically that I would never think seriously of a woman again. And now, this——' and he swept a hand around the room and finished by pointing to the beautiful view from the window ' — is enough for me. To be a good landlord, to do my duty by my tenants, not exploit them, and make Haven's End a fairer, more prosperous place than I found it is all I wish for. My father had neglected it sadly in his last years. Does that answer you?'

Verena rose. 'Yes, James. I am answered. I have not forgotten what your father did to you all those years ago, and I'm sorry that as a consequence you should cut yourself off from possible happiness. I'm also sorry that you're saddled wih this child. You will be kind to her, I hope. She will be alone in a strange land. I understand from Gervase that she was her father's constant companion.'

James laughed harshly. 'And what a father! My own father always shook his head when he spoke of him. First an absentee bishop, and then an absentee land-owner, playing among the ruins of the old Roman Empire. One wonders what the poor child will be like. Well, I am about to find out.'

Verena paused at the door. 'You talked of marrying her off. Had you anyone in mind?'

'Indeed. I thought of our nephew, Emily's son, Frank

Belsize. He will be rich enough to want her for more than her money. He is a good lad, kind and conscientious. A little green, perhaps, but then, Emily is green and his late father was greener, and that will suit an innocent child. He will make a good master for the Silchester lands. I trust you will help me, Verena.'

She walked back to him and kissed him on the cheek. 'Oh, James, I will always help you, you know that. But you could help yourself the most, you know, by coming out of the dismals and being the James you used to be. Perhaps your new ward will bring a breath of young life with her, and bless you with it.'

James's expression was sceptical in the extreme. 'Good God, Verena, that is the last thing I expect from her. A formless child of eighteen, scarce finished with playing with her dolls. No, I shall be compelled to listen to mindless chatter about clothes and hairstyles and be expected to know of the exploits of the latest Minerva Press heroine. Is that what you mean by a breath of young life?'

'Oh, you are incorrigible,' replied his sister severely. 'I expect that you will want me to help you with her, introduce her to the county and to London Society? Rest assured I will do all that I can.'

'Everything but take her off my hands, which you cannot do,' sighed her brother. 'You are a good girl, Verena, you always were, and I do not deserve you.'

'No,' she said, shaking her head. 'You deserve better than me, James, but you are not like to find anyone, sitting here in Wiltshire like St Simeon Stylites up a pole, telling yourself how miserable you are!'

James had to laugh at that. 'St Simeon, indeed! Well, it is to be hoped that Frank takes to her and she to him — and that will be two problems solved. Emily wants him to marry a suitable girl, and soon. Too many of his friends have made unwise marriages or attachments, and he is at an impressionable age.'

'Men are always at an impressionable age,' retorted Verena. 'You should know that. Bring her over soon, James. I am dying to see what kind of offspring old Silchester was responsible for, especially one fathered when he was nearly sixty!'

James watched her barouche bowl down the drive towards the great gates which opened on to the road to Salisbury, and thought, not for he first time, that had he met a woman like Verena he would have tied her to him with hoops of steel; but he had not, and now feared that it was too late to hope to find one.

And, in the meantime, he must prepare to greet Lady Cressida Mortimer, who Gervase Markham had written to inform him would be leaving London for Haven's End at any moment to become a member of his household, and would be accompanied by Miss Sykes and a courier, and man of business in the person of one Hargrove. He must be sure that everything was prepared for her.

Dear God! What a wretched business it was. He had never been entertained by young chits, and the last thing he needed in his quiet and comfortable life was one arriving on his doorstep to destroy his hard-won peace of mind.

No use in repining. He must try to persuade her that Frank Belsize was her fairy prince, ready to take her away — and the sooner, the better!

CHAPTER TWO

Is EVERYBODY mad in England? was Cressy Mortimer's
constant thought. The ritual of polite life in London
society as outlined by Lady Bampton and Miss Sykes
seemed to be designed to make living as difficult as
possible. As for the clothes she was expected to wear,
no one, but no one, could do anything in them. They
were fit only to adorn polite drawing-rooms, to drink
tea in and to take decorous walks, always in company
with Miss Sykes. For, of course, her companion
explained, no young lady was ever expected to be out
unaccompanied, or speak to a man, except in the
presence of others. No young lady apparently ever *did*
anything.

The only prospect of relief appeared to be that she
was to go to Haven's End, to Robert's old friend, Lord
Lyndale. Perhaps she could persuade him that Robert
had brought her up to be self-sufficient, to run things,
to do things, not sit about simpering, or doing fine
embroidery, or reading dull improving books, speaking
only when spoken to. . .

And now, here she was, with Miss Sykes, nearly at
journey's end. Indeed, that good lady, having said to
Cressy, 'I think that we are almost there,' then
exclaimed, violently for her, 'Goodness, Cressy, what
are you doing now?' as Cressy pulled down the coach
window to put her head out to see whether Haven's
End was in sight, which it was.

21

And in doing so, she apparently committed yet another *faux pas*, to add to the long list of those she had already made, for just as she saw the glorious façade of Lord Lyndale's great house come into view Miss Sykes gave a violent tug on her skirts and pulled her back into her seat again.

'Oh, dear,' said Miss Sykes helplessly. 'Whatever will you do next? You are a lady, Cressy; ladies simply do not go on as though they are boys.'

'And a pity they don't,' Cressy replied, exasperated, catching a grin on Mr Hargrove's face, which he suppressed as Miss Sykes glared at him, but which didn't prevent her from adding vigorously, 'For a more boring life than that of a fine lady, I cannot imagine.'

And then, not for the first time since she had arrived in England, she felt betraying tears well up in her eyes. Oh, if only Robert had been younger, had not died and left her all alone, then she might still be in Italy, instead of cold, dull England. Why had he not made the countess her guardian, instead of some old man she didn't know?

Except that the brief glimpse she had had of Haven's End had surprisingly reminded her of Italy, showing her a house modelled on a Palladian villa, to which long wings had been attached. And now, from her seat, steadfastly trying not to cry for the lost past, she could see that they had turned in at wrought-iron gates and were driving up a long sweep towards the house's noble front. Yes, this house might even be in Italy. But it wasn't, and the thought made her feel worse, not better.

Her only hope was that Robert's friend would be like Robert, and would let her behave as Robert did. But

every mile of the journey from London to Wiltshire
had seen that hope diminish.

They were expected. Servants had come from the
house, and her carriage was being stopped before a
long flight of stone steps up to great double doors,
opened to receive them.

A butler appeared and bowed a welcome, before
leading them up the steps, Miss Sykes by her side, Mr
Hargrove a little behind, and the carriages which
formed their train were driven to the stables to be
unpacked.

They were in a huge entrance hall with a high glass
dome, and a tesselated pavement on which was a
mosaic of a dog with the words '*Cave canem*' beneath
it. 'Beware of the dog', and in Latin, too! Her hopes
rose; perhaps her stay here might be a happy one, if the
owner of the house had chosen to surround himself
with *objets d'art* from the country which she loved so
much.

For standing in the hall was an Apollo and beside it
a Diana spearing Actaeon. There was also a rampant
lion, like the one which Robert had unearthed in
Herculaneum, and Cupid kissing Psyche. She could
hardly wait to see the man who owned such treasures.
Who knew, it could even be a meeting of minds; after
all, Lord Lyndale had been Robert's friend and that
must mean something.

But alas, the butler, whose name was March, said
gravely, 'I am afraid that my lord is not here to greet
you. He is spending the afternoon at the Home Farm.
We did not expect you to arrive until tomorrow morning. I shall fetch the housekeeper to show you to your

suite, Lady Cressida. You, sir, I will escort to yours,'
he added to Mr Hargrove.

Well, if they weren't expected, thought Cressy prac-
tically, then this was a well-run house; someone must
have guessed very quickly who the train of carriages
belonged to, for all the servants to have appeared like
magic on the steps of the house.

Mrs Waters appeared like magic, too, a round, rosy-
faced woman who led Cressy and Miss Sykes to a suite
at the back of the house, overlooking lawns and a giant
stretch of water, which had a fountain in its centre
where a wreathed Triton appeared to be blowing water
from a shell.

Oh, yes, it was almost like being in Italy again, if
only the weather had been better. Miss Sykes exclaimed
at the luxury and comfort of the house, and of the room
which she had been given next to Cressy's.

Cressy's bed was a huge thing, with curtains and
hangings in a delicate blue and silver, and there were
three steps up to it, and once inside it, Cressy thought
that it would be more like a room than a bed!

'You would care for some tea, Lady Cressida?'
queried Mrs Waters comfortably. 'Shall I send it up for
you, or would you prefer to take it in the Grand Salon?
It looks out on the gardens.'

'Oh, the Grand Salon, please,' replied Cressy
eagerly. She knew that she was going to like it here. On
the way up to her room she had seen even more
treasures, one of them a statue from Herculaneum
which Robert had sent to his friend. She remembered
it being unearthed when she was quite small. What a
pleasure it would be to talk to someone who knew
about Herculaneum and Pompeii, instead of droning

on all the time about what was proper for a young lady and what was not, as Lady Bampton had done.

Oh, she had meant to be kind, Cressy knew, but she didn't understand that Cressy didn't want to be a proper young lady. Not that she meant to be improper, just that the whole notion of what Society thought was proper was alien to her.

She had just reached this point in her musings when she and Miss Sykes were ushered into the Grand Salon by the footman whom Mrs Waters had sent for them. Tea was laid out on a small table before long windows, going down to the ground, and the view was as magnificent as anyone could wish — although quite unlike Italy despite the cypresses and pines, to say nothing of the statues of gods and goddesses decorating the gardens.

The room was beautiful, too, and there, on the wall, was a painting of the Bay of Naples, which made the foolish tears well up in Cressy's eyes again. It brought back Robert and Caterina and all the happy days which they had spent together.

Mrs Waters brought them more tea, and a plate of little cakes, saying as she placed them on the table, 'M'lord is back, Lady Cressida, and has asked to see you in his study, once you have drunk your tea — in about half an hour, he said.' She looked with approval at the girlish cream muslin gown Cressy had put on, with its little pie frill at the neck and tiny ruffles at the end of its long sleeves.

'Oh, Miss Sykes,' said Cressy. 'You will come with me, won't you?' She felt suddenly and unaccountably shy.

Mrs Waters shook her head regretfully. 'His lordship was most particular that he wished to see you alone on this first occasion. He will interview Mr Hargrove and Miss Sykes later. Mr Hargrove is taking tea in his rooms.'

Everything seemed very well organised at Haven's End, thought Cressy a trifle dazedly, not at all like the easy and comfortable way in which Robert and I went on in Naples. The thought disturbed her a little and disturbed her even more when the same fresh-faced footman, who was to be hers, Mrs Waters said, and was named Sam, led her down a long corridor to Lord Lyndale's study, which was next door to the library, and indeed, opened into it.

The study was yet another beautiful room, lined with break-fronted bookcases, and was hung with architectural drawings. A great desk immediately faced the door, but no one sat or stood there. The only person in the room was a tall man standing at a big window and looking out into the grounds. He turned as Cressy entered, to study her gravely.

Well, whoever he was, he was hardly Lord Lyndale, and Cressy looked interestedly around for an elderly gentleman, but couldn't find him.

Perhaps the man was a secretary and Lord Lyndale was in the library? But when the man walked towards her, Cressy saw at once that, whatever else he was, he was no secretary.

He was beautifully dressed in a black silk suit, with knee breeches. There were thin lines of silver braid around his cuffs and the bottom of the breeches. He wore some sort of order at his throat. His linen was spotless, and his cravat was a work of art.

Cressy had found out about cravats in London. Gentlemen valued them, it seemed, which was another strange and wonderful thing. Fancy worrying about the shape of a bit of linen about one's throat! But she had to admit that this man's was rather fine, as was his waistcoat, striped in black and silver.

But it was his face and physique which were the most remarkable things about him. Not only was he very tall, but he had broad shoulders and was built like the big statue of Hercules which Robert had unearthed in one of the richest villas in Herculaneum. His hair was dark and although one might call him handsome, his face was cold and stern, and his expression severe. His eyes were the most remarkable thing of all: they were a strange amber with dark flecks in them — tiger's eyes. Altogether he was the sort of person whom Robert had always called high-nosed, Cressy thought, with an internal nervous giggle.

She wondered why she felt so nervous. Perhaps it was because of the way in which *he* was looking at *her*. The gentleman, for he was obviously that, bowed to her and said, 'So, you are Lady Cressida Mortimer. Welcome to Haven's End,' but he didn't sound as though he were very pleased to meet her, nor did he say so.

What he also said was, 'What are you looking for so assiduously, Lady Cressida?' for, as she later found, little that others thought or did escaped him.

'I am, of course,' she informed him, a trifle stiffly, for she thought that he was about to patronise her, 'looking for my guardian, Lord Lyndale.'

The strangest expression passed across the haughty face before her. Yes, he was haughty. Some might think him good-looking. Cressy didn't. She thought that he looked proud and condescending.

'Indeed?' he replied. 'And what did you expect to find, pray, when you met him?'

'Robert told me, just before he died,' she was as stiff as he, 'that he had first met Lord Lyndale at Eton and had been a friend of his for many years, and that was why he left me to him, for him to be my guardian, I mean. So I was looking for an elderly gentleman.'

The thin eyebrows arched. Oh, yes, he was about to condescend to her as everyone else had done since she arrived in England. Cressy hoped that she would have very little to do with him. Meantime, where was Lord Lyndale, who had asked her to see him after tea?

'Robert, Lady Cressida?' he uttered. He would never do anything as simple as *say* anything, Cressy thought savagely.

'My father, Lord Silchester. He was Robert to me.' Cressy remained cool and looked around her for her guardian, as *he* plainly saw.

'Did no one in London, Lady Cressida, explain to you what had happened over your father's will?' he asked wearily. Cressy thought that he might be in his middle thirties—she was good at people's ages—but he talked to her as though he were an exhausted ninety, which wasn't strictly true, but thinking so made her feel better. By his icy manner they might well be in the snowy wastes of Iceland, not Wiltshire.

'Only that I had been left as a ward to James, Lord Lyndale, nothing further—and pray, sir, do call me Cressy, everyone else does. I hardly know myself as Cressida.'

He was apparently taking little notice of what she was saying, or was it perhaps too much for he said, stressing her name as he spoke, 'Did no one explain to you, Lady *Cressida*, that your father left you to be the ward of James Chavasse, Lord Lyndale, meaning his old friend, my father? Unfortunately, that James Chavasse, Lord Lyndale, died before your father did, leaving me, also James Chavasse, to inherit not only his title — but you!'

Cressy's mouth gaped open before she exclaimed, in what she later realised was the rudest possible manner, 'Oh, no, he couldn't have made such a dreadful mistake. You're Lord Lyndale! You can't be! I don't believe you!'

'I see that no one thought to inform you of your father's quite understandable error.' Lord Lyndale, Cressy noted, was icier than ever. Perhaps he disliked all women, or perhaps he only disliked young wards decanted on him by mistake. Yes, that was it. Which, now she came to think of it, made matters much better. With luck, she could start back for Italy after all.

'Oh, well, then,' she announced, suddenly cheerful, which surprised James Lyndale more than a little, she was happy to see. 'That's a good thing. I can't be your ward, can I, if you're the wrong Lord Lyndale? So now I haven't got a guardian, and since I certainly don't need one you can arrange for me to return to Italy and go on with Robert's work.'

'Would that it could be so simple,' replied her tormentor sardonically. 'But, alas for both of us, the will was vague. I am James Chavasse, Lord Lyndale, and consequently the law says that I am your guardian. I can assure you that I dislike this turn of events exceedingly, but a man has to do his duty, however unpleasant it may be.'

So, it was going to be unpleasant to be the guardian

of Lady Cressida Mortimer, was it? As was often usual, Cressy's tongue ran away with her on hearing James Lyndale's last unfortunate choice of words. 'Well, I don't want you for a guardian, and that's flat. Most improper, as Lady Bampton would agree. I'm quite sure that Robert would not have left me to the care of a young man — a comparatively young man, that is,' she informed him rudely. But, damn that, as Robert would have said. It was time for truth-telling now.

'Indeed?' James Lyndale was icier than ever. They had apparently passed Iceland and were in Greenland, lost among the snows, almost at the Norh Pole, which judging by his expression they were about to reach at any moment. 'And I don't like rude and ill-mannered little girls. It will be my pleasure to turn you into a reasonable member of society, madam. A pity that you are rather too old for a beating. Your manners would have earned you one, were you a boy.'

'I wish to God I *were* a boy——' Cressy was almost beside herself '—and then people would talk to me as if I had a brain in my head, instead of treating me like a gaby because I *am* a girl. I have been running Robert's affairs for him for the past three years, and people in England treat me as though I were a fool.'

James Lyndale looked wearily at his latest encumbrance. Unknown to Cressy, he already had one ward, and now he had two. And this one a plainish child, he judged, wearing a most unsuitable frock, one designed for a soft and pretty blonde, not a dusky, rather bony termagant. Even Verena might have difficulty in feeling sorry for such a budding shrew as this. Running Robert's affairs, indeed! And to call her father Robert! Well, Silchester had the reputation of being light in the attic, and his daughter's behaviour seemed to prove that reputation to be correct.

On the other hand, he had to admit that shock at the sight and sound of such a wilful child had made him less than kind to someone who had so recently lost her only parent and had arrived in a strange country to live among strangers. He smiled at her in an effort to placate her, but he could see at once that the damage had been done. She was staring at him with a mutinous expression on her face and she had balled her small hands into fists, as though she were the boy she had said that she wished she were.

'My dear.' He was dismally aware that he sounded like an elderly uncle, although that was perhaps better than sounding like an angry father. 'I gather from what you say that your father has allowed you a great deal of freedom while you were living with him in Italy, but you must understand that, in England, young ladies of your great station are expected to behave in quite a different manner. . .'

Cressy interrupted him before he could even finish, saying in a defiant voice, 'Well, then, you must understand that that is exactly why I wish to go back to Italy. Surely you could arrange for Robert's mis. . .friend, the Countess Caterina Franceschini, to look after me? I know that *she* would allow me to continue Robert's work.'

She was rather proud that she had not come out with what poor Caterina really was, since everyone had behaved so *missishly* whenever she had spoken the truth in London about Caterina's relationship with Robert. But no, she could see with a sinking heart that he had no intention of giving way.

'Surely you must understand that sending you back to the Countess Franceschini would be even more improper than the rather strange arrangement which your father inadvertently created when he left you to me? Forgive me, for it is as inconvenient to me as it is to you, but, as I said earlier, we both have our duty to perform, and I certainly intend to perform mine. I trust you to do the same.'

He was judicious to a degree, thought Cressy wildly, as her latest plea for freedom failed to find any response. Such measured pomposity ought to be sitting in court shouting, 'Off with your head' at wretched peasants. By the look and sound of him, he was just the kind of aristocrat whom Robert and she had agreed to detest. No wonder there had been revolutions in Europe with such creatures as James Lyndale about! She had disliked him from the moment she saw him, looking at her as though she were a butterfly on a card, brought in for his inspection.

Well, double horns to him! A favourite exclamation of Caterina's about people who annoyed her, and one which Cressy had never appreciated before. She liked it so much that she almost said it aloud to him, but some relic of prudence kept her quiet. She looked out of the window and did not answer him.

James Lyndale was relieved at her unexpected quiet. Perhaps what he had said to her had struck a chord. Cressy could have told him that it had, but that it was not the chord which he had wished to strike. He decided to continue to be as calm as her true parent might have been with her, except, of course, that her true parent had apparently allowed her to behave exactly as she pleased!

'I think,' he said, trying to be generous, 'that you are tired from your journey, and that the events of the last few months have been a little too much for you. It would be better if we continued this conversation another day when you are feeling calmer. In the meantime, I will have a discussion with your companion, Miss Sykes, about the best way to prepare you to enter Society when the time comes for you to do so. I should like you to meet my sister, Lady Verena Davenport, who will also help you to understand how you must conduct yourself in your new life. In the meantime, my advice to you is to try to accommodate yourself to the desires of others a little. We shall meet again at dinner.'

Yes, with language like that, he ought to be a judge. Cressy stood up, flung her head back and bowed to him. Not a low bow, but one she would give to a parvenu or social pretender.

'Very well. But I warn you, I shall talk as I please. I am tired of trying to be a lady. There must be *somebody* in England who will give me permission to go back to Italy, where I was happy. Perhaps the Lord Chancellor might listen to me. Robert used to say that he had extraordinary powers.'

What a pity that she were not the boy she wished to be, thought James Lyndale, as Cressy walked out of his study, head held high. It would have been so much easier for him to deal with her. As it was, he felt at a gross disadvantage in dealing with a girl child. And what a girl child! It was quite plain that nothing had been withheld from her, and that her benighted papa had treated her as though she were the same age as he was. Become Caterina Franceschini's ward, indeed.

Everyone in Italy and England knew what Caterina was!

He had tried to contest the wardship so cavalierly bestowed on him, but the lawyers had told him that it was useless. He would have to make the best of things. Frank Belsize and his mother must be invited as soon as possible. Verena must arrange for his charge to meet some young girls of her own age with whom she might feel at ease.

And then, as he turned to ring the bell for Miss Sykes and Mr Hargrove to be sent to him, he began to laugh to himself.

What on earth would they all make of Lady Cressida Mortimer? Anything less like the usual young lady who frequented London Society he could not imagine, such a strange mixture of learning and impetuosity as she was. And why was he allowing himself to be so. . . stirred. . .by her? She wasn't even beautiful — or pretty, for that matter.

Cressy, walking desolately along the corridor, Sam behind her like a shadow, was thinking that, of all things, she could never have imagined that she would find herself at the mercy of such a cold-blooded creature as James Lyndale appeared to be.

It must be the dreadful English climate which accounted for all the ice about him. Yes, that was it, the climate. Now, if only he would visit Italy, he might discover that there was more to life than obeying a ridiculous set of rules drawn up by a lot of old women and administered by stiff-necked men like her new guardian, to whom she was tied for the next three years.

* * *

But even a few weeks seemed too long, she thought mournfully, as she left James Lyndale's study a fortnight later. Her troubles had begun on her very first evening at dinner.

She had been sitting opposite to her guardian at table; Miss Sykes, Mr Hargrove, young Mr Gimson, James Lyndale's secretary, and his elderly librarian Dr Soames, were their other companions. Lord Lyndale was still wearing his beautiful black suit — his clothes were perfect, she had to grant him that — and his manner was icier than ever. It soon became apparent that it was not reserved only for her, it was for everyone.

It didn't particularly daunt Mr Hargrove, a middle-aged man with a kind face, who was used to the vagaries of his masters. He was the sort of confidential legal servant who lived only to ensure that all went well in the seats of the mighty. He felt a little sorry for Lady Cressida, who had lived such a free and easy life in Italy but was now condemned to the restricted one of an English young lady of quality.

He only let his pity show occasionally, and certainly not in front of James Lyndale, who struck him as the most complete cold-blooded and cold-hearted monster he had ever encountered. How unfortunate that, of all people, Cressida Mortimer should find herself in his power.

After a time conversation languished. James had tried to put his varied set of guests at ease, but between Cressy's fear of saying anything which she might regret, Miss Sykes's shyness before such a perfect specimen of manhood as Lord Lyndale was, and Mr Hargrove's desire to say nothing which might offend anyone at table, talk dribbled out and came to a muted stop. Even Messrs Gimson and Soames seemed a trifle overcome.

If this were to be his future company at table, then God preserve him! was James's inward thought. The child looked more mutinous than ever. He was uncomfortably aware of Miss Sykes's languishing looks at him — such a fine-looking man, she was thinking — and Hargrove, although a man of sense, was apparently losing it in the face of such an inequality of interests as those present displayed. In any case, Hargrove was leaving at the end of the week to supervise Cressy's estates and he would be condemned, he supposed, to the conversation of the nursery. It was a pity that Lady Cressida was too old to live and eat there.

He had no sooner thought this than Mr Hargrove, in a mistaken attempt to revive the flagging conversation, murmured, 'I note, Lord Lyndale, that you have a remarkable collection of classical statuary and pottery at Haven's End. I believe that your late father was a discerning collector.'

'Yes,' said James briefly, and then, in what he later grasped was an unfortunate effort to include Cressy in the conversation, added, 'I believe, Lady Cressida, that a large part of it came from the excavations which your father conducted at Pompeii and Herculaneum.'

Cressy's face came alive at once. 'Oh, indeed,' she offered, leaning forward, her face growing animated and the mutinous look disappearing, James was pleased to note. 'I helped Robert to choose some of the pieces. The Diana in the entrance hall, for example. Lord Lyndale had asked for an interesting specimen of Roman sculpture of the female form, preferably naked. Robert debated for a long time between that piece and another, equally lovely, and even more interesting. It was the statue of a heavily pregnant woman, a fertility goddess, he thought. It might even have been one of Rhea, who was the goddess always present at the Dionysian orgies. They were fertility rites, too,' she added helpfully and kindly, 'and Rhea was sometimes shown holding a wine cup. A great deal of wine was also drunk during orgies, Robert said.'

She was quie unaware that her table companions were staring at her with expressions ranging from outright shock and horror from Miss Sykes, barely suppressed amusement 'from Mr Hargrove, total surprise from Gimson and Soames, mixed with unwilling admiration for such inapposite learning from the learned Dr Soames, and from James Lyndale an enigmatic eyebrow raised above a stone face from which all expresion had fled.

If the truth were to be told, James was possessed with a terrible desire to laugh at the contrast between Lady Cressida's appearance of innocent if not to say dewy youth, and the learned and improper lecture on which she had embarked. His fear that he was condemned to nursery talk was obviously misplaced and, quite disgracefully, he was not stopping her eager flow of words, for he had an unregenerate desire to know exactly how far Lady Cressida would go.

All the way, apparently, for she then added, 'Robert said he would send the Diana, for he understood that Lord Lyndale wanted it for the entrance hall, and perhaps Rhea was not entirely suitable for that, the English feeling differently about such matters from the old Romans. They were more sensible than we are,' she ended.

'Lady Cressida.' James's voice was as firm as he could make it, and he spoke before Miss Sykes could vent her feelings on her charge. It was hardly the child's fault that her wretched father had apparently considered her to be as old as he was and had hidden absolutely nothing from her. Before she was let loose on Society she must be made to understand that, however appropriate it was for learned old gentlemen to discuss such things, it was not proper for a supposedly innocent young lady.

'Lady Cressida, we all thank you for such an interesting and lucid piece of information. But I am sure you will forgive me if I suggest that it is not quite the subject a young lady ought to raise in mixed company. Perhaps, after dinner, it might be useful if you and Miss Sykes had a little discussion with me about such a delicate matter.'

Cressy came down to earth with a bang. For a moment it had almost been as though she were with Robert again, discussing such interesting matters as how far the worship of Dionysius had extended in Rome, and whether Rhea could be identified with Ops, the wife of the god, Jupiter, another goddess associated with fertility. She had, indeed, been prepared to pass on to such fascinating matters, but now, looking around the table, she realised that she had committed yet another *faux pas*, and, judging by everyone's expressions, a truly dreadful one.

She crimsoned slowly and looked down at the food on her plate which, in one terrible moment, had turned to dust and ashes. She could hardly meet the eyes of the other diners, particularly those of Miss Sykes, who appeared about to faint.

Pagan fertility goddesses, indeed! Pregnant women! What would the child come out with next, and at table, too, and before four men, one of them quite young. They might think that she, Miss Sykes, was responsible for such an indelicate subject for conversation! She must and would assure Lord Lyndale that although she had become aware that her charge knew and spoke of the most outrageous matters, she had not before chattered about fertility rites and. . .orgies!

Remembering this unhappy scene, Cressy went hot all over again. Lord Lyndale had been almost kind, which was surprising, but the outraged Miss Sykes had left her in no doubt of the enormity of what she had done.

Lecture had followed lecture, day after day, until Cressy had exclaimed, 'Why don't you condemn me to bread and water and a stay in Haven's End's little prison and then be quiet about it. I promise never to say the word "pregnant" again, or mention fertility, although goodness knows why you should all make such a fuss about the most natural thing in the world. None of us would be here without it. On second thoughts, why should I keep quiet? It is the rest of you who are behaving foolishly, not I.'

That did it. Miss Sykes, outraged beyond belief, had gone to Lord Lyndale and told him that he must speak to his ward, and severely.

'I trust I need not remind you that she is your responsibility, my lord.' Her outrage compelled her to remind him of his duties.

To be fair to him, he was not annoyed with her, and merely said, with a weary sigh, 'Oh, yes, indeed. I will speak to her.'

So Cressy had been sent to his study again, and there found her guardian, dressed like a gamekeeper, ready to ride around his estates with Mr Lenthall, his agent, but needing to speak to his rebellious ward first. The gamekeeper's clothes made him look stronger and larger than ever, and added to her feeling of being small and unconsidered.

'Lady Cressida,' he began, and his manner, she noted hopefully, was not over-stern. 'What is this Miss Sykes tells me? That you are refusing to submit to her proper authority, and insist that you intend to speak as you please about matters which it has been explained to you are not for a young lady to raise in public.'

His manner had grown perceptibly colder, thought Cressy dismally, unaware that James, faced by her, most unaccountably felt sorry for her. It was not her fault, after all, that she didn't know how to behave. He saw her lower lip begin to tremble, saw the effort which she was making to control herself and not begin to cry, and the strangest feeling swept over him, quite unlike any he had ever had before for anyone.

He wanted to take her on to his knee, take out his handkerchief, dry her eyes, the most beautiful thing about her, and begin to comfort her. . .and after that? Why, after that he would begin himself to instruct her on her proper duties, but as kindly and gently as he could. . .

He came to himself with a start to hear that she was saying, passion in her voice, 'I am not at all interested in any of the things which polite young ladies are supposed to spend their lives doing. Can't you see that it would be simpler to send me back to Italy. . .?' and then, woefully, 'Oh, that will not answer, will it? You can't, I quite see that. . .oh, dear.'

James said, as gently as he could, the desire to protect her still strong in him, 'Suppose you tried a little harder to please Miss Sykes and me? You need not make yourself ill with effort——' this brought a small chuckle from her, and the lip stopped quivering '——but it would make life easier for us all, most of all for yourself. You will have to conform sooner or later, you know; we all do.' And so saying he passed his handkerchief over to her, adding, 'Here, take this, since you seem to be without one.'

'And you?' asked Cressy, when she had blown her nose vigorously, looking up into his face, which she had to admit was very handsome when he was not being stern. 'Did you have to conform? I didn't think men did.'

James motioned her to a chair and sat down himself. 'Of course I did, Cressy, and a hard time I had of it, learning to behave myself.' It was the first time he had used her pet name, and it brought a wan smile to her face. 'Men aren't exempt from discipline, you know. Didn't your father teach you that?'

Cressy shook her head. 'I can't remember discussing discipline with him,' she said slowly. 'Although we discussed a great many topics, that was not among them.'

'Well, it should have been,' returned James briskly. 'And your discipline is to watch your tongue a little. Which, I may add, has been mine, too.'

'Oh, no,' exclaimed Cressy ingenuously. 'I can't believe *that*. You seem very much in control of yourself to me!'

James closed his eyes. They really were a remarkable amber, Cressy saw, now that she was nearer to him than she had ever been. She had never seen eyes like them before, so beautiul and so. . .compelling.

'And that is what I mean about watching your tongue,' he told her gently. 'You shouldn't have said that to me.'

'Why not? It's what I was thinking.'

'If we all said what we were thinking, I tremble to think what would happen to the world,' replied her guardian, a laugh in his voice for the first time.

'Hypocrites,' said Cressy slowly. 'We are all to be hypocrites, then? Is that it?'

James was fascinated, almost against his will. The child, as he had already thought — and this conversation, and the others he had had with her since her arrival, confirmed it — had a mind as sharp as a knife. Due to her unconventional education, no doubt, but the pity was that it was going to make life harder for her, not easier, for there was so much that she was going to have to unlearn — if she could.

He had never thought to find himself a tutor in conduct to a young girl. He must be careful in what he said. If he antagonised her overmuch, they might both be lost in a permanent confrontation. He found himself not wanting that. Before she had arrived, he had thought that she would be a shallow bread-and-butter miss and had resolved to have as little to do with her as possible, but she was so different from his expectations that she was beginning to intrigue him

'No,' he replied slowly, 'not hypocrites. I don't want you to be a hypocrite. The first rule of good conduct is that one should never distress or embarrass those to whom you are speaking. It may be that they are foolish, or wrong-headed, but a true lady should never allow such thoughts to be spoken aloud. She should also try never to hurt those among whom she must live. *That* is not hypocrisy.'

Cressy nodded. She could not answer him. It was easy to deal with him when he was being icy cold, as he was when she had first met him — but kindness! Now that was quite different. He had disarmed her without knowing it.

But she must defend herself, she must. 'I did not know,' she said, with great dignity, 'that what I was saying would be offensive to others.'

'No, indeed,' James agreed. 'Had you said what you did to shock or hurt, then that would have been unforgivable. But I cannot believe that you are unable to think before you speak. You should have asked yourself how Miss Sykes, whom you must know well by now, would feel on hearing such a. . .frank discussion of such. . .earthy matters.'

Cressy looked at him thoughtfully. 'Since, sir,' she had decided on the 'sir' as a mark of the respect which she had so far refused to give him, '*you* would not be shocked if I discussed the customs of the ancients with you, I take it that I am allowed to say what I please to you when I am alone with you. I cannot think that there is much that I could say or do that you would find distressing or embarrassing.'

His reaction to this was so surprising that she was taken aback. He threw back his handsome head — yes, he was handsome, she had decided — and laughed aloud.

'"A Daniel come to judgement! Oh, wise young

judge",' he quoted. 'Do you know to what I refer, Cressy?' For she had gone first white and then red at his unforced response.

'Shylock in the *Merchant of Venice*?' she hazarded. 'But why? Oh, dear, have I said something wrong again?' And her beautiful grey eyes filled with tears.

'Now, "my grey-eyed Pallas",' he replied almost tenderly. 'You are not to be distressed. I simply meant that you are incorrigible. What do I do with a young lady who can verbally outmanoeuvre me at every turn? No, it is not proper for you to discuss such things with an unmarried man, even if he is nearly old enough to be your father.'

Cressy could not stop herself. 'Oh, sir, *that* I do not believe. You must have been far too young. . .' And then she stopped abruptly, as a great blush seemed to have taken over her whole body. 'Oh. . .' she began again brokenly. 'You see how difficult it is? I have never before had to think before I spoke. Robert always encouraged me to express myself. I can see that life is going to be very hard for me.' And she hung her head, only to raise it suddenly to ask eagerly, 'Did you really mean that I look like Pallas Athene? I am sure that you did not, for she was very beautiful and Robert was quite adamant that I wasn't that. Not a bit like my poor Mama, he said.'

James, against his will, was compelled to agree with her. He had seen a portrait of Cressy's mother, done by Romney, and she had had a sad, delicate beauty, beyond compare. He could see a little of her in Cressy, particularly when she, too, was sad. But Cressy, he was beginning to realise, had a character of her own, and was not like anyone at all except herself.

'Come,' he said. 'Let us shake hands on it, my ward. You will try to be a lady, and I will try to be patient with you. There are many interesting topics which you may usefully raise with me that would not bring a blush to anyone's face. We must try to confine ourselves to them. And as an earnest of that, I must ask you if you ride. Because if you do, you might like to accompany me this afternoon. I am visiting one of my tenant farmers who has acquired a new breed of cattle and wishes me to admire them. Come and admire them with me.' And he held out his hand to her.

'Oh, yes!' Cressy was eager. 'Robert said that I was a very Centaur, half-man, half-horse, as I suppose you know. I love riding. The more spirited the horse, the better!'

James closed the amber eyes which were so intriguing his ward. He might have guessed! Of course, Lady Cressida Mortimer would like riding spirited horses, *ventre à terre* no doubt, belly to the ground for the horse, and hair streaming in the wind for the rider.

'I think that I can find a suitable mount for you,' was his answer to that. Best not to start chiding her immediately. 'Off with you. Your new lady's maid may help you to change. I understand that Mrs Waters has given you Catherine Mason.'

'Oh, it is her afternoon off,' explained Cressida, 'and Miss Sykes is visiting the Vicar's wife this afternoon. But that is no matter. I always dressed myself in Italy. I won't take long, I promise you.' And she was off, half of her mourning over her need to be proper and the other half excited at the thought of being on a horse again. Her guardian had told her to meet him on the sweep before the house.

James watched her go. Now, why had he saddled himself with the chit? Was he taking his duties so seriously that he proposed to make a companion of her? Surely not! He was merely sorry for the child. The sooner Frank Belsize arrived, and Verena, who had promised to visit him to help him with Cressida, the better. He could go back to the orderly way of life which had satisfied him since he had inherited.

And why did that life suddenly seem so sterile?

CHAPTER THREE

CRESSY slid, breathless, from her horse at the end of the afternoon. Somehow, she had not committed any *faux pas* great enough to earn a reprimand from his haughty lordship. There had been two small untoward incidents which had disturbed her a little but, reviewing the afternoon, she was happy with herself for the first time since she had arrived in England.

Running upstairs to change, she had thought with delight of wearing boy's clothes again. She always wore boy's clothes when she rode with Robert, or when she was excavating with him, they were so much more convenient than skirts.

But suddenly, fishing them out of one of the many trunks which had accompanied her from Italy, and which had remained unpacked, she stopped. Staring at them, she went slowly red and thought, Oh, no! I'm sure that they will cause another brouhaha. Miss Sykes had told her the other day that ladies in England rode side-saddle and wore discreet riding habits to do so. She had also told Cressy that the heavy bottle-green skirt and jacket and the little black leather boots, bought in London for her just before they had left, which she had stared at, saying, 'But not for summer wear, surely?' would do well for riding at any season of the year. Yes, there were sure to be recriminations and wailings if she wore breeches and rode astride. Lord

Lyndale would look down his proud beak at her and she would be in the dungeons of his esteem again.

So she discarded the breeches and put on her new habit and sailed decorously downstairs, trying to walk, not to run, another sin for which she had been reprimanded. She arrived at the front of the house to find James and his land agent and a pair of grooms, one leading a depressing-looking creature fit only for an old woman, which she was sure would be hers, and, of course, it was.

'Very *comme il faut*,' remarked James approvingly. He had been wondering what outrageous turn-out the impossible child would arrive in, and he was happy to introduce this elegant young woman to youngish Mr Lenthall, his agent, before helping Cressy on to her horse, not allowing the groom to do so.

It was then that the first odd thing happened to Cressy. So odd that she withdrew her hand from his as though she had been stung. For, on his touching her, it was as though in some extraordinary way a spark passed from him to her which ignited in her the strangest feelings. They were everywhere and nowhere, but finally seemed to settle in the pit of her stomach, a place which normally never troubled her.

She flushed and looked away. Whatever could be the matter with her? Had touching her hand had the same effect on Lord Lyndale as on herself? She could not tell. His face was as impassive as ever, the haughty mask which always annoyed her, because it told the world of his total self-control.

James had, indeed, felt the strange spark, and cursed to himself as he did so. Was it possible that he had been without a woman for so long that to touch this fledgling child was causing him to feel the most unwanted emotions, given who and what she was?

Sternly repressing the wave of desire which had passed over him — for he knew exactly what the sensation was, as Cressy in her innocence didn't — he mounted in his turn and the three of them, followed by the two grooms, rode off on their tour around the estate to arrive at Farmer Martin's acres to inspect his new herd.

Cressy wondered for a little what had happened to her. She had an accurate theoretical knowledge of what passed sexually between men and women, of what occurred in marriage — and out of it — for her father's instructions to her had been frank and graphic. Lord Silchester believed that such things should not be hidden from young women, so he had hidden nothing from his daughter.

She had, however, little or no understanding of the feelings and emotions involved in human love, and was, indeed, rather puzzled as to why anyone should want to perform such an unlikely act, and want it so passionately that common sense frequently flew out of the window where it was concerned.

She sounded knowledgeable, but the impression she gave was a false one, as her guardian was becoming aware. James, indeed, was wondering whether he should ask his sister to have a frank talk with his ward, but what sort of frank talk? He thought it might be beyond Verena's capacities to explain to Cressy the difference between theoretical and actual knowledge. It was certainly beyond his. He was beginning to be worried about where and how such a conversation might end!

Looking sideways at him, Cressy thought that he looked sterner than ever and was unaware that she was the cause of it. And then she forgot all about her strange feelings in the pleasure of seeing the animals and the dairy and inspecting the calves, which she found charming.

Mr Lenthall found Lady Cressida Mortimer delightful in her charming naïveté. It was not that she was beautiful or even conventionally pretty, but he found her frank enthusiasm for everything she saw most attractive. She asked such intelligent questions, and if he was a little surprised to be asked about the details of cattle breeding by an eighteen-year-old girl, he soon forgot his surprise in telling her about milk yields and the proper pasture for assuring that the yields were high.

James was sardonically amused to watch Lenthall, a dour man with a dour wife, succumbing to the unusual charms of his ward. It was obvious, too, that Stephen, her groom, as well as Sam, her footman, was only too happy to serve her, and he had already noticed that all the servants liked her, because in her frank way she was considerate of them and spoke to them in terms of happy equality in such a way that they did not take advantage of it.

All in all, Lady Cressida Mortimer, he thought, appeared to please everyone, except her equals, all of whom were hard put to it to see that she did not say, or do, anything which might damage her reputation irretrievably.

But nothing untoward happened during the rest of Cressy's happy afternoon, and after she had drunk a cup of new milk, she rode back to Haven's End on her docile steed. She had already decided that on their return she must ask her guardian to provide her with something a little more lively. When James handed her down, she again had that strange quivering sensation pass over her and end in her stomach. She must be sickening for something.

She was about to ask him what it meant, when the discretion which she was slowly learning told her not to. And then, she again forgot about it, as well as about asking him for a better mount, because it was apparent as they reached the sweep in front of the house that Haven's End had visitors. Strange servants were bustling about, and looking towards the stables Cressy saw that two travelling coaches were being unpacked. A handsome curricle, picked out in red and white, with an unfamiliar groom up was being driven slowly along the front sweep. As well as the coaches, there were two small chaises, and all of them, apart from the curricle, had their arms emblazoned on their doors.

'Who is it, sir?' she asked James as they walked together into the house. James's emotions were strangely mixed. It was some years since so many visitors had arrived together at Haven's End, and although he knew that they would help him to entertain his unwanted ward he also knew that he had much rather have been left in his solitude.

He sighed, and replied stiffly, 'I think, by the arms on the coaches that we have two sets of visitors. My nephew, Frank Belsize and his mother, my sister Emily, and my other sister, Lady Verena Davenport and her husband. Now you will have some company of your own age, for Verena is much younger than I am, and you must mind your manners, my dear, as my old nurse used to say. Yes, it will be useful practice for you among friends before we let you loose on Society!'

He makes me sound like a performing bear, thought Cressy resentfully, but her feelings about visitors were quite different from those of James. A young man of her own age and a lady who was not so much older than she was might perhaps not be so ready as m'lord and Miss Sykes to keep her in the straight and narrow way! She could hardly wait to meet them.

Alas, she was sent to her room to change, and all the time that Cressy dressed herself she was in a fever of expectation, mixed with a strange shyness. Perhaps they would not like her! Perhaps, in common with everyone else she had met in England, except the servants, they would find her forward.

She stared at herself in the mirror before going downstairs. She had put on a gown of white sprigged muslin with a pale blue ribbon bound high under her breasts, carefully tied into a bow with the ends falling gracefully down her back. The neckline was heart-shaped and even more discretion was added by a wide ruffle.

Mason had dressed her hair high on top of her head, with a few ringlets hanging down, and Cressy thought that the whole effect was quite becoming. Now if only her conversation could match her gown! She really must try not to embarass anyone, as *he* had advised. She tried to walk slowly downstairs only to meet Miss Sykes, her face harassed, coming in the opposite direction.

'Oh, there you are, Lady Cressida. We have visitors. I see that you have attired yourself correctly.' Miss Sykes said this last in a fashion which suggested to

Cressy that she was usually accustomed to seeing Cressy dressed in skins *à la* Ancient Briton.

'I see that I, too, must prepare to meet our visitors. I think that you should wait for me, my dear.'

'Oh, no,' exclaimed Cressy, all good resolutions forgotten. 'Lord Lyndale said that I was to come downstairs as soon as I was presentable.'

'Just like a man,' sighed Miss Sykes. 'Nevertheless, I think that it would be more *convenable* if you waited for me.' So it was some time before she and Miss Sykes arrived in the Grand Salon where the new arrivals were gathered to take tea and a light collation — dinner being put back a little for the sake of the chef, who had not prepared for such a large party.

The room seemed full of people to Cressy. *He*, as she now thought of him, was there, looking quite superb in grey pantaloons, a bottle-green jacket and a cravat of such splendour that Cressy blinked at it. His hair was dressed *à la Brutus*, and he was wearing light slippers with small silver rosettes. She wondered acidly how many servants it had taken to produce such a rapid transformation from the gamekeeper she had arrived home with. She and Robert had barely changed their clothing once a day, let alone twice or thrice as these people seemed to do — but she had to own that her guardian looked magnificent.

Seated side by side on a low couch were two ladies. One, Lord Lyndale's older sister, Emily, was comfortably middle-aged, wearing a deep blue wool gown, trimmed with fine lace, and her hair dressed in the fashion of twenty years ago. It really needed powder to finish it off, but Cressy was not to know that. She had a kind expression and smiled at them as they entered.

The other lady was very like *him*, but her face was soft where *his* was hard, and her black hair cascaded in light curls about her face, instead of being cut short. She had amber eyes, too, and altogether she seemed a softer, kinder soul. Her dress was charming, a high-waisted amber silk — to match the eyes, one supposed — with a minimum of trimmings.

James performed the introductions to his sisters, the Ladies Emily Belsize and Verena Davenport, and the latter, always an impulsive creature, rose and hugged Cressy, giving her a whiff of a delicate wild rose scent.

'Let me look at you, child,' she said, and held her off. 'Yes, I remember your Mama, and you certainly have a look of her, does she not, James?' appealing to *him*.

Before he could answer, a young man who had been standing in the big window strolled forward and murmured, 'Now, my dear aunt, you are not to monopolise our new friend. I trust you, sir,' and he smiled at his uncle, 'to introduce me to her before the rest of the county has had the opportunity to cut me out.'

James smiled at him, and then at Cressy. 'Come, Frank, eagerness is one thing, good manners another.' Which was exactly the sort of pompous statement he was given to, thought Cressy disgustedly, for she could hardly wait to speak to the young Apollo who stood before her.

He was as tall as Lord Lyndale and had a distant look of him. But where James was as dark as night, he was fair and as bright as day. He was well built, and dressed, like his uncle, to perfection. He was young, not more than twenty-three at the most, and had an eager lively face, with laughing blue eyes. Oh, she was sure that she was going to like him, but would he like her? Cressy had no illusions about herself, she knew that she was no beauty, but the bright eyes the young Apollo turned on her were admiring.

'Let me introduce you to my nephew,' said James calmly, for, after all, had he not asked Frank to visit Haven's End in the hope that he would fall headlong for Silchester's heiress and she for him? That being so, why did he feel such reluctance to make them acquainted? 'Lady Cressida Mortimer, my ward, allow me to present Mr Frank Belsize of Belsize Park in Northamptonshire, come with his Mama, my sister, to meet the new member of my household.'

So that was what she was, just the latest member of his household! And why, for a moment, was the bright day dimmed as Frank bowed and smiled at her, and his uncle strode to the hearth, to smile benevolently, if a trifle sardonically, at them?

'Lady Cressida,' murmured Frank, and bowed low, as though to a member of the Royal Family, rising to show her his eyes brimming with mischief. 'My Mama tells me that you have been living in Italy, assisting your Papa in excavating Pompeii. How fortunate that you have been rescued from such a dry-as-dust fate to come to England to enjoy yourself as you ought.'

Cressy found herself prey to conflicting emotions. It had *not* been dull in Italy, but she supposed Frank might think so. She was about to put him right about that, and about Herculaneum being her father's interest, not Pompeii, but perhaps she ought not to tell Frank that. *He* might think it impolite.

Instead she answered, 'Oh, I was not bored all the time, Mr Belsize, and Italy is very beautiful,' which was not at all the thing she would have said to him a month ago. She hoped that *he* was listening with approval. 'And pray call me Cressy. Rob. . .my father always did. I hardly know myself as Cressida.'

'Lady Cressy. Charming,' was Frank's reply to that. 'And I refuse to be Mr Belsize. Call me Cousin Frank or Frank, I beg of you. I insist that we are honorary cousins.'

If Cressy was being subjected to contrary emotions, adoring Frank Belsize's appearance, but finding his understanding a trifle lacking — excavating being dull, indeed! — James Lyndale found himself in the same condition.

On the one hand, he had arranged for Frank to be present to enchant his ward — a most suitable marriage — and on the other hand, he was thinking, What a damn'd puppy he is. The poor child deserves better than *that*.

'Herculaneum,' he found himself saying. 'Not Pompeii.' It had not escaped his notice that Cressy had been on the brink of correcting Frank and informing him briskly how happy she had been to dig up ruins with her father and that the ruins had been at Herculaneum, not Pompeii. And while he would normally have commended her for her restraint, how strangely annoying it was that the first time that she *had* exercised it, it had been for the benefit of his damn'd ignoramus of a nephew. Frank really deserved to be set down.

'Herculaneum?' echoed Frank, a little puzzled as to how it had arrived in the conversation. He had already forgotten his early ingenuous remark about Pompeii.

'Herculaneum,' offered James, a trifle captiously. 'It

was Herculaneum Lady Cressida's father was busy excavating, not Pompeii.'

'Oh, that.' Frank was cheerful. He had not excelled at the classics at Cambridge, being too busy introducing a tame bear and a monkey into the lecture hall when he should have been listening to his Professor discoursing on the delights of Livy and Horace: a feat for which he had been sent down. Not that there was any harm in him, as his fond Mama so frequently said. 'I'm afraid all ruins are the same to me,' he offered apologetically to Cressy, who was staring reproachfully at James. How dared he put Frank down so rudely almost immediately after he had spent so much time telling her that she was to do no such thing! She would make a point of reprimanding him over it as soon as she could. After all, *he* had not spared her! Fair was fair, no doubt about that. It was not poor Frank's fault that no one had seen fit to give him a proper education.

And then she registered what Frank had said, and since it seemed that James could say what he pleased, then so would she, but gently. 'Well, they're not,' she told him helpfully. 'All the same, that is. And when we have a few moments to spare, after we have taken tea, perhaps,' for the double doors had opened and a procession of servants had entered carrying tea boards and plates of sandwiches and cakes, 'we can repair to the library where there are some excellent folios, and I can explain to you how different ruins can be, and why they are important.'

James, standing near them, nearly disgraced himself by laughing out loud. The mere idea of Frank Belsize being entertained, in a library of all places, by an eighteen-year-old chit! Wonders would never cease.

But he underestimated his man. The strange charm which Cressy exercised on so many was beginning to work on Frank.

'I say,' he bubbled eagerly. 'Would you? Would you really? It would be most amazing kind of you. I'm afraid I was a fearful dunce at Cambridge; my own fault I assure you, I never attended. I know that I should have done, but I could never bring myself to do it. Now . . .if you were my tutor. . .'

Cressy was saved from further *faux pas* on the lines of, 'You have been to Cambridge and have never learned anything!' and, 'Oh, if only I could go to Cambridge and listen to the Professors as Robert did, *I* shouldn't waste *my* time,' by the entry of Fred Davenport, who had been organising matters in the stables, and was consequently a late arrival to the tea-party.

So Fred had to be presented to Lyndale's ward, which meant that the cheerful Frank had to retire a little, and enabled Cressy to say quietly to her guardian when he offered her a plate of sandwiches, 'Pray why, sir, when I am told not to embarrass people, and consequently refrained from embarrassing Frank, did you feel the need to do so? It is the outside of enough if gentlemen may do as they please while I am to put my conversation in hobbles.'

James looked down into the grey eyes which were throwing daggers at him, and the devil which had got into him earlier got into him again.

'It is all your fault,' he said. Good God, he afterwards thought, I was flirting with her! 'You have infected me with your dreadful example, and I find every now and again I have a similar urge to correct and instruct those around me as you do.'

This piece of nonsense came out so solemnly from his stone face, as Cressy thought of it, that she was quite unhinged and began to laugh, a gay, pealing sound which rang around the big room and turned every head towards her. There was something so delightfully artless and frank about her, and her laughter reinforced this impression.

And then her laughter stopped and Cressy gazed back at her guardian, and grey eyes met compelling amber ones. And all the breath was knocked out of her body. But before she could fully understand what was happening to her, Miss Sykes was upon her, saying agitatedly, 'Oh, my dear, do guard your tongue. No lady ever. . .ever. . .laughs aloud as you have done. Pray apologise to your guardian. I do not expect you to apologise to the whole room for, after all, it is plain that you know no better.'

Surprisingly, her guardian put up his hand and said, apologising himself to the startled Miss Sykes, 'No, I beg of you, do not reproach Lady Cressida. It was I who misbehaved after she had conducted herself with total correctitude, and I who should apologise to her. And it was I who caused her to laugh, so I must ask your forgiveness for leading your charge astray.'

Both Cressy and Miss Sykes gazed at him, openmouthed. To hear him confess a fault, even though he had spoken with his usual air of cold self-command, was as though God himself had come down from the heavens to admit that he might have been in error over such trifling matters as creating a world of men.

'Oh, I do beg your pardon, Lord Lyndale,' twittered

Miss Sykes. 'I had not meant to reflect on *your* conduct, no, not at all, far from it, I am sure that you always behave. . .' and she ran out of words at the enormity of what she was saying to one of the Lords of Creation who ruled her world.

'I wish,' said James, a trifle ruefully, 'that I could agree with your kind sentiment. Particularly as I have myself just fallen below the level of good conduct expected from a gentleman. And may I add that this afternoon Lady Cressida does you credit in every way.' He put up his glass to survey Cressy, adding, 'Her turn-out, so appropriate, and her conduct, until I distracted her, so irreproachable,' and he bowed to them both.

Well, thought Cressy crossly, I like old Sykes, but this is too much; she had absolutely nothing to do with my appearance, nor with my determination to try to be that puling thing, a lady! But I suppose that I had better not say so. And how dare a man who I dare swear is not yet forty speak in such a pompous and elderly manner? What will he be like when he is old if he can carry on like this before he gets there!

James had almost felt Cressy bridle, and could guess why she had done so, but his speech had achieved its purpose. Miss Sykes was already smiling at him and had begun to preen herself a little, her recent discomposure forgotten.

'So kind,' she gushed. 'Yes, I flatter myself that Lady Cressida is vastly improved. So teachable, I find.' And she gazed fondly at her charge, so that Cressy mentally gnashed her teeth and almost resolved to behave exactly as she had been used to do before she had arrived at Haven's End. Only the thought of all the excitement and trouble it would cause prevented her from turning back into Robert's unregenerate daughter on the spot! Teachable, indeed!

And then, as she seethed, she caught the tiger's eyes on her, and saw his mouth twitch, and it was plain that James knew exactly what she was thinking.

'Oh, indeed,' he said blandly to Miss Sykes. 'I could not agree with you. I am sure that Lady Cressida, under your tutelage, will become a perfect model for a young lady's book of etiquette before the month is out,' and Miss Sykes, bowing and nodding, moved away gratified, her recent *faux pas* quite forgotten.

'Oh, how dare you?' raged Cressy to James. 'You know perfectly well that I have no desire to be any such thing, but. . .'

'But,' interjected James smoothly, if a trifle rudely, 'I have just given you an example of how little consideration it takes to make those around us happy. I know perfectly well that you dressed yourself, but look what a few kind if untruthful words did for her self-respect. Only take heed of what I tell you and you will achieve perfection.'

'Perfection!' Cressy spat savagely at him, trying to keep her voice low while she did so. 'In your opinion only one person at Haven's End possesses that quality, and that is yourself, as well as the most consummate self-love. I wonder that you don't travel a few feet above the ground to demonstrate to the full your angelic, omniscient and omnipotent nature.'

James's eyes began dancing much as his nephew's had done during this impassioned speech, but Cressy was too blind with anger to notice any such thing. 'Not at all,' he replied gravely, 'most inconvenient for me, I tower over people too much as it is. Another few feet higher would disgust. By the by, I do admire your choice of adjectives when angry, and wish that they were demonstrated on a more worthy cause than myself.'

Why that should defuse her own anger Cressy had no idea, then or later. Dreadfully, she began to laugh again, and this time it was Verena, who had been watching them in some surprise who came over, and said severely to her brother, 'Whatever can you be at, James? First I thought that you were berating your ward, and then you inspire her to laughter. The poor child will not know how to please you, so contrarily are you behaving. Come, my dear, let us take a turn about the gardens, and leave Fred and James to talk politics. I know that they are dying to do so, or so Fred informed me on the way here.' And she skilfully removed Cressy from the room and began discussing the glories of the garden with her.

Later James wandered absentmindedly into the library — or so he pretended to himself, being unwilling to face the true reason why he was going there. He tried to think of something to ask Dr Soames, but couldn't think of anything and decided instead that he needed to look up a reference in a book. But which book?

Oh, damn it, leave that. A man had a right to wander into his library without reason. Which was all a hum, all of it, because he didn't want to confess to himself why he so urgently needed to be in the library, which was that he wanted to see Lady Cressida Mortimer instructing that ass Frank Belsize in the wonders of classical civilisation. And even then he couldn't be

honest with himself, for the truth was that he simply
wanted to be with her and resented Frank being alone,
barring the hovering Dr Soames, with Cressy.

He refused to examine his mind's workings and the
way in which his ward was turning from an encumbrance with a formal title into a sylph with a nickname!

There they were, in the far bay window, and, yes, Dr
Soames *was* hovering, worried, doubtless, that the
young people might damage his precious folios.

No worry about that. At Cressy's command, Frank
had carefully lifted a giant volume on to an oak and gilt
stand and was listening earnestly, head bent, an
expression of the gravest attention on his face, to
Cressy's exposition of the differing wonders of the
ancient world. Even Dr Soames had a slightly stunned
expression on his face on hearing such an erudite
disquisition coming from such unlikely and pretty lips.

'So,' concluded Cressy, a trifle breathlessly, her
finger on the page of the book before her, but happy to
do for another what Robert had so often done for her,
'I am sure that you can plainly see that ruins are all
quite different, according to the period in which they
were built, the place in which they were found, and the
varying natures of the people who lived there.'

Frank was not looking at the page Cressy indicated,
but at the glowing face of the girl who was speaking to
him.

'Oh, quite,' he said, turning all his youthful charm on
her. 'Now, if I had had you for a tutor instead of those
dry-as-dust old men, why, I might even have made
Senior Wrangler instead of being such an idle dunce.
Rome and Greece were quite mixed in my mind, but
you have made it all plain.'

Ass! thought James furiously. You haven't got a mind if you don't know, or have forgotten, that only mathematicians, not classicists, can be Senior Wrangler. Aloud he remarked in his coldest voice, 'Then it's a pity, Frank, that you didn't make up your mind earlier to use it a little at Cambridge, and save your poor father and mother a great deal of grief.'

'Oh,' said Frank mournfully. 'You have the right of it, Uncle. But then, I wasn't like you when you were a young man. I didn't feel inclined to devote my days to study and please my masters. Perhaps age will bring me wisdom, seeing that I lacked it a little in youth.' And he smiled engagingly at Cressy. 'Further instruction from such a charming tutor while I am here will surely bring me up to scratch!'

So, thought James, now internally white-hot with rage, I am an old man who was dry-as-dust in youth, and Frank intends to repair the neglect of years in the next few weeks! I doubt if studying in here with Cressy is all that he intends to do with her.

'Well,' he said icily, trying to keep his voice calm, 'I am sure that we shall all be charmed to learn that you intend to turn over a new leaf. I must point out, however, that my library is not the place to introduce bears or monkeys should you become bored with your studies again.'

Cressy looked up, her face alight with interest. Frank, introduce monkeys and bears to the library? Whatever could her guardian mean by such a statement? 'Why should Frank bring such animals here?' she enquired politely.

Before his uncle could answer, Frank said ingenuously, 'Oh, Lady Cressida, I am ashamed to say that when I was young and foolish and became tired of trying to keep up with my lessons, I was stupid enough to attempt to enliven them by introducing some livestock to the fellows who were teaching me. Of course, I shouldn't do anything like that now, and I'm sure that *you* won't bore me. Quite the contrary.'

'So it is to be hoped.' James was stiffer than ever. Whatever could be the matter with him? He had always quite liked Frank, despite his silliness. He was in agreement with his sister's belief that there was no harm in Frank. Foolishness, yes, but malice, no.

Cressy was also wondering whatever was the matter with James. Her guardian's amber eyes had an expression in them which she had never seen before, and she could almost feel the waves of anger coming from him. What could he be so cross about? Surely he was pleased with the manner in which she was entertaining Frank? She had been so careful to say nothing to which he could take exception, so perhaps it was Frank who was upsetting him. But it was James who had introduced monkeys and bears into the conversaion, not Frank.

What Cressy did not ask herself was why she was so aware of her guardian's feelings, so much so that she could almost feel the self-control which he was exerting to be polite to poor Frank. He wheeled away abruptly and said tersely to Dr Soames, who had been a somewhat puzzled witness to the little scene, since even he had noticed that m'lord was quite unlike himself, 'Dr Soames, I wonder if you would be good enough to track down for me that Board of Agriculture report which I was reading recently. I wish Lenthall to study it before he attends the Duke of Bedford's show this summer.'

'Certainly, m'lord.' Dr Soames busied himself with turning over a pile of solander boxes in one of which the report had been filed.

Covertly James watched Frank and Cressy. They were now laughing together. Not much instruction going on there, he thought nastily, unless it was Frank instructing Cressy in how to flirt. Yes, that was it, for Frank had now taken Cressy by the arm and was leading her out of the library.

Oh, be damned to that! Who knew what the young pup might get up to with her once he had her on his own? He had no business to be leading her off with no duenna, no kind aunt or protectress in sight — and she so young and innocent, for all her theoretical knowledge of life. It was his duty to protect her.

With a muttered oath, James ignored the Report which Dr Soames had found and was proffering to him, and strode out of the room after the misbehaving pair.

'Frank!' he almost shouted in a parade-ground voice which had Frank turning to stare at him and Cressy looking frightened. She had seen and heard her guardian annoyed several times, but he had never once used a voice like that before her.

James cursed himself as he saw her reaction to his anger and immediately moderated his tone. 'Frank,' he repeated more gently. 'I particularly wished to speak to you.' What about? he thought wildly. I never really wish to speak to Frank about anything and, God knows, this evening I wish to talk to him less than ever.

Inspiration struck. He said, 'I understand that you recently spent some time at Westerley Park with the Openshaws. They have recently improved their estate and I wondered whether you had had any discussion with them on the matter. I was thinking of developing the north fields beyond the present park boundary. You might like to come to my study to inform me of anything you have learned. We can ring for Lady Cressy's companion to accompany her to the garden, where I believe my sisters are enjoying the evening air.'

Frank looked a little bemused. Yes, he had been at the Openshaws', and both Gilly Openshaw and his father had ranted on at boring length about what had been done at Westerley. With luck, he might remember a little of it, but he wondered why his uncle should want to talk about it with him when he could afford to engage experts. He was not such a fool that he was unaware that James did not have much respect for his intellect. But he was an obliging young man and obediently led Cressy to the study and, rather wistfully, watched her disappear with her duenna, for that was what Miss Sykes obviously was.

And James, having parted the young people, thus nullifying his hopes before Frank's arrival that they would come together, and perhaps marry, was condemned to the teeth-drawing conversation which prising any solid informaion about estate improvement from Frank would inevitably prove to be.

'M'lady?' Cressy was being dressed by Mason, the lady's maid who had been found for her. She didn't like calling her Mason, it seemed very short and impolite, but Mason had refused to be called Kitty. 'Wouldn't be proper, m'lady', so Mason it had to be.

'Yes?' said Cressida, as her maid turned her about in order to fasten the big bright yellow satin bow which

went with her cream muslin day dress. 'What is it,
Mason?'

'Sam, the footman, he's my brother, m'lady. He said
that when you were abroad you spent your time with
your Pa digging up things.' She hesitated. You never
knew quite where you were with the gentry, perhaps
Lady C might think her forward, but she had never
been stand-offish like some, so she ploughed on.

'Sam says that some of those pretty little statues in
the drawing-room are what you and your Pa dug up
abroad and sent to the old lord. Sam says that he
thought that you might like to know that he and Pa
found some like them when they were ploughing
Plover's meadow. Pa's a farmer, you see, and Ma liked
them and put them on our mantelpiece; imitating the
gentry, she was. And they dug down and found some
funny old ruins, and Pa ploughed round them after
that. Sam wondered if you would like to see them.
Stephen, our brother — he's your groom — could take
you there.'

Cressy suddenly became even more keenly aware
that the servants around her not only had lives of their
own, but minds as well. And what was even more
interesting was that Sam must have taken an interest in
the treasures of the house in which he worked, and that
he had drawn a connection between what he and his Pa
had unearthed and the little objects which she and
Robert had sent from Herculaneum.

'A Roman villa,' she breathed. 'Oh, Mason, suppose
it were! What a find.'

'Roman,' said Mason doubtfully. 'And who might
they be, m'lady?'

'People from Rome in Italy who lived here many

hundreds of years ago,' replied Cressy, ever willing to instruct. Oh, suppose it were true. She might become as famous as Robert if she were able to unearth a real treasure on her own.

And then reality struck. For sure, her guardian would never allow her to grub among old stones in a Wiltshire field. It wouldn't fit anyone's idea of what was ladylike, least of all his.

She looked at Mason, whose rosy face wore an anxious expression. She was doubtless worrying whether she had said something impertinent.

'Oh, I do thank you for telling me of this, Mason. Now, tell Sam to say nothing to anyone else, least of all to my guardian. And yes, Stephen shall take me there, but he is not to talk about that, either. You do understand.'

'Oh, yes, m'lady,' said Mason fervently. Like all servants, she knew more about her masters than they thought, and all the servants knew that Lord Lyndale, and everyone else for that matter, disapproved of Lady Cressy's life in Italy where she had grubbed up pretty objects from the earth. Why they should was a mystery, it seemed no more strange than many other things the lords of their world did, but there it was.

'Good.' Cressy gave Mason the dazzling smile which quite transformed her face. Mason thought that m'lady was changing from the rather thin, plain girl who had arrived from Italy—perhaps all that grubbing up had worn her out—and was becoming quite pretty. Her clothes were having to be altered, too, because she was growing a bosom and hips. Perhaps it was good English food which was doing the trick; everyone knew that foreign food was disgusting.

Cressy galloped downstairs, forgetting her resolution to behave herself and glide about gracefully *à la* Ladies Emily and Verena, and it was just her luck, she thought bitterly, that her guardian was at the bottom, dressed *à point*, not in his country clothing, and who raised a languid quizzing glass to stare at her as she slowed down on seeing him.

'Forgetting ourselves today, are we?' he enquired coolly.

'We?' said Cressy, looking about her. 'I thought that I was alone.'

'Come now,' James dropped the glass. 'You know perfectly of what I speak. Practice makes perfect, Lady Cressida, in etiquette as well as in life.'

He spoke more like a book of maxims every day. How could he be so handsome, so much what you might expect a man to look like, and yet talk like a prosy old dowager? He was bloodless, quite bloodless, thought Cressy savagely.

Aloud she said, 'I think that you have forgotten what it is like to be young, sir.' There, that should settle him.

It did. Told twice in two days that he was an old man, once by Frank and now by his ward, had an extraordinary effect on James. Damn it all, he was not yet quite thirty-seven; he had not fallen into his dotage. And his body knew that he was not in his dotage. He thought that he had subdued it, made it behave itself, that he was its master, but a pair of bright eyes and a figure which while not perfect was good were beginning to undo him.

By all that was holy, how could this impertinent plainish chit have such an effect on him? He had woken in the night for the first time in months, nay years, to find himslf in the grip of desire. His dreams had been confused. There had been a veiled woman in them, and he had chased her down corridors and into a garden like the one at Haven's End, and there, beneath a statue of Diana, he had caught her and borne her to the ground.

And as he had readied himself to take her, he had woken up, panting, in such a state as he had not been since he had been a boy, finding out for the first time the urgent demands his body could make. The woman had been faceless, until the last minute, when he had pulled away the veil, and there, beneath him, was Cressy. The shock of it had woken him, he was sure.

It must be having her near him, that was all. Any woman would surely do. But, if so, why had temptation never struck before? He had not been such a hermit these last five years that he had not been in company with women far more desirable than Silchester's impossible daughter without working himself into such a lather. Yes, it must be propinquity. . .it could be nothing else.

'Sir?' he heard Cressy saying anxiously. 'Sir?'

James came to himself with a start. He realised that he had been standing for a few moments, silent.

He recovered himself quickly. 'I was expected to behave myself when I was young. I see little sign, my ward, that you are trying to please either myself or Miss Sykes,' and in his annoyance with himself, and with Fate which had destroyed the happy privacy in which he had been living, he knew that he was being unfair to her.

'Oh,' wailed Cressy, 'and I have been trying so hard to be good. You know I have. And people's idea of

how a girl should behave is so different from what
Robert expected of me that you can have *no idea* of
how difficult it is for me. Oh, it is too bad.' And she
felt a strange desire to cry over his displeasure. What
was it about him and Haven's End that was causing
this? She had never cried when she had lived with
Robert, and despised those girls who turned on the
waterworks at the slightest provocation.

James saw the trembling lower lip and cursed himself.
He found that he had the most extraordinary desire to
stroke the soft pink cheek, to kiss the tender lips, to
murmur into her small ear, There, there, do not be
distressed, I did not mean to be harsh to you. Pray do
not cry, I beg of you.

Instead he said, as coldly as he could, for by God he
must do something to stifle these unruly thoughts, 'That
may be so but, nevertheless, you are a young woman
and should behave as a young woman ought,' which
was a damn'd old-maidish speech, he knew, but would
have to serve. 'And now let us go into breakfast. I
believe that we were both on our way there. No more
sermons, eh?' And he offered her a frozen smile which
was all he dared muster.

No more sermons, indeed! Why, they never stopped,
and Cressy fumed all the way into breakfast. Only
Frank, up unaccountably early, as both his Mama and
his uncle commented, was able to restore her spirits by
his cheerful nonsense.

'And what's to do today?' he asked cheerfully, looking about him as he brought his laden plate to table. 'I
thought a ride this morning would blow the cobwebs
away. Do you ride, Lady Cressy?'

'Oh, yes,' she replied eagerly, aware that James was

looking suspiciously at them. 'Rob. . .my father and I always rode every day. The best of exercise, he always said, after walking.'

'Splendid,' said Frank, his mouth full of cold roast beef. 'Then we shall ride together this morning. I shall show you all my favourite places here and you shall tell me when we return all about the Greeks and Romans. A fair exchange, eh?'

Cressy's response to Frank's offer was all the warmer because she was aware that for some reason her guardian was not best pleased by it. Well, pooh to that. And when he said, glacially, 'I shall not be able to accompany you. It is my morning with Lenthall and I must not put him off,' she felt a small pang at the thought of his absence, which surprised her more than a little.

'Oh, that's no matter,' said Frank carelessly, buttering himself another roll. 'I shall be able to do the pretty without you, Uncle.' And he gave a half-wink at Cressy.

She had never met anyone like Frank before. She had, as James had thought, lived in a world of old gentlemen, and young men had not been part of her life. She did not quite know what to make of him. She spooned jam on to her own roll and tried to avoid James's eye. The tiger was feeling cross again this morning, and why? she asked herself. He surely could not mind her riding out with Frank and the two grooms, for the rest of the party who were up declined the exercise.

'Oh, by the by,' announced Frank insouciantly, throwing down his napkin as he rose. 'I hope you don't mind, Uncle, but I have asked an old friend to come and stay here. You have enough bedrooms to quarter an army, and although he was once in the army he's out of it now, so won't be bringing his regiment along to overtax you.' And he laughed heartily at his own joke.

James looked up from his breakfast, which was neither as frugal as Cressy's nor as large as Frank's. Cressy wished that she could despise him for being a glutton, but he wasn't that, she had discovered.

'It all depends on whom you have asked, whether I am pleased at the news.'

Frank make a face. 'It's Barrett Dumaine,' he replied. 'I met him at Brighton last year and we get along famously. I know you'll like him.'

'I can't say that I have ever heard of him.' James was thoughtful. He was not sure that any friend of Frank's would be quite the sort of person whom he wished to be introduced to Cressy, but love for his sister and a certain exasperated affection for Frank kept him quiet, until Frank remarked cheerfully, 'Oh, I don't suppose you do know him, Uncle. He came upon the town long after your day was over.'

Cressy knew even before Frank had finished speaking what effect such a tactless offering about his age would have on James, who seemed to be feeling his years since Frank had arrived. Her guardian rose to his feet, threw down his napkin, and snorted at Frank, 'I am not quite decrepit yet, Frank, even though you choose to think so. I have never come across the name Dumaine in all my long years in Society and out of it.'

'Oh, he's from Jersey — some old family there. Was with the Light Bobs in the war. Sold out after Waterloo.'

James stopped at the door. 'Since you have already invited him, asking me for permission for him to come here is a little after the fact. I will tell March that we are expecting another visitor.'

'What's with him these days?' Frank asked his mother once James had left, surprise written on his open face. 'He bites my head off every time he looks at me. I thought you said that he was most particular that I should come with you on this visit. He don't behave like it.'

'You are not,' replied his fond Mama, 'perhaps quite as respectful to him as you ought to be, although I must admit that Lyndale has never before stood on such ceremony with you.'

'Not like the old fellow at all,' agreed Frank, compounding his offence, although fortunately James was not in the room to hear him. 'Pity Luke ain't here yet; he always knows how to get round uncle. Luke's my uncle's other ward,' he informed Cressy. 'Probably thinks two wards one too many, eh? Never say die, though? Ready to ride out as soon as breakfast has gone down?'

Cressy could hardly contain her pleasure at the invitation. It was not so much that she particularly wished to ride with Frank, but that she might be able to persuade him to take her to the ruins of which Mason had spoken.

'Oh, yes,' she responded eagerly, so eagerly that Frank rose to make for the stables to tell them that he and Lady Cressy Mortimer would be off within the hour and to have the horses and grooms ready for them.

Later she skipped out in her new riding habit, Miss Sykes trailing behind, reminding her that she must behave like a lady and not a hoyden, particularly since neither of James's two sisters wished to accompany them, so that she would be without a lady to advise her.

'Oh, goodness,' exclaimed Cressy, giving Frank a dazzling smile, which made his heart lurch. 'Oh, goodness, there will be two grooms and four horses with me. Difficult for me to do anything really untoward, I would have thought. Do tell me what I might be doing—so that I may avoid it.'

There was no talking to the child, she had a tongue which could cut steel when she felt like it. Miss Sykes grew even more mournful at the sight of Cressy being friendly and cheerful with Frank and one of the two grooms, and would have been even more mournful if she could have heard what she was saying.

'Oh, Mr Belsize. . .'

'Frank—do call me Frank,' interjected that young man eagerly.

'Frank, then,' responded Cressy, using her eyes on him with devastating effect, although she was unaware of what she was doing, sexual artifice not being yet her line. 'Frank, before I ask a favour of you over this afternoon's ride, pray what did you mean by my guardian's other ward? No one has said anything about him to me.'

'Oh, he's a distant cousin, both parents dead. Great fellow, Luke, about your age. Strange my uncle didn't tell you of him. He's at Cambridge—not like me, the professors all love him. He don't take dancing bears into college. You'll meet him when he comes down this summer.'

Well, that explained Luke. Now all that remained was to suborn Frank. No great task, that, thought

Cressy cheerfully. It was plain that, pleasant though Frank was to be with, he was not the shrewdest of young men. She began her campaign immediately.

'I must tell you that Stephen here,' and now the groom got the benefit of her eyes, 'knows of a field not far from Haven's End, where his sister, my maid, says that they have dug up the most interesting little statues. I hope you may agree that we should ride there. If you are truly interested in furthering your knowledge of the classical past, it will be the most valuable experience for you.'

Frank Belsize, who had never thought to find himself agreeing enthusiastically to such an unlikely suggestion, replied with great vigour, 'Oh, if that is so, yes. Nothing like a ride having a purpose, I always say. Lead on, Stephen, or whatever your name is. It's not too far away, I hope; mustn't tire Lady Cressy.'

'Mason, sir,' replied Stephen quietly. He knew his place even if Lady Cressy didn't appear to. 'And no, sir, it's not far. I should be happy to take you and Lady Cressida there.'

'And I should like to see the little statues your sister says that you found,' offered Cressy eagerly, before Stephen gave her a lift into the saddle and they all rode off, Stephen having agreed that Lady Cressy should see the statues which graced the farmhouse's mantelpiece.

James, trapped in his study, watched them from the window. He could see Cressy, respectably dressed for once in her deep blue habit, a little bicorne hat on top of her dark chestnut curls, giving her a rakish, almost naval look when coupled with the brass buttons on her habit's front and up her sleeves. That idiot Frank was as well turned out as usual—which was perhaps the most you could say for him, the rest of him, including his mind, being so splendidly null.

Did he really wish to marry off such a bright spirit as Cressy to such a dunce? The idea of the marriage which he had thought up so enthusiastically before Cressy arrived seemed the most horrible mistake, now that he had met her and seen her with Frank. Whatever could he have been thinking of? She needed somebody older and steadier to guide her, to encourage her to use her good mind in a manner which would not cause offence, to initiate her gently into marriage. . .

James came to a full stop. Dreadfully, his thoughts were leading in a direction which, however much it pleased his poor starved body, troubled his intellect and his sense of honour. He looked up, saw himself in a small oval mirror, and recognised his own harsh sternness of face and body compared with Frank's softer — admit it, man! — more youthful looks. Naturally a young girl would be attracted to someone nearer to her own age, even if her conversation with him would smack of the nursery compared to that to which she was so obviously used — and which an older, more seasoned man could supply her with. . .

And what about Barrett Dumaine? Who the devil was he? He would write at once to his cousin, William Lamb, for information about him. The mere idea of some idiotic crony of Frank's — or some toady of his; he was sure that Frank would attract toadies — paying court to such an innocent child was anathema to him. He would urge both Verena and Miss Sykes to keep their eyes fimly on her lest she come to harm. A guardian had his duties to his ward and he intended to perform his to the best of his ability.

The subject of his thoughts had arrived with Frank and the two grooms at the field which Farmer Mason had ploughed, only to uncover the remains of something which had been hidden for centuries. He had left that part of the field fallow the year after the discovery and simple curiosity had led him to grub away at the ruins.

It was immediately apparent to Cressy that something remarkable lay in the soil of the Wiltshire countryside. She gave an interested exclamation as she slid off her horse, not waiting for Frank or Stephen to help her to dismount.

Neither did she wait for them to accompany her while she scampered, as quickly as her habit would allow, down into the hollow already created by the amateur efforts of Farmer Mason and his sons.

She plumped down on to her knees, pulled off her gloves and began to examine what had been revealed, pushing away the soil, careless of what such an act might do to her hands. Face aglow, she looked up at Stephen and Frank who had followed her, Frank looking dubiously at the ravaged field. There appeared to be very little to see, except pieces of dirty broken stone and soil thrown up in heaps.

His dubious look even extended to Cressy. 'I thought. . .' he began.

Cressy was not so naïve that she did not know what Frank was thinking. She rose, dusting down her hands. 'You thought,' she said shrewdly, 'that you were going to see a proper Roman villa, with marble columns, even if broken down, and a red roof! No, this is, by all appearances, only the floor of the villa; everything else has gone long ago. I wouldn't be surprised if some of the stone and marble is now in the walls of the houses roundabout, perhaps even in Haven's End. That happened in Italy, you know. But there are sure to be lots of exciting pieces left in the ground.'

'So, what do we do?' asked Frank, a trifle glumly. 'Dig them up?'

Cressy considered. 'I would like to. But you know that Lord Lyndale would never let me. Why,' she asked Stephen who was standing by, looking after their horses, 'why did your father not tell Lord Lyndale he had found this?'

'Didn't want to lose the whole field,' replied Stephen bluntly, but Lady Cressy seemed to be able to extract truth from those around her, and he would have spoken to none other of *them* after such a fashion. 'Begging your pardon, m'lady, but our Kitty had no right telling you of this, but now she has done. . .' And he shrugged his shoulders.

Cressy considered again. 'Well,' she said thoughtfully, 'seeing that your father would not be happy for Lord Lyndale to be aware of his discovery, and from all that my guardian has said to me, he would cetainly not allow me to excavate this site, then let it be our secret.'

'Oh, yes,' said Frank, a trifle relieved that nothing further seemed to be required of them, other than to dutifully admire a damaged field and retire.

'But,' began Cressy, 'your father didn't just plough it in when he found it. I collect that this part of his farm wasn't cultivated until the land was needed during the late wars, so he must have been a little intrigued by what he had found. Would he mind, do you think, if we began to dig up what is left? We needn't tell Lord

Lyndale,' she added. 'He will just think that we are out riding.'

'Well, my Mama or Aunt Verena would be bound to tell him if they came with us,' Frank offered.

'Oh, when they do, we won't ride this way.' Cressy had discovered in herself an aptitude for innocent deceit when dealing with Italian peasants and the workers on Robert's sites. It seemed to be coming in useful in Wiltshire, too. 'Of course,' she said to Stephen, 'we should have to ask your father's permission when you take us to see his finds.'

She continued enthusiastically, 'I'm sure that he would be delighted if we found something truly remarkable. And think of what it would mean to discover how people lived in Wiltshire so long ago.'

Frank was more interested in people who lived in Wiltshire in 1818, particularly one girl who seemed to become prettier every time you looked at her. What really made him agree to Cressy's wishes was the thought of putting one over on his uncle, who seemed stiffer than ever, if not positively unkind, on this visit.

And so it was decided after they had all drunk tea in Farmer Mason's best parlour and admired the new pianoforte which he had bought for the daughters still at home to learn to play on. Seeing the two statuettes and the small blue glass bottle which the Masons had already unearthed made Cressy more determined than ever to develop the site. Farmer Mason needed little persuasion to keep the proposed work secret. Allowing Cressy, Frank and Stephen, as well as his two younger sons and one or two of the farmworkers—when he could spare them—to play about on the field occasionally meant that he needn't have hordes of foreigners from outside the county invading his farm. Besides, deceiving his lordship rather appealed to him than not.

'After all,' Cressy told him earnestly, just before they all rode back to Haven's End, 'think how pleased Lord Lyndale will be if we unearth a real treasure.'

What she didn't say aloud was how wonderful it would be to put one over on her guardian, although it was not in those indelicate terms she thought of what she was doing. Rather, she thought along the lines of, It's all he deserves for being so harsh with me, and being so critical of poor dead Robert. Riding home, she felt truly happy for the first time since she had arrived in England.

CHAPTER FOUR

'OH, LOOK!' Frank exclaimed to Cressy. 'I do believe that my friend, Barrett Dumaine, has arrived already.'

They were riding along the drive and could see the evidence of a visitor before the entrance. A small chaise, a groom leading two horses, a curricle with a tiger up and driving and a tall man were standing before the bowing butler and a group of footmen. Before Frank and Cressy arrived at the entrance, the party had dispersed, the man had been ushered into the house and the chaise and curricle were being driven to the stables to be unpacked.

'He was Captain Dumaine when he was in the Army,' explained Frank. 'Uncle was a bit put out that I had invited him—never minded me having a friend here before.' He forgot to tell Cressy that previous friends had been school or college fellows of his, all from families well known to his uncle.

Really, thought Cressy, mounting the main stairway to her room, my guardian is a complete stick of a man, for all his good looks. First he's unkind to Frank, and now he objects to his friends. She found Frank a jolly companion of a kind which she had never met before and was prepared to be charmed by his friend.

It was perhaps unfortunate that she met James at the top of the stairs. He had had a hard day, not eased by the knowledge that Cressy was jaunting about the countryside with Frank.

'You have enjoyed yourself, madam?' he enquired glacially, the amber eyes not warm at all today, Cressy noticed with a sigh.

'Indeed,' Cressy replied. 'Most invigorating. I see that we have a visitor. That will make life here a little livelier,' she ended. She knew that she was being provoking, but for some reason could not help herself. She dearly wanted James to unbend, to show her the man behind the stern mask, and perhaps annoying him would do that, if being compliant didn't serve.

'Oh, indeed,' replied James, stiffer than ever, far from unbending. 'Any friend of Frank's is sure to please those for whom pleasure consists of one long round of empty entertainment.'

If Cressy had had any doubts about the propriety of concealing the dig from him they flew away on an instant. Let him try calling *that* empty entertainment when he finally saw what they had done between them. Perhaps Captain Dumaine could be persuaded to help them.

'Exactly how do you wish me to behave, sir?' she enquired sweetly. 'First you reprimand me for behaving as seriously as a young man might, and now, it appears that I am to be condemned for enjoying the life of idle pleasure which seems to be a young woman's lot. It would assist me greatly if you chose to write out for me a list of those actions of which you would approve. So far you have confined yourself to informing me of those which you do not!'

This piece of gross impertinence, to her surprise, brought about the unbending for which she had wished. It did not answer the question, which was, Why did she so ardently wish him to unbend?

'My dear,' said James, and to her further astonishment he took her hand, grubby from the examination of the ruin, and kissed it. 'I sometimes think, against my will, that you are a nonpareil. What kind of nonpareil I hesitate to decide. Were you the boy you so obviously wish you were, I would advise the law as your destination. Such an ability to dissect and nitpick — if you will forgive the word — would ensure you the most rapid promotion. No, I will not write out a list for you, you impertinent baggage, and you will cease from roasting me on every occasion on which we meet. In return for that, I will try to be a little more patient wih you.'

'And cease to be so cross with Frank all the time,' responded Cressy daringly, pushing her luck.

'Oh, my dear, you may wish to be a boy, but you are all woman,' riposted her guardian. 'Give you an inch and you take an ell. On second thoughts, you may take a woman's reward,' and, unable to restrain himself at the sight of such charming animation as she presented, he leaned forward and kissed her rosy cheek. He would have liked to bestow the kiss on her smiling lips, but restrained himself at the last moment.

Again, as he touched her, that strange *frisson* of delight shot through Cressy. And it was all the more extraordinary, she thought later, that she should experience such a sensation, for when Frank had handed her down after their ride his touch had had no such effect. So it wasn't simply a man touching her that caused such an odd thing to happen, since it only occurred with *him*. What could it mean?

And the kiss! The effect of that was even odder. For Cressy wanted most fervently to kiss him back. And because he had lifted his head again and he was so tall that she couldn't easily kiss his cheek even if she stood on tiptoe, she took his hand and kissed the back of that instead. Which had a dreadful effect on the pair of them. They looked at one another and drowned in each other's eyes.

'No,' exclaimed James in a stifled voice, snatching his hand away as though a snake had bitten it. What could he be thinking of? And the poor child in her artlessness had responded as though she had been kissed in the nursery—giving him such a light peck in fair exchange. She could have no idea of what she had done to him. No idea at all.

Cressy was far too interested in wondering what the kiss had done to *her* to consider what it might have done to her guardian. And the look which they had exchanged, why should that have made her shiver and given her a feeling of such yearning, the kind of feeling which she had sometimes experienced when she had looked at something very beautiful or heard something moving? Strange what effect a pair of amber eyes could have on her.

She shook her head and willed away the odd tremblings which had followed their encounter. 'Excuse me, sir, I must go and change for dinner,' she announced, astonished to find that her voice had lost its usual cheerfully robust tones and had come out like a little girl's quaver.

James, usually percipient where women were concerned, quite misread Cressy's tremblings and her change of voice. There, he had frightened her! What a brute he was. First he bullied the dear little thing because she had been brought up so strangely by her eccentric father — which was no fault of hers — and then he virtually assaulted her.

He watched Cressy gallop away, both hands clenched by his sides, willing himself not to follow her. How in the world had it happened? In a few short weeks she had turned from an unwanted encumbrance into a woman whom he apparently only had to see to desire. He shied away from the tenderness he felt towards her and tried to persuade himself that only the effects of continence and propinquity lay behind his feelings. . . Meantime there was this unwanted visitor whom he must see. Another young upstart near to her own age for Cressy to look at as she looked at Frank.

Barrett Dumaine's manners were excellent. He was as polished a fine gentleman as you could hope to find, and now you could find him at Haven's End, thought James sourly after dinner was over. He had seen Cressy's eyes widen a little when she had been introduced to him while they were waiting for dinner to be served.

Cressy, indeed, was in a strange state of confusion. The cool, objective and intellectual world in which she had lived with Robert had disappeared, and she had been shot into one where all the guidelines by which she had lived had disappeared.

Dressed in one of her new gowns, peach-coloured silk, quite close-fitting, with a fine amber net overdress floating above it, a silk flower in her hair, she entered the drawing-room to find Frank's friend there, and the sight of him was another shock. He was as tall as James, in his late twenties, and was as handsome as one of the

statues which she had left behind in Italy. Not
Antinous, perhaps, but Narcissus.

His look for her, as they were introduced by an
enthusiastic Frank, was admiring.

'Now, old fellow,' Frank had said to his friend earlier,
'you are not to cut me out, mind. But she's a little
jewel. Not much to look at, at first, but she grows on
you. And clever.'

Barrett Dumaine looked sideways at Frank. 'Didn't
think you liked 'em clever,' he offered. 'Got the distinct
impression you liked the other sort.'

'This one's different,' said the besotted Frank, wondering for the first time whether it had been a good idea
to ask Barrett here. His reputation with women was a
formidable one, but Cressy was not the kind of girl his
friend usually made a dead set at. He forgot, being rich
himself, that as a titled heiress Cressy was certain to be
Dumaine's target even if she had been as ugly as the
pig-faced woman whom they had once seen at a fair —
and Cressy was far from being that.

'Lady Cressida,' Barrett said, 'most honoured to
make your acquaintance,' and he took her hand and
kissed it. Interesting, thought Cressy, I quite liked that,
but I didn't feel at all as I did when James touches or
kisses me. It was the first time that she had called him
James in her mind. Before he had always been *he*, or
my guardian.

Aloud she said, 'Most happy to meet you, Captain
Dumaine,' remembering that Frank had called him
that.

'Oh, no,' he replied, still holding her hand, with
James behind him thinking furiously, Puppy, the
damned puppy, as he did so. 'Not Captain, I beg of

you. I sold out after Waterloo; my soldiering days are over.'

'Mr Dumaine, then,' replied Cressy, who was rapidly learning the arts of polite conversation. 'Have you been in this part of the country before?' How easy it was to talk nothings. Did men really want women to talk nothings? She supposed that they did.

'No, Lady Cressida, this territory is all new to me. I propose to reconnoitre it as soon as possible. Dare I hope that you will be my guide when I first ride out in it?'

Cressy prepared to give him an eager yes. He seemed such a charming young man, a Frank with more brains, perhaps. Now, how did she know that? Before she could do so, James intervened as politely and coolly as he could. He did not like the way in which Dumaine was eyeing Cressy. His instincts told him that Barrett Dumaine was too good to be true, something not quite right there. Why should a man of such obvious experience trouble with the likes of Frank, unless it was for what he could get out of him?

'I shall be happy to ride out with you myself, Dumaine,' he said, his voice pitched mid-way between interest and boredom, but the expression on his face gave him away to his ward, who had already learned to read his smallest change of mood.

What is he cross about now? Is it something I have done? Surely not? And he cannot know about the site, she thought guiltily.

After dinner, Captain Dumaine, for everyone called him that despite his graceful objections, was even more charming. He was now bending over Verena, discussing Kean with her, comparing his acting with Kemble's.

Verena considered that Kean had more fire than
Kemble, but thought that there was something vulgar
about Kean, too showy by half.

Dumaine managed to disagree with her without in
any way disturbing the happy relationship which
seemed to be springing up between them. He was
equally agreeable when Frank suggested a game of
Speculation, involving Dumaine, himself, Cressy and
Verena. Fred Davenport had gone to sleep and Lady
Emily excused herself on the grounds that she must
finish the piece of canvas-work on which she was
engaged — she had been finishing it, she announced, for
nearly two years now, and this must really be the end.

Cressy had never played Speculation — nor any other
harmless game for that matter — so Frank proposed to
teach her, but was immediately cut out by his friend.

'Come, Frank, you must allow me to instruct the
Lady,' said Dumaine, giving Cressy his friendly smile.
James, who was supposed to be reading *The Times*, but
was watching the young people instead, had the dubious
pleasure of seeing Cressy's happy face turned trustingly
towards Dumaine — James refused to call him
Captain — having reached the kind of rapprochement
with him, in about fifteen minutes of the clock, which
James had not achieved with her in several weeks.

But then, Barrett Dumaine was not her guardian
who was required to see that she behaved with propriety at all times — he was more likely to be instructing
her to forget about propriety, given half a chance.

In a pause in the game, Barrett Dumaine murmured
to Cressy, turning his fine blue eyes on her just as she
was speculating whether she preferred them to amber

ones, and said, 'I believe that you said earlier that you ride, Lady Cressida?'

'Oh, yes,' replied Cressy eagerly. 'Every day, if the weather is suitable.'

'Excellent,' he replied. 'There is no better exercise, as I am sure you will agree. You will ride with me tomorrow?'

'Now, Dumaine,' said Frank, breaking into the conversation. He could see that his friend was, as usual, going to make off with the lady, but not if he could prevent it. 'I can't have you monopolising Lady Cressy.'

'Lady Cressy.' Dumaine's beautiful voice made the words sound like something from an Italian opera. 'Oh, I like that better than stately Cressida. You will allow me the pleasure of calling you Lady Cressy, I hope,' and his eyes stroked her as well as his voice.

Against her will almost, Cressy found herself responding. He was charming after a fashion which she had never met before. 'Of course I will allow,' she said gaily, her expression giving Barrett Dumaine exactly the message which he wanted to receive fom her.

'Excellent,' he said again. 'Then Lady Cressy it shall be, for now and evermore.'

'Look here, Dumaine,' began Frank, a trifle crossly, 'you never let me finish. I was about to say that if you are riding out tomorrow then we must make a party up, for I should most certainly like to accompany you, and perhaps others may.'

This was not at all to Cressy's liking. If everyone came then there could be no further exploration of the archaeological site and she most desperately wanted to start work on it.

But none of the others, except James, expressed a

wish to accompany them. To his internal annoyance, he could not offer. He was expecting the agent from his northern estates to arrive with his accounts and the matter could not be put off! He was compelled to listen while Cressy, Frank and. . .that upstart puppy made their plans for the morrow.

When the game ended he flung down *The Times*, of which he had hardly read a word, and said to Cressy in a voice which brooked no denial, 'My dear ward, I would like to take a turn with you on the terrace. We have hardly spoken together today, and there are some matters relating to your father's estate and its disposition of which I wish to speak to you.'

'Now?' queried Cressy, a trifle dismayed. For the first time in her short life she was encountering the delights of having two personable young men squabbling over her favours, and she was only too happy to enjoy such a novel experience.

'Now.' James's reply was as dour as he could make it. 'The matter is urgent, and I shall be fully engaged tomorrow.' And he rose, holding out an arm to her in such a fashion that she could not refuse him.

Barrett Dumaine's eyes as he watched the pair of them walk through the glass doors into the garden were speculative in the extreme. He hardly heard Frank's exclamation, 'Poor Cressy. He talks to her as though she were a soldier and he a sergeant-major.' He was too busy wondering what were the true feelings of that haughty swine, James Lyndale, towards his youthful ward.

Cressy expected James to begin to speak once they were out on the terrace. It was a balmy evening with a rising moon. The scents of early summer flowers filled the air. There was a great fall of lilac not far away. Its delicate flowers were black in the moonlight.

She shivered. It was touching James which caused the shivers, she thought wildly. And when he spoke in his coldest voice, she shivered again.

'Madam!' Cressy knew at once that he was cross because he only called her madam when he was cross. 'Madam, I am sure that you will not object if I offer you a few words of wisdom.'

Which meant, of course, that he thought that she *would* object. She decided to annoy him, using the megrims of a fine lady, tossing her head, raising her brows, pursing her mouth, just like Caterina when she was trying to provoke Robert, something she had never done before. 'I thought that we were to discuss matters relating to Robert's estate,' she announced airily.

James could hardly admit that the reason he had given in order to take her on to the terrace was not a true one, merely a ploy to snatch her away from over-importunate young men.

Instead he said, 'We shall come to that in a moment, madam, if you will have a little patience.'

He heard her breathing change. Cressy wrenched her arm away from his and turned to confront him.

'Oh, I do believe that story about Robert's affairs was all a hum! You really meant to bring me out here to ring a peal over me, and I have done nothing. It is you who need a reprimand for deceiving everyone as to your true motive, particularly me. I've a good mind to cut line and go in again, on my own, if need be, and then what will everybody think?'

'Oh, madam, I see that Frank and Dumaine have

been educating you in fashionable slang, if nothing else,' was his only response to that.

'At least they don't tell me fairy-tales to entice me on to the terrace in order to begin to admonish me, and then have the impertinence to ask me to "have a little patience". My patience is beginning to be in short supply, sir.'

James was frosty. 'I find it difficult to believe that you ever had any, except for Greek and Roman artefacts.'

'Of which, sir, you are not one!'

They were in their usual situation, face to face, defying one another. James sighed, and looked away from her. She was temptation itself in the moonlight, Greek fire shooting from her eyes. He said, trying to make his voice kind, but, oh, he knew how dangerous that might be, 'Pray listen a moment. I would advise you to be on your guard against the flatteries of handsome young men. They do not usually have the interests of rich and pretty young women in mind. . .'

'Frank, sir, is rich himself, and your nephew. You are not referring to him, I trust.'

'But Barrett Dumaine. . .'

'And he is Frank's friend, and, by his manner and his general turn-out, is rich himself. Pray, sir, exactly who are these handsome young men whom I am to view with suspicion? I should like to know. Are they to be found inside Haven's End, or outside of it?'

'If you would but listen to me for a moment, and not interrupt me. . .' James began, hardly knowing where his next sentence would take him. Between his feelings for the pretty and witty minx opposite to him, and his sense of propriety, which told him that whatever else he did he must not begin to make love to a ward who was half his age, plus the blind jealousy which overcame him when he saw her with other men, he was almost beside himself.

'Yes, sir—and what after that. . .? I can scarce endure the wait for the potent piece of advice which you are about to offer me.' For James had fallen silent in the middle of his last sentence; and this last offering coming from a face, which if not beautiful, was on fire with passion, undid him. For love was a mixture of attraction and opposition, and when these two came together, it was like fire sparking from two sharply struck stones.

'This,' he found himself saying, all common sense, all prudence gone. Everything he had ever wanted in a woman was concentrated in this vivid and clever child, and he took her in his arms and brought his mouth down on hers—and God damn everything!

If merely touching James had had such a strong effect on Cressy, it was as nothing to being kissed by him. No one, apart from her old nurse, and occasionally Robert, had ever kissed her before. Certainly no young man, or boy, had ever been close enough to take such a liberty with her.

She was drowning in a sensation which had taken over her whole body, a sensation so strong that for a moment the world swung about her, and in an instant, everything had changed. It was as though this passionate kiss was something for which she had been waiting all her life, and its effect on her was so powerful that it frightened her.

Nevertheless her hands went up to meet behind her guardian's head, to hold him nearer to her, and for a moment they were so close that his masculine scent mingled with her feminine one to give her added pleasure, every sense being involved in lovemaking, she was beginning to find. And then her analytic mind, which had not been wholly destroyed by these new sensations, said to her, So, this is why men and women kiss and mate! Robert never properly explained that to me.

The thought was horrific, for it told her what the inevitable end was of what she and James were doing, and also told her that she could not resist him. From the moment they had first met, when he had looked at her, disapproval and dismay riding on his face, she had been attracted to him. Worse, on every occasion on which they had met, she had sparked at him and defied him to protect herself from that knowledge. Because she felt for him as she did, Frank and Barrett Dumaine were pale shadows of men compared to him.

She dropped her hands, and gave a low despairing wail, for this must stop, or she would be lost. Venus, the goddess of love, had placed her finger on Cressy's lips and marked her for her own, but she must resist her. For James might desire her, but he could not love such a young and raw thing as herself, whom he so constantly reproached. Robert had tried to tell her of the difference between lust and love, but until she herself had loved, she could not understand that difference. And now she did.

James, coming to his senses, immediately let her go for very shame. He had not been so thoroughly roused for years, and only the sense of honour which had supported him through good times and bad prevented him from continuing to make love to her. He knew,

beyond a doubt, from the evidence of her first passionate response to his kiss that were he to go on, she
would, after some hesitation, go with him. He also
knew, like Cressy, where that would end, if not tonight,
then at another time, but soon.

Seduction had never been his game, and to seduce
his young and innocent ward, a virgin. . .what a low
villain he would be.

'I am sorry,' he said stiffly, turning away from her,
for he knew that the evidence of his arousal was marked
on his face and body. 'That was a mistake. I had not
intended to do any such thing. My wits must be
wandering.'

Cressy did not know whether she was glad or sorry
that he had stopped.

No, she knew. Sorry! Sorry! Sorry! He had rejected
her. He thought her young and foolish and she was
dreadfully ashamed of her first passionate response.
And to put her arms around his neck and try to pull
him closer! What would he think of her? But he had
rejected her! He had no right. She would show him
how little she cared for a man who had begun what he
did not mean to finish.

The contrary desires which roared through her were
as strong as those which James was suffering, even if
they were different from his.

'Oh,' she exclaimed, and was shocked at the shrill
tones which baffled passion had created. 'No, your wits
were not wandering. No, not at all. You were merely
demonstrating the manner in which young and handsome men might behave towards me, even if you are
neither yourself. Most illuminating.' And she scrubbed
her lips violently. She would not let him know how

passionately she had desired him. 'I suppose that you have been too long without a woman. Robert once explained to me that that was a bad thing for men.'

There, if that did not put him down, nothing would. She saw his face change and for one delightful but shocking moment she thought that he was about to lunge at her and finish what he had begun, here on the terrace, with all his guests but a flimsy glass door away.

Cressy was right. The insults hurled at him by the rosy lips which he had just kissed with such fervour nearly undid James completely.

Oh, damn her, damn her, indeed, even if she had the right of it. She knew how to slip the knife between a man's ribs, and demean his manhood at the same time. What innate qualities which being a daughter of Eve conferred on her had brought her to sexual maturity so quickly? It would serve her right if he gave her the best punishment for such monstrous impudence. He forgot that he had been worrying about her virginity and the difference in age between them in the moments before and after all his restraint had fled.

'Be careful, madam. I must inform you that there are some things which a lady must not say.'

'Madam, madam,' she mocked him fiercely. 'And may I inform *you* that there are some things which a gentleman must not do. Now you may take me in, before your guests begin to think that young and handsome men are not the only creatures that rich and pretty young women ought to be warned against.'

There was nothing, absolutely nothing to be said to that, James confessed glumly to himself, so he put out his arm and added, belatedly, 'We had best speak of your father's estate some other time.'

'With others present,' remarked Cressy nastily, unable to stop herself, 'seeing that that, combined with our isolation, seems to have had such a remarkable effect on you.'

'No, madam, on both of us.' James was equally nasty. 'Seeing that you co-operated most enthusiastically with me at the beginning. But I admit that, being old and ugly, I ought to have set you a good example. I apologise and will try not to let such a thing occur again.'

Oh, I scored a hit, a most palpable hit, was Cressy's inward answer to that. But why did she feel so unhappy that her barb comparing him unfavourably with Frank and Barrett Dumaine had sunk so deeply as to provoke his last comment. And it was a lie. He was neither old nor ugly, simply the most impressive man she had ever met, and when they were not fighting with one another their minds met nearly as closely as their bodies had so recently done.

But when they were indoors they were both so stiffly proper, and James's expression was so dour, that no member of the party could possibly have suspected what had so recently occurred on the terrace. Except for Barrett Dumaine, that was. His experience of life and love was such that he read both Cressy and James correctly, and set himself to working out how he might profit from his knowledge.

CHAPTER FIVE

'YOU learn rapidly, my dear.' Lady Verena Davenport had been instructing Cressy in the art of canvas work, and she had begun working on a study of tulips in a graceful vase which she had drawn on to the canvas, the canvas and wool being supplied by Verena, who had exclaimed over the excellence of her draughtsmanship.

'Oh, Rober. . .my father had me taught by a painter when he discovered that I had a small talent for it,' Cressy had replied modestly. 'I used to draw all the most interesting pieces we unearthed, as well as the scenery around the villa we lived in, just outside Naples. He used to know Sir William Hamilton who was a real connoisseur of the arts.'

She did not add that, to the genuine admiration of both Frank and Barrett Dumaine, she had drawn the small treasures they had discovered in Farmer Mason's field, as well as some of the beauties of the Wiltshire countryside. She had unpacked her colours, brushes and paints from the trunks which had come with her from Naples. So far she had worked only in water-colour. She had been too shy to fetch out her oil-painting equipment, and had done nothing at Haven's End, so that James and his family were unaware of her talent.

Now she coloured, looked shyly at Verena and said, 'I like canvas work, it is so soothing. I don't have time to think and I can forget all the wrong things I seem to do. Proper behaviour seems beyond me.'

Lady Verena put out an impulsive hand to touch Cressy's. 'Oh, my dear, you must not worry overmuch about that. I know that you found life in England difficult at first, but I meant it when I told you that you learn quickly. You have improved since I arrived here. But do not trouble overmuch about checking what you say. You have a delightful spontaneity and you never say anything truly shocking.'

'But I did when I first came here, and Lord Lyndale said. . .' began Cressy, a trifle nervously.

Lady Verena sighed. It was a source of mild distress to her that her brother and his ward were so much at odds. It was not that they spoke to each other coldly, but that these days they rarely seemed to speak together at all. In any case, James seemed to be at his haughtiest with all his guests. He was back to the stifled distress which he had shown when Jane Forster had betrayed him, and she wondered what could be causing *that*. She had thought him recovered.

'You must not heed my brother's manner overmuch, my dear. It is his way. He is cold towards everyone, not merely to yourself. And I have to say that he has reason, so far as women are concerned. His first love had a tragic end, and later, when I thought that he had recovered, he proposed to a false friend of mine who left him at the altar. He was only a younger son then, and she found a richer husband. It is no wonder that he is cold.'

Cold, thought Cressy, attempting to stifle a hysterical giggle which tried to burst to the surface when she heard this. Was he being cold towards me when he kissed me on the terrace? Surely not! And such a kiss! For on reflection Cressy had come to understand that James's kiss had been no ordinary one — although how she knew that was another mystery; she seemed to be surrounded by them. But poor James. She wondered what his first tragic love had been, but delicacy told her not to question Verena.

Not for the first time she wished that her mother had not died so soon after her birth. She could have asked her about some of the problems which were puzzling her. She looked sideways at kind Verena. She knew how much she loved her brother, so she could not ask her what James's contrary behaviour towards her signified.

'Oh, that does explain matters a little,' was all that Cressy could say. 'Has he always been so stern and strict, or did he become so after his misfortunes?'

'It is because he has such high standards,' sighed Verena. 'And, since he lives up to them, it is difficult for us lesser mortals to criticise or defy them.'

The hysterical giggles were threatening to surface again. High standards, indeed. What sort of high standards caused a man to assault his ward was a question which she would have liked to ask but dared not.

She concentrated instead on filling in one of the tulips on her pattern and listening to Verena, who began to talk about the London season and what her come-out would involve.

'My brother thought that perhaps you ought to wait another year before I introduced you to the *ton*, but I have told him that now that I have met you I consider that this year would not be too soon. As I said earlier, you learn very quickly, and so I informed him.'

'And what did he say to that?' asked Cressy, fascinated.

'Oh,' replied Verena doubtfully, 'he didn't say anything, merely growled at me — he really does worry me, you know,' she added sadly. 'I shouldn't be telling you this, but you seem such a sensible grown-up little thing that I can't refrain from saying that I have never seen him, even in his worst days, quite so down in the dumps.'

His worst days! What could they be like if his more recent behaviour was that of his best days? This was being unfair, Cressy knew, because until the scene on the terrace his annoyance had been reserved for her; now it seemed to be caused by everyone. Frank and Barrett Dumaine in particular were the subjects of his greatest displeasure.

The only thing was that lately he had retreated to his own suite of rooms, leaving Verena and Fred Davenport to be his host and hostess at dinner and elsewhere. He had spoken to Cressy at length only once and that was to keep up the fiction that he needed to discuss with her the disposition of Robert's affairs.

Cressy sighed again, so that Verena looked up sharply and remarked, 'What is it, child? Is anything troubling you?'

'No, not at all,' lied Cressy. For, when she had thought about James's withdrawal from Society, she'd realised that she had been unhappy at losing his company. In the month before Frank and Barrett Dumaine had arrived, she had felt that she was coming to better terms with him.

They had played chess together and he had questioned her about Robert's work and had been interested and amused to learn that she had been instructed just like a boy, being taught Greek, Latin and French from an early age by a clergyman who had settled near Herculaneum.

'What, no Hebrew?' he had asked her, raising his eyebrows comically, to have her reply seriously, 'Oh, Rob. . .Father thought that I would have no real need for it, so I was instructed in mathmatics and natural philosophy instead, together with a little of the physical sciences.'

'Only a little?' James had murmured naughtily, fascinated by the play of humour on her grave face as she began to understand that he was roasting her gently.

'Enough is as good as a feast,' she threw at him cheerfully, for she had begun to notice that, stern though he might be with her, he was amused by the way in which she sparked at him. But then, there was nothing to that, for Robert had always wanted her to speak her mind and encouraged originality of thought and speech in those who surrounded him.

'You will be thought as witty as Lady Granville,' he said, 'when you arrive in Society, but only if you repress a tendency towards the outré in your conversation.'

'And she is never outré?'

'Oh, in private, I understand, and in her letters,' said James carelessly, 'but in public she is a model of decorum as befits the wife of a politician and diplomat.'

'I'm not sure that I would wish to marry either a politician or a diplomat if that put too much of a brake on my speech,' offered Cressy thoughtfully, 'and to marry someone who was both at once would tax the behaviour of a saint.'

'Which you are not, my child,' said James rising. It

was one of the first occasions on which they had both begun to grasp how deeply they were becoming attracted to one another, although neither was yet ready to acknowledge that fact.

Oh, I do miss talking to him, thought Cressy sadly, coming back to the present and realising that she had been staring blankly at her canvas work for some minutes.

She glanced surreptitiously at Verena who, being lost in her own thoughts, had not noticed that Cressy had gone astray in hers.

I do believe that being poor Cressy's guardian is throwing him into such a lather, Verena concluded to herself. Such a pity. Why cannot he see what a dear girl she is beneath that odd mixture of learning and naïveté which her father's education has produced in her? When I first came here, I thought her quite plain, but she grows on you in the strangest way.

The dear girl put down her canvas work and exclaimed restlessly, 'I wonder what is keeping Frank and Captain Dumaine so long? They said that they would be back for a ride this afternoon, but,' and she looked at the clock, 'there will not be time now. Oh, it is too bad, I had hoped that today we might. . .' And then she stopped. She had hoped that they would go to the site, for yesterday Stephen had brought her a message that the two labourers working on it had uncovered something which she ought to see.

She had nearly forgotten that Verena must not know what was being done on Farmer Mason's land, and it was fortunate for her that Verena, usually sharp, had failed to notice that she had not finished her sentence.

Cressy put her canvas work carefully away in the bag

which Verena had given her to keep it in so that it should not become soiled. Verena had already been made aware that, unconventional though Cressy was in many ways, she had been taught to be thorough and methodical in all that she did. Like James, in fact, she concluded with some surprise. Remarkable that they don't seem to deal well together.

She watched Cressy walk decorously across the room with some amusement, only to see that decorum disappear as Frank and Captain Dumaine came in, both in high spirits and a little out of breath.

Cressy surveyed them a trifle crossly. 'You promised,' she told them reproachfully, 'that we should go for a ride this afternoon, but the afternoon has gone. You broke your word to me.'

Both men began to speak together, Frank, for once managing to get his oar in first. 'Oh, Cressy, you must forgive us, but we were brought word of a mill over towards Devizes and the opportunity was too good to miss.'

Barrett Dumaine, who had been composing a much more tactful speech in his head, gave a short laugh at the expression on Cressy's face.

'A mill, Frank? Whatever can you mean?'

Captain Dumaine spoke before Frank could plunge them both deeper into the mud.

'A mill is a prizefight, Lady Cressy. I know that you will think it frivolous of us, but we could not miss the opportunity of seeing the Bromley Bear take on the Chelmsford Slasher, and we thought, given that the bout took place this morning, that we should return well in time for us to be your escorts, but, alas, the

roads around Devizes were jammed with every convey-
ance you can imagine. . .'

'Exactly so.' Frank was only too happy to support his
friend's version of what had taken place, and even saw
fit to embroider it a little. 'We were fearful that
Barrett's curricle might be damaged in the crush, so we
were compelled to take matters slowly. I'm sure that
you will forgive us. We have both wanted to see the
Chelmsford Slasher in action.'

'And did he win?' If Cressy's question was offered a
trifle satirically, Frank missed the satire completely, but
Barrett Dumaine did not.

'Of course,' he said smoothly, replying before Frank
could. 'Need you ask? Thirty rounds and he was put
down twice, but the Bear cried pax in the end.'

'I am happy to learn that your day was not wasted,'
was her only reply to that.

'Oh, it was wrong of us, I know.' Captain Dumaine
stepped forward, and took Cressy's hand to lift it to his
lips. 'You will forgive us, I hope. We promise to take
you to Farmer Mason's site tomorrow without fail. And
tonight we shall teach you to play whist,' and he kissed
her hand again.

It did not have at all the same effect on her as James's
kisses did, but he was a handsome man and the admiration in his eyes warmed Cressy. He never criticised
her lightest word as her guardian frequently did, and
his constant flattery was beginning to please her. He
was careful never to overdo it, and if Cressy had found
Frank a happy companion when she had first met him,
she was finding Barrett Dumaine a happier one.

So James thought that night, when he walked into
the drawing-room after dinner to find Cressy being

taught to play whist after a fashion, which involved a
great deal of laughing and high spirits. It also involved
Captain Dumaine holding Cressy's cards for her and
bending over her to reinforce the instruction which he
was offering.

James, who had spent a hard day in Salisbury with
several lawyers and a representative of the Cathedral in
a matter involving a dispute over land which Haven's
End and the Cathedral both claimed, was not best
pleased at the sight.

Miss Sykes was hardly carrying out her duties, he
thought. Far from acting as a brake on impropriety, she
was smiling at the young people enjoying themselves,
and Verena, who might also have been expected to
keep all proper, was too busy being part of the merri-
ment to restrain it.

He might, unwillingly, have agreed to Frank courting
Cressy, but it had not been his plan to have such a
dubious character as Barrett Dumaine after her. He
had even, James noted coldly, managed to win over
Verena, judging by the way in which she was co-
operating with him.

'What exactly are you all at?' he asked in a voice
which seemed to have travelled from the Arctic wastes.

Every face turned towards him after a fashion which
made him appear a gross intruder in his own home.

'Oh, sir,' exclaimed Cressy, seeing that no one else,
for their varying reasons, saw fit to answer him. 'I am
being taught to play whist,' and in an effort to mollify
him she turned on her new-found arts, and said as
winningly as she could, 'I must confess that, with so
many assisting, I do not seem to be learning very much.'

James wanted to answer, Oh, yes, you are, and you

are learning all the wrong things, but said instead, 'If you wish to play a game correctly, particularly such a difficult one as whist, then I suggest that a calmer atmosphere might be more conducive to success.'

Everyone's expression told him immediately what a pompous ass he sounded but, between jealousy and desire, he seemed to be losing more of his senses every day. He had the impression that without so much as moving a muscle, Barrett Dumaine had trumped his ace, so to speak, before the game had even begun.

'Pray, what do you suggest, Lyndale?' said that gentleman smoothly. 'I am sure that we should all be grateful for the advice of such a seasoned expert as yourself.'

Cressy was not the only person to think that James looked as though he were about to burst with anger at such a cavalier reply. He was also enraged at being addressed as 'Lyndale' by such an upstart swine.

Used to organising and dominating those about her, an art which she had found little opportunity to practise at Haven's End, Cressy said as quickly as she could, 'Oh, if you are an expert, sir, then pray instruct me, I beg. I am sure that Frank and Captain Dumaine would be grateful for your advice,' and she gave her newly learned heart-stopping smile at them all.

To refuse such an offer would brand him boor, so James unwillingly complied and pressed Fred Davenport, a noted player, into the game, thus successfully sidelining Frank and Dumaine.

Frank retired looking sullen, but Captain Dumaine never lost his charming smile and begged Miss Sykes to play the piano for him. 'But quietly so that we shall not disturb Lady Cressida's lesson.'

Cressy looked over the top of her cards at her guardian's lowering face. She thought that he seemed tired and rather sad, and wondered what could have distressed him. She almost missed her turn to play, and he reminded her coldly, adding, 'Now, my ward, if you wish to learn to play whist, you must really give the game your whole attention. It is no time to go woolgathering.'

Woolgathering! Why, she had only been worrying about him, and what a mistake that was. He needed no one to worry about him, that was for sure. She then proceeded to give her whole attention to the game, to such effect that she and her partner, Fred Davenport, easily beat James and Verena — Verena not being a very expert player. Fred had announced that he never partnered his wife. It was a recipe for marital disaster, he said, so James was deprived of a chance to partner Cressy.

If he had wanted confirmation of how quick her mind was, and the speed with which she grasped whatever she was taught, he had it during this first rubber of whist with him. Captain Dumaine, after listening for a time to Miss Sykes perform, came over to watch them, and he, too, was astonished at how rapidly Cressy acquired the requisite skills to enable her to support her more experienced partner.

Captain Dumaine clapped his hands together. 'Bravo, Lady Cressy,' he exclaimed. 'As Frank would say, what a girl you are! Who taught you to reason and count so successfully?'

'My father,' said Cressy demurely. She had almost cured herself of saying Robert, and was happy to pay tribute to his teaching of her. 'He said that because I was a girl was no reason for me to behave like a halfwit. He thought most women were halfwits,' she explained to the company. 'And I must say,' she added in a burst of misplaced confidence, 'that since being in England, I can quite see why he did. It must be the way in which women are brought up. I cannot believe that we are so very different from men in the way of understanding, but if women are treated like idiots, it is small wonder that they behave as though they are.'

This declaration of the Rights of Women amused most of the company, but had the worst effect possible on her guardian, Cressy saw with a sinking heart. Oh, dear, after behaving herself so well for so long, it was plain that she had blotted her copybook again. A moment's reflection should have told her that what she was saying was not at all *comme il faut*—but she had not taken a moment to reflect.

Before he could speak, she said rapidly, 'Oh, sir, I know that I should not have said that—even if I thought it—and I do apologise to the company if I said anything to offend,' and then she spoilt that pretty speech by adding ruefully, 'But I cannot say other than that I am of the belief that my father had the right of it!'

Captain Dumaine gave a crack of laughter and Frank and Fred Davenport both added their laughter to his. James blinked, his mouth twitched and then, he too, was laughing, with Verena joining in. The only persons left in the room who were not laughing were a shocked Miss Sykes, and Frank's mama, who lay fast asleep on the sofa, a picture of happy contentment.

Captain Dumaine caught Cressy's hand again, to kiss it. 'Oh, Lady Cressy, you are a wonder. I vow that when you do go to town you will be all the rage.

Coming from such charming lips, little that you say could cause offence. And after coming to know you, why, I shall never talk down women's understanding again.'

What a creeping and crawling snake you are, thought James, his own laughter stopping at the sight of that cur handling Cressy so carelessly. And she was enjoying it, yes, she was, her face alight, transforming her seeming plainness into something rare and precious — like her wit.

He had never thought to fall in love with a witty woman nearly half his age, but he knew now what was wrong with him. But in honour, he could not court her himself, such a child as she was for all her cleverness. He must, instead, see that no fortune-hunting swine, as he thought Captain Dumaine to be, should have the opportunity to despoil her. Lady Cressy, indeed!

'And now Frank and I demand a rubber with you and Lady Verena,' said Captain Dumaine, reluctantly letting go of Cressy's hand. 'And I insist that you partner me, Lady Cressy. No, Frank, do not protest — you were too slow. You must learn to take your chances, as I have often told you.'

'You never give a fellow a chance,' complained Frank, and then, realising that he was hardly being polite to his aunt, added hastily, 'but a pleasure to partner you, Aunt Verena.'

And now it was the turn of Verena's lips to twitch, but she sat obediently down, to be comprehensively carved up by Captain Dumaine and Cressy who made a formidable pair.

'Pity we weren't playing for money, Lady Cressy,' commented Captain Dumaine, pulling the cards together at the end of the game. 'We could have made a small fortune.'

'Oh,' said James, who had been leaning against a pillar, watching the game with a sardonic smile. 'Do but give me Lady Cressida for a partner, Dumaine, and I shall be happy to take on you and my sister any time at all—now, for instance.'

'Oh, James,' wailed Verena, 'are you determined to have me on the losing side on every occasion.'

'No, indeed,' was James's reply. 'For I am going to wake up Emily, whom you will allow is a much better player than you are, and she may partner Captain Dumaine. What do you say, Dumaine?'

'Why, that I am on, Lyndale,' smiled that gentleman, seeing no way out, and confident of his own abilities to carry any lady through. He had never heard that Lyndale was a card player. 'Shuffle and cut the cards and may the best pair win.'

They all sat down to play, Emily having been shaken awake by Verena to struggle up, saying, 'Oh, Philpot, is it morning already?' in the mistaken belief that she had been in her bed.

She was always prepared to play whist, however, and, like Verena, had succumbed to Captain Dumaine's charms. Everyone loves him but me, was James's sour thought. If he fails to win Cressy's fortune, he can always try to breach Emily's middle-aged defences, for she was smiling her pleasure at partnering him, and informing James that she intended to give him and his novice partner no quarter.

Verena watched the players. She saw that James, his face a mask of concentration, was treating the game with the utmost seriousness and that Barrett Dumaine was no less involved. It was as though the two women did not exist, being merely supernumeraries in their duel. Even Frank, lounging in his armchair, normally unaware of the deeper nuances of the world in which he lived, sensed the strange atmosphere surrounding the game.

But neither Cressy nor Emily Belsize wished to be supernumeraries, and Cressy, studying her cards no less seriously than James and the other pair, was not sure whether she wished to win the rubber or not. And then she looked at Barrett Dumaine, and for the first time one of the talents which Robert had fostered in her, the talent to read men and women a little, a talent which had hibernated in England, caused her to wonder whether everything about him was as fair as his face and body.

Of course she wanted to win! But, better than that, she wanted James to win, and looking across the table at him, at his expression of acute concentration on the game, she knew that she loved him. More, just as when he had first kissed her on the lips and the world had swung about her and for a moment had changed completely, it did so again — and for good this time.

She paused, thunderstruck, and then became conscious that the others were staring at her. It was her turn to play. She brought her wandering wits back to the game, extracted a card from her hand and played it to win the trick. She half expected approval for what she had done, only to see from James's expression that she had made a dreadful error. His card had already taken it. The trick had already been won.

'O. . .o. . .h,' she almost stammered. 'Forgive me, I lost the game for a moment.'

'Play like that, my ward, and we shall lose the rubber completely if you waste your cards on one already taken trick.'

'I promise not to do it again,' she answered him remorsefully, but, of course they lost the game which they would otherwise have won. It was a bad start to their enterprise, and one which she inwardly vowed to remedy, if possible.

After that she played with all the concentration which Robert had taught her to bring to everything she did, and halfway through the rubber she saw not only Barrett Dumaine's eye on her speculatively, but James's, as she began to demonstrate a surprising mastery of the game. Emily, as James had suggested, was no mean player and there was little to choose between James and Captain Dumaine, James shading the odds in his favour a little perhaps.

Her play became more daring as the points on the score which James was keeping mounted on their side until finally, when she had trumped Barrett Dumaine's ace on the final trick, they had won.

'What a splendid rubber of whist,' announced Emily enthusiastically. She was quite oblivious to the undercurrents beneath an apparently idle evening's play, and her best compliments were reserved for Cressy. 'What a bold game you play, my dear. Quite superb. I must compliment you.'

'Oh,' said Cressy gaily, forgetting herself completely in the joys of having won a game with, and for James. 'Rob. . .my father always said after I had played a good hand that, in whist, as in life, who dares wins. . .'

And then she stopped as she saw the expression on the faces of both men, and although he was behind her and she could not see it, Frank's expression mirrored theirs.

'Indeed!' James's voice was at its grimmest. 'Do I collect that you have played whist before, then? I was under the impression that you were a novice who needed instruction.'

Cressy licked her lips. Captain Dumaine's expression had changed to one of high amusement, but as for James, no such thing. '*I* never said that I could not play. No one ever asked me whether I could; *you* were all determined that I could not. Then I thought that no lady would ever embarrass the company by informing them of what an error they had made. I was merely trying to live up to your instructions about my conduct being entirely *comme il faut* on all occasions, sir.'

This exercise in sophistry had no effect on James. By his expression he obviously considered it a piece of gross impertinence. Fortunately, Captain Dumaine came to Cressy's rescue by asking in a voice choked with amusement, 'And exactly how long have you been playing whist, Lady Cressida, for surely your performance was not that of an amateur.'

Cressy avoided looking at James and answered the Captain as cheerfully as she could. 'Oh, Robert taught me when I was twelve. He was a stern master and after that I played with him and the Count and Countess Franceschini every night until the Count died, and then we brought the Countess's brother into the game. He was a first-rate player, better even than Robert. We had some famous rubbers, I can tell you. We used to play for money.' She had forgotten all the precepts of good conduct which had been drummed into her for weeks at Haven's End in telling of her happy memories of days gone by. Her father had become Robert again.

Captain Dumaine was laughing outright by now. 'Wait 'til I get back to town and tell them how I was rooked by a female cardsharp who has not yet reached her years of discretion. Better not let her loose at White's or Watiers, Lyndale. And, by the by, who is Robert?'

'Her father,' said James curtly. 'Whom she has been expressly forbidden to refer to so cavalierly.'

'*He* never minded me calling him Robert, in fact, he instructed me to do so,' said Cressy spiritedly, in for a penny, in for a pound being her motto in the face of James's intransigence.

So, thought James, the minx had deceived, not merely himself, but all of them, including the fly Captain into the bargain. Oh, I shall have to be stern with her or shall I kiss her before them all, and then where should we be?

Aloud James said, 'Well, in future, Lady Cressida Mortimer, you are instructed to tell the truth about your many accomplishments. Suppose we had been playing for money? Your conduct would then have been shady to say the least.'

'All's fair in love and war,' Cressy announced gaily. 'Besides, Robert used to say that only fools sat down to play without sounding out the true nature of the opposition.'

'Robert said far too much about everything,' was James's riposte to this further outburst of impudence, a remark lost in the gale of laughter which Cressy's remark provoked from all the company except himself.

Cressy then did something which disarmed everyone,

including James, for she could not bear to have him
take her in despite over anything so stupid as a game of
whist. 'Pax,' she said, like a frank schoolboy, holding
out her hand. 'I did not mean anything by what I did,
and it was you who suggested we make up a four and
by then I had gone too far to retreat.'

James took the offered hand, but not to shake it.
Instead, he kissed it, not lingeringly as Barrett Dumaine
had done, but gently and briefly.

'Pax, indeed,' he said. 'I cannot rebuke you overmuch after you have offered me such a gallant white
flag,' and the amber eyes were warm again, Cressy
noted with relief.

Other eyes were more speculative. Barrett
Dumaine's suspicions of the true relationship between
Lyndale and his ward were simply reinforced, and
Verena, head lifted from her tapestry, read James's
face correctly.

Oh, no! Poor James. Not after all these years. To
begin to feel again, something for which she had always
hoped, but for such a child. Surely a doomed love.

Cressy took back her hand. She wanted to stroke it
where his lips had touched it, but the eyes of the
company were on her, and instead she made him a
great curtsy, one fit for the Prince Regent himself when
she was presented to him.

'I shall try to remember your wise precepts, sir,' she
offered him, smiling as she rose.

'Until tomorrow,' replied James. 'You forget, I know
you, madam,' but this time there was no hint of
reproval in the madam, it came out almost lovingly.

'Oh, tomorrow is another day.' Gaiety bubbled in
Cressy's voice, joy shone in her face. For the moment

she knew that she loved him and for the moment she knew that that untold love gave her pleasure. Her growing maturity had already informed her that on the morrow it might give her pain.

Tomorrow would be another day; tonight was for enjoyment, and enjoy it she did. Barrett Dumaine laughing and talking with her, cutting out both the aggrieved Frank and the jealous James, could only appreciate her. Oh, she was becoming a prize worth winning, not only for her unbounded wealth, but for herself — she was a girl of real quality. And if James had told her that she was a nonpareil, Barrett Dumaine thought so too, and his eyes informed her of his admiration.

The days flew by. Cressy found that love gave her spirit wings, and her happiness spread itself over her two young cavaliers, as well as over James and his sisters. Never mind that she could not confess her love to him, or to them, that it was doomed to die aborning as some poet had once said; simply to know that she loved him was enough.

There were times when the knowledge made her sad — but then she drew on her store of wisdom, learned from Robert. She tried harder to please him, and told herself that perhaps, if she did, he might come to feel for her what she felt for him — and then she laughed at herself.

But pleasing him did not mean that she gave up her independent spirit, or informed him of the dig, or avoided Barrett Dumaine whom she was beginning to find a pleasant friend. He was not so brash as poor Frank, was well informed and had a nice line in bantering conversation of a kind which Cressy had not met before.

Watching them at play around Haven's End, James began to be aware of a feeling of suppressed excitement about the three of them and began also to wonder what was causing it. Daily they rode out each afternoon, passing his study window, and he began to notice a curious thing. When they rode out alone, just Cressy, Frank, Dumaine and the three grooms, they always took the same direction, north, but when Verena joined them—Fred and Emily rarely rode—they never went that way, striking off south, east or west, but never north.

Some sixth sense informed him that something odd was going on. One afternoon when they had all returned from their trip to the north, the party's spirits were so high that Verena commented on them when they finally arrived back in the drawing-room.

'One might have thought that you had found Ali Baba's cave and its treasures,' she said. James, who had been working that afternoon with Lenthall, had just brought that gentleman in, ordering tea and muffins for the company at four o'clock. Cressy was on her high ropes, Frank and Dumaine no less so.

'Oh, a ride with Lady Cressy is always an adventure. With her we manage to combine the picturesque and the antique,' replied Captain Dumaine gaily, which brought him a reproving stare from Cressy. She had already noticed that there was a recklessness about him, not only in the way he took fences and rode over ditches, but also in the nature of his conversation. Sometimes it verged on the improper, but never quite reaching it, always being saved by his friendly grin.

Now he was taking a chance that James would not guess that they were engaged in clandestine activities.

James caught Cressy's look, and if his ward was beginning to read him, he was beginning to read his ward. Something was up, but what?

'A muffin?' he asked, proffering the plate to Dumaine. 'You look as though you need food after your labours. But I had not thought that the direction in which you ride provided any useful examples of the antique. The picturesque — yes, I can agree with that.'

It was a shot in the dark, yet he thought that he had found his mark, but what mark? Dumaine gave him a brief sharp glance, but was too fly to say anything, contenting himself with accepting a muffin, and giving Cressy a significant look, which James also intercepted.

Cressy, indeed, was annoyed that Captain Dumaine should leave them open to question. She said, her voice as sweet as poured honey, 'Oh, sir, you forget. There are the ruins of Armfield Abbey for us to enjoy. We have been reading about it in your library. Dr Soames is a mine of information.'

Now why should he think that that guileless stare, that innocent eye cocked in his direction, was there merely to deceive? His only comfort was that, in the company of Frank and the grooms, Cressy and Dumaine could not be enjoying a secret tryst.

Honour and decency forbade that he ask the grooms what they were involved in, although he was sure that, however reluctantly, they would tell him. He must try to discover for himself what naughtiness his ward was committing, what deceit was being practised on him that should cause them all to be enjoying such private glee.

He offered Cressy his haughtiest stare and dismissed
the hovering Miss Sykes with, 'I would have a word in
private with Lady Cressida, if you please, Miss Sykes.'
He was always courteous with those who served him
and Miss Sykes had developed quite a *tendre* for him.
She gave him a melting yes and left Cressy to be
devoured by the tiger — who led her to his study.

Privately she cursed Barrett, as she had begun to call
him to herself, for it was plain that what he had said
had in some ways aroused James's suspicions, and the
tiger was on the prowl.

'Sir?' she said, and looked at him with all the
artlessness which she could command.

'You are happy here, my ward?'

'Oh, yes,' and her face told him that she was speaking
the truth. 'I thought I would not be, everything in
England being so different, but my enjoyment is different, too.'

'And you enjoy riding out with Frank?'

'Indeed,' she answered, but she could not quite meet
his eyes. She suddenly felt sorry that she was deceiving
him, and wished that she had told him what she was
doing, even though she might have risked him forbidding her to carry out the excavation. But she had gone
too far to turn back, and involving Frank and Barrett
Dumaine had compounded the offence.

And then she thought, best perhaps to tell him, after
all, and she opened her mouth to do so, just as James
unluckily said, 'I hope, however, that you have remembered my warnings about young Dumaine. I have heard
from a friend of mine, and while he knows nothing
directly to his detriment, he tells me that there is no

doubt that he is fortune-hunting for a rich bride. You would do well to be careful with him.'

All Cressy's good resolutions and the desire to tell him the truth about her jaunts to the Masons' farm flew away. 'You would do better to trust me a little — sir,' she replied, fire in her eyes, insolence in her voice. Love him she might, but she would not have him reproach her over Barrett Dumaine, by no means.

They were back in an instant to the hostility of their earlier days, for James, his suspicions fired by he knew not what, and reinforced by jealousy and the manner in which she had spoken to him, said in his most haughty voice, 'You would do well to pay attention to what I tell you, madam. Were you a little younger I would consider confinement to your room to be a suitable treatment for you. As it is, I must ask you to be discreet in your conduct at all times.'

Oh, he was impossible! She had, apart from the deceit over the site, done nothing wrong, and she had encouraged neither of her suitors — for she knew that they were both that — to believe that she felt anything for them. And they had always been chaperoned by the grooms and the labourers who worked on the site under her directions.

The little objects on Farmer Mason's mantelshelf had grown in number, and that afternoon the party's excitement had been sparked off by the uncovering of a fine piece of mosaic pavement. Even Frank had been inspired when the last soil had been brushed away to reveal a dog and the Latin words '*Cave canem*' beneath it. It was an even more splendid specimen of the art than the one in Haven's End's entrance hall.

'Beware of the dog!' Frank had exclaimed, dim

memories of afternoons spent translating and constru-
ing Latin returning to him. Cressy had clapped her
hands together and had congratulated the labourers for
the care which they had taken in uncovering it. The
mosaic was nearly as fresh as it had been all those
centuries ago, before time and chance had covered it
up, to lie unknown in Farmer Mason's field, until his
plough had found it.

And *he* thought that she had spent the afternoon
flirting with Frank and Barrett when they had been
most seriously examining their find. The two young
men had even taken off their fine jackets to help the
labourers so that the whole of the glories of the
pavement might be seen.

'Oh,' she exclaimed. 'I am always discreet, and what
you think that we can be doing when there are three
grooms always with us. . .' And she tossed her head as
though she had spent her whole life being an idle and
saucy young miss in society drawing-rooms.

Despite himself, James began to laugh. The toss
suited so ill with Cressy's usual forthright behaviour,
and he found it hard to be severe with her when it was
taking him all the strength of a strong mind not to kiss
her on her charming lips. How strange that it was her
defiance which roused him most. The fire in her eyes,
the fire in her voice, both were enough to bring him to
fever pitch — and at the most inconvenient times, too.

'But you will think a little of what I say?' he begged
her, because, wonderfully, it was almost a plea he was
making.

Only for her to defy him the more. 'I always think of
what you say. Whether as a consequence I shall act
upon it is quite a different thing!'

What a mind she had—and at only eighteen. What would she be like when she had reached maturity? But would she ever possess the maturity of judgement to go with the mind and the wit? Protection was what she needed, and if he could not be her lover, then he could be her protector—if she would so allow.

Cressy knew that she was being naughty, but she could not help herself. Whenever she was with James, she still wished to provoke him. In their earliest days she had done so because she had been annoyed with him, as the man who could bar her from the freedom of thought and action which she had always enjoyed with Robert. Now her provocation was because she wished him to react to her, to melt the cold aloofness with which he had treated her since the day when he had taken her into his arms. She wanted to see the tiger's eyes flash at her, even in anger, because that was better than being ignored.

And now she had made him laugh, and even when he reacted to her last riposte by saying, as they moved back to the drawing-room, 'Madam, I beg of you to consider your actions before you commit them. As to conversation, I doubt that I shall ever persuade you to think before you speak.' Cressy could not be angry with him.

'Oh,' she said airily, suddenly aware that Barrett Dumaine's keen eyes were on them again, and now she must disarm *his* suspicions. 'I assure you, sir that everything I say is most carefully considered. You will excuse me, I trust,' and she moved away to say to Frank, 'If you like, Frank, we may go to the library to look up the reference to Pliny the Elder dying in the eruption of Vesuvius, which brought about the destruction of both Pompeii and Herculaneum.'

'Oh, indeed,' replied Frank, who had become Cressy's most faithful slave, and would have assented cheerfully to anything she ordered him to do—even something as unlikely as looking up a Latin text years after he had happily thought himself rid of the cursed language altogether. 'By all means, let us go and see old Soames; the very man, to be sure.' He made for the door in his mistress's wake, with Captain Dumaine, a sardonic look on his handsome face, following him.

'So good for Frank,' sighed Frank's mother sentimentally, 'to be with someone as serious and steady as dear Cressy. He is quite reformed. Captain Dumaine, too. What a dear child she is.'

'Not such a child these days,' remarked Verena, looking sideways at her brother. 'She is growing prettier every day, and so much more in command of herself.'

James gave a dry laugh. 'You do surprise me there, Verena. I would have thought that she has always been in command of herself, too much so for her own good. What she needed to learn was to accommodate herself a little more to the wishes of others.'

'Not like you to be a stick, James,' was Verena's equally dry response to him. She took him by the arm and led him away out of Emily's hearing, to say 'You cannot be serious, James, in wishing Cressy to marry Frank. A most unsuitable match. She would tire of him in a week. It is plain that she indulges him as though he were a child—to marry them would be a recipe for disaster.'

James looked down at his nose at his sister. 'I suppose that you think Barrett Dumaine would be a better prospect — seeing that, as everyone here has fallen in love with him, then it is only fair that someone should win the prize of his hand, and Cressy being the only one available who is single and young enough. . .'

Verena broke in, gazing at him in wonder. 'Whatever can you be at, James? It is not like you to be so wild. You will have me thinking that you have an eye on the girl yourself.'

'Have an eye on a barely fledged hoyden of eighteen! You must be light in the attic, Verena.' James knew that his anger with his sister stemmed from the fact that she had put an inconvenient finger on the truth.

Verena shrugged. 'You know best, my dear,' she answered him in a voice which begged leave to doubt any such thing.

By this time Cressy and her two cavaliers had disappeared into the library and James was compelled to suppress a wild desire to follow them. There was, though, little that they could get up to in the library, with Dr Soames there to oversee them.

And then, his sense of humour and his common sense returned with a rush. How in the world could he be so stupid as to imagine some kind of wild orgy was going on while Frank solemnly looked up a reference he did not understand in a language which he had never learned to translate? He, James, was the one who was light in the attic, not his sister. Best, perhaps to try to forget the child altogether — but he knew that he couldn't.

CHAPTER SIX

'LADY CRESSY.'

Cressy was seated in the shade of a large tree overlooking the site of the newly excavated villa. She was sketching in water-colour the view before her, and had not heard Barrett Dumaine approaching. He threw himself down on the grass before her and said lazily, 'You will allow that I worship at the feet of the artist?'

They had reached the point in their work where the entire floor and the broken pillars of the villa had been revealed. Earlier the labourers and Cressy had been sorting through a pile of earth for hidden treasure, but they had stopped at lunchtime and afterwards Frank had gone to sleep on the other side of the tree.

The night before, he and Captain Dumaine had driven over to a friend of Dumaine's who had a small country house a few miles from Haven's End, and they had spent the evening drinking and gambling in an all-male party. They had been invited to stay on, but both of them had their reason for returning to Haven's End and the reason was Cressy.

But they had not fallen into their beds before three in the morning and both of them, as Cressy had already pointed out, looked the worse for wear. The three grooms had brought along a picnic and bottles of ale. Frank and Dumaine had shudderingly declined the food, but had killed several of the bottles of ale and the aspect of the whole party could only be called unbuttoned. The sun shone relentlessly down, and altogether 1818 could only be described as a most satisfactory year after the rain and cold of 1817. The harvest, Farmer Mason had told them, would be good in Wiltshire. There should be few food riots in the county this year, he had added.

But food riots were far from everyone's mind, and Cressy, adding a solitary cloud to her sky, perhaps an augury that the storm which had been threatening was drawing near, answered Dumaine as lightly as he had spoken to her, 'You may worship where you please, Barrett, but I warn you, goddesses rarely respond to their worshippers, and when they do, the worshippers usually regret it!'

'I am sure I shall not,' was his only reply to that, and he continued to banter lazily with her, both of them sharing their amusement at poor Frank's snores. The labourers had stopped work and were now sitting in the shade of the hedge devouring their own food.

'We are a fit subject for Stubbs or Morland,' commented Dumaine, who, as Cressy had rapidly discovered, was by no means a fool, and possessed an odd store of knowledge denied to Frank. He had already told her that he owned some barren acres and a ramshackle house in Wales, and had been candid about his relative lack of means.

Cressy felt that she ought to like him more than she did. She thought that perhaps she found him a little too charming, a little too easy. She had been used to sterner men. Robert had been stern. He might have been patient with her, but he had always been demanding. She was not used to compliments and particularly not to idle ones.

Nevertheless, she enjoyed being with Barrett Dumaine, and tried not to let him believe that she cared for him as more than a friend. She was not sure that she was being successful. He was a man who was used to female admiration. He might find it difficult to believe that not every woman was ready to lay her heart at his feet.

I wonder where all this knowledge of men and women is coming from, thought Cressy. Perhaps Robert's teachings are beginning to make some sense at last, or it could be living with strangers, or perhaps falling in love with James. It isn't always comfortable, but it is useful.

The painting drew to its conclusion. The idyllic scene, fit for the brush of a Constable or a Gainsborough, grew even more idyllic as the labourers, their lunch over, like Frank began to doze. Only Cressy and Dumaine were left to enjoy the sun, the blue sky and the drifting clouds. . .

James Lyndale had determined to discover what his ward and her companions were up to. He had seen them ride off before instead of after lunch, and an apparently idle question to Barker, his head groom, had brought the answer that the the young people had taken a picnic with them and would be staying out a little longer than usual. 'It being such a fine day,' he added.

'Oh, of course,' replied James, apparently idly. It would never do to let Barker know of his suspicions. 'Saddle Paris for me, will you,' he ordered. 'I have a mind for a ride myself. No, I don't need a groom. You've no notion where Lady Cressida and her party were bound for?'

Barker had learned the art of useful ignorance long ago. He shook his head. 'Somewhere thataway,' he said blankly, waving a hand towards the north. And then, seeing that it would not do to antagonise m'lord over-much, added, 'Over towards Farmer Mason's, mayhap.'

He watched his master ride out alone and walked back to the small group of interested stable hands, who had been wondering how long m'lord would allow Master Frank and the Captain to monopolise his ward.

'Off to find out what they're all at,' commented Barker to his best hand, Jonas. 'Thought he'd be after 'em one day soon.'

'The Captain sweet on Lady Cressy, eh?' laughed Jonas. 'Master Frank can't take his eyes off her.'

Barker laughed in his turn, and thought, but did not say aloud that Master Frank and the Captain might not be the only ones sweet on m'lord's ward.

James, unaware that, as usual, his servants were following the game of his life nearly as closely as he was, rode off towards the Masons' lands. He automatically noted that everything he saw was in good order. Mason was a sound fellow and was quick to take up any improvements which James or his agent suggested.

He was beginning to wonder whether he was going in the right direction when he reached the brow of a small hill, and saw below him the field in which the excavation was taking place. He also saw the spreading tree beneath which his long sight informed him, his ward was sketching, Barrett Dumaine lying sprawled indol-ently at her feet.

He spurred his horse to ride on, his face grim. So, he had found them, but what were they doing? His curios-

ity was aroused by the large scar on the field's surface.
His anger was aroused by the sight of Dumaine lying
half-asleep at Cressy's feet. He could see no sign of
Frank. And then, as his path curved down the hill and
he drew nearer, he saw him at last, sleeping beneath a
tree, and an unwilling grin grew on his face. He might
have guessed. Frank had, symbolically, surrendered the
field to his friend.

Finally, almost upon them, he could see the full
extent of the excavation, the broken pillars, the mosaic
floor, the heaps of soil and laid out on a blanket the
few damaged artefacts which had been found that day —
a small green bottle, the remains of a statuette and
several jagged pieces of metal.

Cressy heard him first. Dumaine was by now half
asleep, and she turned her head to see James upon
them. His expression, she thought ruefully, was not
reassuring.

He called to Stephen to take his horse as he swung
down from it, and Stephen, half asleep, jerked fully
awake to obey him and lead the horse away, leaving
James standing facing Cressy and Dumaine, whose
after-lunch rest had also been disturbed. Dumaine sat
up, then lazily rose. He, too, had read James's
expression and knew that the day of reckoning was on
them.

James spoke to his ward as though Dumaine were
not there.

'Lady Cressida, what is this?' He waved a hand at the
villa, a hand which also took in the whole organised
site, including the grooms and the workmen who had
begun to stir, all except Frank who slept placidly on.

Cressy licked dry lips. His question had been put

quietly, but she had no illusions as to his suppressed anger. 'You may see, sir, quite plainly, what it is,' she replied as coolly as she could. 'It is the remains of a Roman villa which Farmer Mason discovered by accident in his field. He thought, knowing my interest in such matters, that we might like to excavate it. He lent us a few of his men when he could spare them, to do the heavy digging. And, oh,' she was suddenly eager, forgetting her fear of his anger, 'it is the most splendid site, and we have found such interesting things. Robert would have been pleased with me, I think. . .' She fell silent at the sight of the growing thunder on James's face, for the tiger's eyes were flashing their warning.

'Yes, I can see that you have been excavating a building—Roman, I believe, from the mosaic floor— and that you have been doing so for some time.' He paused. Common sense told him that he did not want a scene before the amused Dumaine, who had been a party to the deceit which had been practised on him. 'I also understand that neither you, nor Mason, nor Frank,' and he stared at his still prostrate and sleeping nephew, 'have seen fit to inform me of what you have been doing on my land.'

Still conscious of Dumaine behind him, enjoying his discomfiture, James paused for a moment and then continued, keeping his voice as level as he could, 'I don't propose to discuss the matter with you here and now. It is not a fit subject for public debate,' and that he thought, successfully disposes of any right of Dumaine's to speak of the matter.

'If you will awaken Frank,' he continued, voice still level, 'I think that you might all call it quits for the day and return to Haven's End where I can speak with you

privately.' His anger, barely reined in, anger created by
the knowledge that she should deceive him with such a
pair of idle fribbles as Frank and Dumaine, finally
overcame him.

'On second thoughts,' he grated, 'I think that I shall
wake up Master Frank myself.' He walked over to
where Frank lay, still sleeping peacefully, and kicked
him sharply in the ribs with the toe of one highly
polished boot.

'Hey, what's that, Dumaine? What the devil do you
mean by that?' And Frank sat up indignantly, clutching
his side, to meet James's baleful stare. 'Oh, Uncle,
what are you doing here? Was it you who gave me such
a damn'd dirty blow? That's no way to wake a fellow
up, I can tell you,' and still grumbling he hoisted himself
to his feet.

'So you have been party to this. . .' James said,
waving his hand again at the scene. The labourers and
the grooms had retreated to leave their betters to their
business.

'Oh, yes.' Frank was eager. 'Splendid, ain't it? At
least so Cressy says. Dog on the floor down there,' he
finished obligingly. '*Cave canem*, you know. Latin came
in useful after all. . .' He ended on a dying note,
suddenly aware that, for some unaccountable reason,
James was furiously angry with the whole party.

'Ain't going to be cross with Cressy, are you, Uncle?'
he enquired a little anxiously. 'Done a famous job here.
Kept the men in order, organised us all. Just like
Herculaneum, she says. Found lots of little bits and
pieces, too.'

'No doubt, and now, I think, work is over for today.

You will oblige me, Frank, by returning to Haven's End with the rest of your party as soon as possible.'

Frank looked from his uncle to the silent Cressy. 'Not my party, Uncle. Cressy had the honour of finding the site and she knew how to dig it up, not Barrett and me. . .' He seemed to realise by his uncle and Cressy's expressions that he was not saying quite the right thing. 'Not that Barrett and me weren't other than happy to do our bit,' he ended gallantly. 'Wouldn't like you to think that we weren't willing, by no means.'

Cressy closed her eyes at Frank's clumsy explanations which, designed to make matters better, had only succeeded in making them worse. She had not spoken since James had woken Frank. Being found out was much more unpleasant than she had supposed it might be. When she had begun the excavation in secret, hiding what she was doing from James, it had seemed a joke, a good way of getting back at him for his treatment of her, for his refusal to allow her to return to Italy. But then, their relationship had changed and now she wished that she had not begun to deceive him.

Every day that passed, however, had made it harder and harder to confess her misdeed to him, and besides, the thrill of the chase was on her. She was doing alone what she had only done before with her father. To the delight of uncovering such a treasure was added the delight that she was able, without supervision, to organise successfully an archaeological dig. After that she had not wanted to tell James of the site, because she was fearful that he would forbid her to go on, and she could not bear the thought of that.

Another thought struck her as she began, mechanically, to obey him, to pack up her painting equipment.

She looked up at her guardian and said, 'You are not to be cross with Farmer Mason. . .'

'Oh, I realise that you suborned him, too. Quite an effective little schemer, are you not, my ward? Did Robert teach you that, as well as all your other little tricks?'

'It was your fault,' Cressy began angrily. 'If you had not been so unkind about Robert, and what we did in Italy, I would have told you. . .' She fell silent. She could not fight with him before Barrett Dumaine and Frank. The tears were falling at last as she resumed her packing. James had walked over to her small easel and was looking at her painting and then at her.

'Another talent,' he said quietly. 'You thought fit to hide this from me as well.'

Worse and worse. Cressy could see quite plainly that she had hurt him badly by her deception. How could she persuade him of her true remorse at what she had done? He wouldn't believe her. He probably thought that she had passed her time at the site in laughing with Barrett and Frank about what a splendid joke it was to deceive him, when the truth was that she had been so engaged in the joy of discovery that she had temporarily forgotten him when she was working there.

Stephen and the grooms had begun to pack up the remains of the picnic and stow them in their saddle-bags. Their frozen faces betrayed that they were well aware of the dissension among the gentry, but were pretending that it was passing over their heads.

Cressy, her packing finished, walked over to the labourers and said in her most efficient manner, 'Work is over for today. I suppose you had better report back to Farmer Mason, but before you do, here is something extra for your pains,' and she pulled some coins from the purse which she wore at her waist.

The men's leader pulled his forelock, and, collecting their spades and picks, they set off towards the farmhouse. Barrett Dumaine, who had kept quiet out of policy, walked over to Cressy and said quietly to her, 'Good girl, Lady Cressy. They deserved their *pourboire* for working over and above the call of duty.'

Cressy was grateful for his sympathy, for she was only too keenly aware of James's hard stare on her back. He had walked away from the party and was looking down at the excavated site, his face an impassive blank. Only Frank, puppying about, was missing the nuances which Barrett Dumaine's antennae was picking up. As James turned back to remount, he walked over to his uncle, saying in his candid and open manner which always disarmed criticism, 'I say, Uncle, you are going to look at what Cressy's accomplished, surely. Can't miss the dog, you know — splendid specimen. Cressy says there aren't many mosaics uncovered anywhere as good as that.' And he pointed to the floor below them.

To refuse in the face of Frank's simple-minded innocence would be churlish. James shrugged and allowed himself to be led down the small pathway to the new level of the exposed site. Before him, the soil now completely cleared away from it, was the mosaic in all its glory. The dog's head was thrown back, teeth exposed, and its tail was erect. The colours on the pavement were as fresh as though they had been laid down yesterday.

It was, indeed, James reluctantly conceded, a splendid specimen and its uncovering would make the name

of any antiquarian fortunate enough to have discovered
it. Farmer Mason and Lady Cressida Mortimer between
them had pulled off a coup which many would envy.
And Cressy had seen fit to exclude him from partici-
pating in it. That hurt. It hurt him so much that it
surprised the hard man he was. To have confided in
Frank and Barrett Dumaine and not in him. . .

'What a fine fellow he is.' Frank was eager precisely
because he could understand the Romans liking a dog.
To think of the flim flam in Caesar and Livy, to say
nothing of that dead bore Horace, which he had been
made to study, and all the time the Romans had been
jolly good fellows who had liked dogs and horses and
hunting and all the things which amused Frank — or so
Cressy had told him.

James decided to be gracious. 'I agree with you.
Whoever designed that pavement knew all about dogs.'
He looked up at Cressy who stood slightly above him,
and said, unwillingly but truthfully, 'I had not thought
to see so excellent a specimen of mosaic work outside
Italy itself. Your labourers and you are to be commended for the care which you have shown in uncovering it.'

His words eased Cressy's sore heart a little, but she
did not delude herself. She was still in the basement of
James's esteem when she had wished to be in the
attic — or perhaps even the clouds above the house. She
nodded her thanks, unable to speak, when remorse and
distress had worked such an effect on her. They stayed
with her all the way back to Haven's End, where in the
stable yard, James asked her in his grimmest voice to
attend him immediately in his study.

Frank stared after him as he made his way into the

house. 'And what's the matter with *him*? he enquired
of Cressy. 'I would have thought that he would have
been on his high ropes to have had such a discovery
made on his land, and instead he's going on as though
he'd lost his inheritance in a card-game!'

Cressy was suddenly exasperated by Frank's obtuse-
ness. She had previously been a little amused by it, and
because Frank was such an honest young man, if
simple-minded, she had been prepared to bear with
him. But now her temper snapped.

'Oh, Frank! Do you never have any notion of what is
going on around you? Of course he's angry. Anyone
would be angry. We have been deceiving him for over
a fortnight, and that destroys his pleasure in what we
have done.' And she marched off after James, her head
held high, prepared to take her medicine.

'And now she's in the boughs as well as my uncle.'
Frank was nearly as exasperated as Cressy, and was
appealing to his friend. 'Has everyone run mad today?
What a to-do about nothing.'

'Not exactly nothing,' replied Barrett Dumaine
patiently. He, for one, understood the cause of the
distress of both James and Cressy. So, the high and
mighty Lord Lyndale was hot for his ward, and his ward
was no less hot for him. So much for his own hopes of
netting the heiress.

But he knew that Cressy was as proud as her guardian
and if the man was fool enough to overdo his anger —
why then, there might still be a game to be won, and
he, Barrett Dumaine, might win it.

Cressy pushed open the study door, feeling exactly as
she had done when as a child she had misbehaved

herself with her tutor, middle-aged and stern Mr
Brooke, and had been sent to Robert to be corrected.
Robert's tongue had been as sharp as James's and she
had learned to bear it — Robert despised crying girl
children. But, oddly, James's sharp tongue always hurt
her more than Robert's had. She decided to puzzle out
that conundrum when James had finished ringing a peal
over her, for she was sure that he was going to and that
the peal would be both loud and long.

He was standing by the window, behind his desk,
looking out over the park and the drive down which he
had watched the three of them set out for Farmer
Mason's field. The look he gave her was not so much
angry as weary and disillusioned, which surprised her.

She is so young, James thought, watching her enter,
her head still high. I am a fool to feel for her as I do.
There can be no future in it. Like a child, she hardly
understands what she is doing. She must grow up a
little and then find someone nearer to her own age to
be her companion through life. I would always expect
too much from her, and that is a burden which she
ought not to bear.

But when he saw her woebegone face these sensible
resolutions flew out of his head. Hurt though he was,
he wanted to take her in his arms and comfort her. But
he must not, and, in order to stiffen his resolve and
blunt the temptation which she offered, he decided to
be as hard as he could with her.

'You know why I am angry with you, I suppose,' he
began, his face set in its sternest lines, the tiger's eyes
cold and cruel.

'Y. . .y. . .yes. . .' faltered Cressy, all her bravery
leaking out of her. Oh, he hated her for what she had

done, she was sure of it. He would never learn to love her now. She wanted most desperately to cry, but would not. 'I shouldn't have excavated the villa after all that you said to me about my life with Robert and its unsuitability as a guide for conduct in England.'

'That too,' agreed James, trying not to look at her, addressing the Titian behind her head instead. It showed the flaying of Marsyas, an apt symbol for what he was about to do to Cressy to exorcise his love for her. 'But the real wrong thing which you did was not the excavation of the villa, but the deceit which accompanied it. *That* was the wrong thing. And you compounded the lie of omission which you were practising by drawing poor silly Frank and Barrett Dumaine into it, as well as Farmer Mason, the grooms and the men who worked for you. Barrett Dumaine knew quite well that what you were doing was wrong and my feelings towards him are not improved by his conduct, either.'

Cressy's head dropped lower and lower. She could not excuse herself. She could not even tell him that she had had qualms of conscience about her trickery once she had got to know him, once she had—think it, Cressy, think it, be honest with yourself—fallen in love with him. But she had lacked the moral courage to do so, and Robert had always said that lacking moral courage was the worst sin of all. Speak the truth and shame the devil, he had said more than once to her when he was training her to be his successor.

'I never meant to commit such a massive sin,' Cressy faltered. 'It seemed such a small one when I began, and if I am truthful. . .'

'Yes,' replied James coldly. 'By all means be truthful. It will be a most gratifying change of habit for you.'

'If I am truthful, I did enjoy deceiving you at the beginning. I thought it served you right for not letting me go back to Italy, and then. . .'

'And then. . .' prompted James mercilessly.

'And then I was sorry, but I didn't know how to tell you. I thought that you would be angry with me, and I couldn't bear that.'

'So you went on deceiving me, and encouraging my servants and my tenants to do the same. I hope that you all enjoyed yourselves while you were doing so. Otherwise it would have been a greatly missed opportunity.'

For some reason, this last remark stung Cressy and restored her ability to argue with him, and make her feel that she had been wrong to capitulate so completely to him. What if she had been naughty? The sin had surely not been so massive after all. It was his hurt feelings which were making him so censorious. He was committing the sin of pride, and need not be so hard on her. She told him so.

James stared at her. 'Do I hear you aright? You have the impudence to inform me that we are quits, because, if you deceived me, then my anger at the deception may be dismissed, because it is only hurt pride which is causing me to reprimand you?'

'Yes,' said Cressy rebelliously. 'You see, if we follow my argument to its logical conclusion, you are no better than I am. You are only angry with me because you thought that we were laughing at you — and that is hurt pride.' She stuck her chin into the air and defied him as hard as she could.

She might love him, but she was damn'd if she was going to submit tamely to his reprimands. How dare he adopt such a high moral tone with her, when he was no better than she was?

James's expression was merciless. 'If you were a boy, Lady Cressida Mortimer, I would thrash you for your impudence. Do you understand me, madam? But since you are a young woman that is forbidden me. You will go to your room and stay there until I tell you that you may leave it. Miss Sykes will be the only person allowed in to speak with you. I am supposing that you corrupted your maid, Catherine Mason, as well as her brother, Stephen, the groom, so for the time being their company shall be denied you. If you behave like a naughty child, you shall be treated like one.'

It broke his heart to speak to her as he did. No matter. He must not encourage his own passion for her, nor that which she had begun to show for him the night he had kissed her. To treat her harshly would mean that she would come to dislike him and that would be for the best, for both of them.

Cressy's lip trembled. Frank and Barrett Dumaine would be sure to understand that she was being punished like a naughty child, and now it was *her* pride which was hurt. But there was one thing which she must say, and damn the consequences.

'Please,' she burst out. 'You may punish me, but I hope that you will not dismiss Mason or Stephen, and as for Farmer Mason, he is as innocent as they were. Don't be hard on him.'

James's mouth twisted a little. 'Oh, I doubt that, I really do,' he said drily. 'Their innocence, I mean. I should imagine that deceiving me was as good a trick for them as for you. But I have to bear in mind that you used your position, so much above theirs, to subvert them, and so I shall merely give them a talking to and a warning not to do it again. Your case is the worst, you must own.'

Cressy did, but did not like to say so. Her heart was nearly breaking. She had never thought that she could feel so distressed about anything. She had forfeited everything by deceiving him. He disliked her for what she had done, and had not been backward in letting her know it.

She wanted to go back to Italy. Haven's End, which she had begun to feel was home, was home no longer. She wanted to be away from him, from everything. Frank and Barrett Dumaine meant nothing to her; her whole world had collapsed around her.

She could not stay here, she could not. She wanted to dig a hole deeper than any which she and Robert had ever dug, and bury herself in it. Instinctively she knew that she had hurt James by her conduct, and, however defiant she had been to him, nothing could wash that away. To retreat with dignity was all that was left to her. She bowed to him, straightened up to meet his inimical stare, a stare which, unknown to her, took James all of his resolution to hold steady.

He watched her leave the room, and his heart went with her, whatever his lips said, but Cressy was not to know that.

Take 4 Love on Call

Mills & Boon Love on Call romances capture all the excitement and emotion of a busy medical world... A world, however, where love and romance are never far away.

We will send you four LOVE ON CALL ROMANCES absolutely FREE plus a cuddly teddy bear and a mystery gift, as your introduction to this superb series.

At the same time we'll reserve a subscription for you to our Reader Service.

Every month you could receive the four latest Love on Call romances delivered direct to your door postage and packing FREE, plus a free Newsletter packed with competitions, author news and much more.

And remember there's no obligation, you may cancel or suspend your subscription at any time. So you've nothing to lose and a world of romance to gain!

FILL IN THE FREE BOOKS COUPON OVERLEAF

Your Free Gifts!

Return this card, and we'll send you a lovely little soft brown bear together with a mystery gift... So don't delay!

FREE BOOKS COUPON

YES Please send me four FREE Love on Call romances together with my teddy bear and mystery gift. Please also reserve a special Reader Service subscription for me. If I decide to subscribe, I will receive four brand new books for just £7.20 each month, postage and packing free. If however, I decide not to subscribe, I shall write to you within 10 days. The free books and gifts will be mine to keep in anycase. I understand that I am under no obligation - I may cancel or suspend my subscription at any time simply by writing to you. I am over 18 years of age.

EXTRA BONUS

We all love mysteries, so as well as the FREE books and Teddy, here's an intriguing gift especially for you. No clues - send off today!

9A4D

Ms/Mrs/Miss/Mr _____

Address _____

_____

Postcode _____ Signature _____

Mills & Boon Reader Service
FREEPOST
P.O. Box 236
Croydon
CR9 9EL

SEND NO MONEY NOW

CHAPTER SEVEN

JAMES was writing a letter to the *Gentleman's Magazine*. After Cressy had gone to her room he had sat for a long time with his head in his hands. Well, that should dispose of any love she had for him and no mistake. It did not dispose of his for her.

The rest of the day he spent clad in sackcloth, dust and ashes, although no one else but himself knew that he did. It was like saying goodbye to his youth and his hope of a normal life. He would never marry now.

He explained Cressy's absence by saying coldly to the company when he went in to dinner that she was not feeling very well and would keep to her room. He had sworn the trembling Miss Sykes to secrecy in the hope that he might deceive everyone as to why she was really there.

He deceived no one, judging by the expression on everyone's face. Dinner was a strange, silent meal. It was as though in some strange way Cressy had become the social lubricant of their lives. Her presence, her *joie de vivre*, the carefree enthusiasm which she brought to everything she said and did had been the reason for the house-party's success. She had spread happiness wherever she had gone.

He thought of the villa and the pavement, of Frank's improbable enthusiasm for the mosaic of the dog. Cressy had certainly touched something in him which no one had touched before. Frank had spent dinner

staring reproachfully at his uncle for his treatment of
Cressy. He had been like a death's head at a feast.
Well, if Cressy had given Frank sensibility, a genuine
feeling for another, she had certainly accomplished at
least one miracle. Which he knew was a lie — the state
to which she had reduced himself was another.

Dinner had been early, as was usual at Haven's End.
The storm which had been threatening all day was
drawing nearer. He bent to his task again. The letter
was to tell the editor of the magazine that an antiquarian discovery of great note had been found on the land
of the Earl of Lyndale, the letter writer; that it was
currently being excavated and when the excavation had
been completed the writer would forward a proper
report, with diagrams and illustrations, all by the main
author of the discovery, the Lady Cressida Mortimer,
daughter and only child of the late Earl of Silchester,
himself an antiquarian of note who had assisted in the
unearthing of Pompeii and Herculaneum, near Naples.

It was Barrett Dumaine who had told him of the
careful drawings which his ward had made of the
objects unearthed on the site. That she had chosen to
confide in Dumaine and not himself was the cause of
further pain to him.

Late in the afternoon he had also spoken to Farmer
Mason, who, having learned from his workmen of
m'lord's arrival and his anger on discovering that the
site was being worked without his knowledge, had come
to make his apologies.

James had listened to him wearily. He was too
emotionally spent to reprimand the man overmuch. He
waved a hand at him when Mason had finished his
halting effort to exculpate himself, and said coldly,

'You made a mistake, Mason, as you have freely owned. The Lady Cressida is an impulsive child. Let us leave the matter there. I am sure that you will not err after such a fashion again.'

And that was true enough, he thought with grim humour. Mason was hardly likely to find another villa on his land, and another wilful child to behave as Cressy had done.

He put down his pen and sighed again. The letter was the least that he could do for her. She deserved the credit for seeing that the villa and the small treasures which it had contained had been unearthed so carefully, and he would see that the work went on. Once she had served her sentence of banishment, the pair of them would oversee it. In future, all would be carried out in proper form.

Duty having been done, he should have felt purged, but instead he merely felt empty. He had extinguished the light which had illuminated Haven's End, and he felt like a murderer or a prospective suicide, for he had extinguished his own reviving light, too.

There was a sudden violent knocking on his door. He raised his head, surprised, called, 'Enter,' and there was Miss Sykes, agitated, a piece of paper in her hand, and behind her Frank and Verena, their faces white and anxious. Barrett Dumaine stood at a little distance, a sardonic observer.

'Good God, what is it?' he exclaimed. 'Is the house on fire?'

Miss Sykes was for once no longer timid.

'Oh, m'lord. It is dreadful news I bring you. Lady Cressida. . .' Her voice faltered.

Frank, impatient, pushed her on one side. 'For God's

sake, madam, tell him, don't flap at him. No time to lose.' He was straightforwardly blunt with his uncle, his pleasant face hard. 'You must know, sir, that you have driven her away by your unkindness, no, your cruelty. Miss Sykes went to her room to find her gone. You had apparently ordered the door to be locked, God knows why. The window was open and a note was left on the bed. Read it, sir, read it.' He unceremoniously took the paper from Miss Sykes's hands and thrust it at his uncle who, judging by the way Frank was speaking to him, was uncle no longer.

James stared at the tear-stained scrap of paper on which was written, 'I can no longer stay where I am not loved or wanted. I shall try to find my way back to Italy. My guardian will be happier when I am gone.'

He crumpled the paper in his fist and the face he turned on Frank and the rest was unrecognisable. 'Gone? How can she be gone? Why should she go?'

Frank sneered at him. 'Oh, you of all people should know, sir. You drove her away, did you not?' And he broke into sudden passionate speech. 'I should have told her that I love her, that I would marry her. I would have let her excavate fields if she wanted to, that I would!'

James hardly heard him. 'You say that she is not in her room — and that the window was open. Never tell me that she left by it.'

'But that's exactly what she must have done, my lord,' said Miss Sykes breathlessly. 'Some of her clothes have gone and she went down to the stables and ordered young Thomson to saddle Mercury for her, and he had no more sense than to obey her.'

'Gone on Mercury.' Whatever was the matter with

him that he should echo only what others were saying? The enormity of her departure and those dreadful words, 'My guardian will be happier when I am gone,' ran through his head. 'Thomson saddled Mercury for her, you say? Has he any idea which way she went? And how long ago was this?'

'No idea where she went,' said Frank. 'And it must have been earlier this evening. Barrett and I met Miss Sykes as she came downstairs in a fluster a few minutes ago and Barrett suggested that we go straight to the stables before we told you—she couldn't get far on foot, he said.'

Again he was the last to know what she was doing. And if he thought that he had been hurt before, the pain then was nothing to this. He had succeeded better than he knew in driving her from him. He had driven her away for good, and now she was lost in the Wiltshire countryside, riding away from Haven's End in the growing dusk, at the mercy of any rogue or cut-throat who might come across her. . . She had been so determined to leave him that she had taken leave of her common sense as well.

He must not take leave of his. He shook his head, aware that Frank was staring at him curiously, struck by the sight of his usually decisive uncle standing there bereft and helpless, the piece of paper still in his hand.

'She is probably making for the main road to London, to pick up the stage-coach,' offered Barrett Dumaine. 'We were only talking of it yesterday. She was curious to know how ordinary people travelled around England. She would leave Mercury at the staging post there. Either at the *Red Lion* outside Andover, to the east, or

south to the *Sun in Splendour* beyond Salisbury. But
the *Red Lion* is the more likely.'

'And the stage does not pass through either of them
until tomorrow,' said James, relief in his voice, 'and the
Mail coach will not go through until midnight.' He
turned to call for his valet to bring him his boots. 'We
must go after her. I am sure that you are right.'

Nothing about him betrayed how frantic he was
inside. He found that he was still holding Cressy's
farewell note and pushed it into the breast pocket of his
coat. It was all that he had left of her.

He felt rather than saw Barrett Dumaine's keen gaze
on him. Dumaine had already sent for his riding boots,
as had Frank, and the three men prepared to ride out
after the missing Cressy, with three grooms in
attendance.

The temptation to chase after her immediately without taking thought was strong in them all, but before
they mounted and set off, James held a short council of
war. 'Frank,' he ordered. 'Take one of the grooms and
make for the road beyond Wells. It is a possibility that
we have not considered. Dumaine, you make for the
Red Lion and I'll set out for the *Sun in Splendour*.
Whichever she makes for, she will have to stay over-
night. I can hardly imagine she'll try to make for
London on horseback.'

'She's such a gallant girl,' declared Frank rudely to
his uncle. 'I can imagine her trying to do anything. A
pity she was driven to this at all.'

James held his rising temper in check. Pointless to
bandy words with his nephew when there was a head-
strong girl to discover. 'And if none of us finds her?'
added Frank. 'What then?'

'No point in dashing around the countryside with our heads on fire,' said James. 'Back to Haven's End for all of us, but keeping a watch on the way. She might have lost herself before even reaching a posting inn, whichever she was making for. And then we must send out as many of the estate workers as we can round up to look for her. Pray God it does not come to that.'

'Like trying to find a needle in a haystack,' said Barrett Dumaine quietly. 'You were in Spain at the same time as I was, Lyndale; needless to tell you how hard it is to find someone in open country when you have no idea in which direction they have gone. . .'

'Luck,' said James savagely. 'Luck is what we need. Pray God one of us has some before the worst befalls her.'

'Amen to that,' replied Dumaine, still sombre, and then they were all mounted and were off, Verena, Emily and Miss Sykes watching them go.

'Poor silly child,' sighed Emily, as the riders disappeared from view. 'Whatever could have possessed her to do such a reckless thing?'

Verena could have told her, but chose not to do so. Frank had informed his mother and herself of James's anger over the secret excavation of Farmer Mason's Roman villa, and Verena was sure from the way in which Cressy looked at and spoke to her guardian that to be reprimanded severely by him would be devastating.

'I shall pray for her,' said Miss Sykes simply. 'I am certain that, if asked properly, God would not let harm come to her. She is such a good-hearted little thing beneath her wild manner. Lord Lyndale is right to try to tame her, but I think that at times he is a little over-severe, if you will pardon my criticism of your brother, ladies,' she added, fearing that she might have offended.

'I think,' said Emily, briskly for her, 'James is severe with everyone around him. Why, he is even severe with my Frank, and a better, kinder young man never existed. I know that he is not clever, but he has a good heart, and I don't think James values that enough. The same thing goes for Cressy. Oh, I do hope that they find her and soon, but Wiltshire is so large and Cressy is so small. . . I will pray, too, dear Miss Sykes.'

'And I,' added Verena. 'I am only sorry that Fred's gout does not allow him to ride out with the others.' She put her arm in Miss Sykes's and they all went into the house to watch and wait. 'Which is the usual role of women,' Verena said, 'and I sometimes think is harder than actually doing something. I would rather be out with James than sitting here doing nothing and trying not to think of the worst.'

The thunder which had been threatening but distant all day had come nearer with the evening, and was now loud and insistent. The occasional lightning flash lit up the surrounding countryside as James, beginning to feel distraught, stood in the yard of the *Sun in Splendour* and debated with himself. No unaccompanied young lady, indeed, no one at all, had arrived at the inn to wait for the stage or the mail coach. Stephen, whom he had chosen to accompany him, stood by their horses, a worried expression on his face. Like all the servants at Haven's End, he liked and admired Lady Cressy, 'a good plucked 'un' being the general verdict on her. He disliked the thought of her being out somewhere in the growing dark.

'It's always possible,' said James slowly to him at last, 'that she did make for one of the other two inns where she could have boarded a stage. But she's always shown great common sense about practical matters. This is the nearest staging post, so this is the one which she was most likely to make for. . .'

He fell silent, before resuming, 'If she didn't make for the Wells or Andover routes and isn't here, then somehow she went astray on the journey, perhaps lost her way. The road she would finally take to join the main London highway is at best only a track, and in its worst places is barely that. Did she ever come this way with you before?'

'Once, m'lord,' said Stephen after thinking a moment. 'When the ladies were with us. Not as far as this, of course, but we rode along the byway and she asked me where it led to. I told her to the main highway to London, and later I heard her asking Captain Dumaine about the coaches which ran along it, and the way the staging posts were organised. Lady Cressida was always interested in how things worked, m'lord.'

'Yes.' James was brief. 'So, if we are right, and I take it that you agree with me that this is the direction in which she must have come, then she must be somewhere between here and Haven's End. Now, seeing that we travelled by the only route which she could have taken, and saw no sign of her, then the chances are strong that she lost her way. I suggest that we start off together, then split up and take different routes home across country, trying to keep our eyes open for any sign of her.'

He thought of Dumaine's needles in haystacks and did not know whom he could curse the most for their present predicament, himself or the wilful child lost somewhere in the hinterlands around them. 'At least she is unlikely to have crossed the main highway.'

Stephen nodded, and added in his practical fashion which would one day ensure him promotion, 'May I suggest, m'lord, that we part at the end of the good track which leads straight on to the highway. She would hardly be likely to have lost her way on that — more like the middle bit deceived her.'

James accepted this piece of advice gratefully. He and Stephen parted where the byway petered out to little more than a green lane, and a narrow one at that. The road had once been a cattle track, but was long disused.

Thunder rolled overhead as he struck off to the left, Stephen having gone to the right, to find himself in scrub and heathland with stands of trees punctuated by the occasional open space. He was not yet quite back on his own land, but he knew that years ago there had been attempts to farm this part of Wiltshire, but that the attempt had failed. There was the occasional derelict farmhouse overgrown with weeds and bramble, mute evidence of man's one time occupation.

The rain which had threatened all evening began to fall. He cursed under his breath. A strong and gusty wind had sprung up and he was riding into the teeth of it. Thunder, now overhead, rolled and the occasional lightning flash showed him momentarily every detail of the landscape in a livid light. In the name of God, where could she be? And out in this! It was imperative that she be found.

* * *

Cressy was sitting in the lee of what had once been a farmhouse. She had no idea where she was. She had thought once or twice that she recognised certain landmarks seen on one of her rides, but once she had lost her way she had been sure of nothing.

Everything had gone horribly wrong. Sitting in her room, full of the most intense grief which she had ever experienced, for Robert's death had been a different sort of sorrow, not burning and bitter like this, it had been easy to decide that she would run away to London, try to buy a passage to Italy—and try also to forget James, if that were possible.

She had gone to her trunks and fished out the boy's clothes which she had worn when working in the excavated sites with Robert. For money she had a hidden purse in which were enough sovereigns and guineas to get her first to London and then on to a ship. She had been hoarding them ever since Mr Coutts, the banker, had given them to her when she had first reached London. They were for her personal use, her pin money, he had said with a smile.

Even then, sitting in his office, waiting to be delivered like a parcel to old Lord Lyndale, as she had thought, there had been some dim scheme at the back of her mind that she might run away and somehow reach Naples again.

But at Haven's End, after the first few weeks of misery, she had found happiness of quite a different nature from that which she had experienced in Italy. Improbably, the source of that happiness was her unexpected guardian.

She had smashed that happiness by her own folly and now she knew that, whatever she felt for him, he obviously felt nothing for her but contempt, and the knowledge had been too much for her. Italy was her haven, not this beautiful house in England, and to that haven she would return to continue alone what she and Robert had started together.

She would appeal to the King of the Two Sicilies, who was a friend of the Franceschinis, if her guardian tried to have her returned to him, and if that failed she would petition the Lord Chancellor, or the Prince Regent himself. . . The thunder rolled to interrupt her musings, a wild wind ran across the grass and the rain at last came down, so that she scrambled for refuge into the ruined farmhouse.

Her flight seemed to have been doomed from the beginning. Oh, it had started well enough with the poor young stablehand, mesmerised by her peremptory orders, allowing her to take out Mercury, one of James's second-run horses. She would not steal one of his fliers; that would be wrong. Riding along in the dim evening light, thunder rolling in the distance, growing ever nearer, disaster had struck. Mercury had caught his right foreleg in a rabbit-hole when she had unaccountably strayed off the track into the wilderness, and had fallen lame. Thank goodness that it had not been Hector or Paris she had stolen.

After that she had dismounted and walked him along, looking for the lost track as she did so, but she had been uneasily conscious that she was probably getting further and further away from her destination, the *Sun in Splendour* on the road from Salisbury.

Huddled in the lee of an inside wall out of the rain — she had already tethered Mercury to a tree when she had finally decided to stop walking for very weariness —

she waited for the morning. Her humiliation was complete. She was lost, her flight had not been successful and now she must hope that one way or another she would either be found by James and Frank, whom she was sure would come after her, or when dawn broke she might, fortunately, find the byway again and reach the London road and the *Sun in Splendour*, even if she had to walk there.

Cressy grimaced. Common sense told her that the likelihood was that she would be followed and returned to Haven's End, her tail between her legs, to await whatever punishment her guardian thought fit.

For very weariness despite herself she began to doze, at first her head upon her knees, until, lulled by the sound of the rain, she propped herself against the wall to sleep in earnest.

James, swearing to himself, gradually becoming soaked despite his protective coat, was growing more and more desperate at the thought of Cressy lost in the downpour. A sudden flash of lightning directly overhead, and consequently coincident with a deafening crack of thunder, lit up the whole landscape for him so that it was as bright as day. In that split second before darkness descended again he saw Mercury, tossing his head, showing the whites of his eyes, but securely tethered to a tree.

It was enough. Through the darkness James made for where he had glimpsed Mercury, saw the ruined farmhouse and guessed that his lost ward must be there. At least she had found shelter from the storm, as now so would he.

He tethered his own mount, and stepped over the

broken wall, to see Cressy half-sitting, half-lying there, asleep.

Relief fuelled his rage. How dared she sleep while he and Frank and Dumaine, all half out of their minds because of her reckless folly, quartered the countryside in the year's worst storm looking for her!

He made for the corner where she lay, knelt down and shook her awake. Cressy, eyes opening slowly, looked up at him, and murmured 'Oh, you have come for me, my darling,' and rested her head on his chest, to sleep again.

She had been dreaming. One day she had gone to the Masons' farm and there had been a wise woman there, sent for to bless the newly pregnant wife of Farmer Mason's eldest son, not long married. She had burned herbs in the fireplace, placed her hands on the girl's stomach, bent her head to listen, and then said confidently, 'A good strong lad, Maister Mason, and no mistake.'

She had looked up to see Cressy staring at her. She had gone into the farmhouse for a cup of new milk, leaving Frank and Dumaine outside drinking ale with Rob and the grooms, as was their habit at the end of the afternoon's work.

'Eh, a pretty young maid we have here, and a good day to you.' The wise woman made naught of gentry and she rose and handled Cressy as familiarly as she would have done one of the milkmaids, taking her by the chin and turning her head this way and that.

'Ripe for marriage, my sweeting — let Granny show you your true love,' and she had handed Cressy a small muslin pouch filled with fragrant herbs. 'Wear that, my little dear, when you sleep, and see your true love's face.'

Mrs Mason had looked troubled by the familiarity, but Cressy had smiled. She had met wise women in Italy and they had been even less formal than the goodwife. She took the offered pouch, but she had not worn it when she slept, for Cressy was a child of the new Enlightenment, taught by Robert, and did not believe in magic and spells.

She had put it in her trunk to sweeten its contents and when she pulled out her boy's clothes, it had fallen out of them and she had thrust it into her breeches pocket almost absent-mindedly, and forgotten about it.

But in her sleep she had entered a strange world which she had never seen before. She was standing on a stone floor, wearing a plain white gown, belted with a purple sash. A woman spoke to her, but Cressy could not tell what she had said. She only knew that she was waiting for someone, but who that someone might be was unknown to her. She had turned and walked down some marble steps on to a mosaic floor this time, with urns of flowers standing on it. . .

For some reason she had looked down at the floor, and there was a dog worked in the mosaic, its head back and its tail held high. *Cave canem*, it said beneath him. The dog was hers, and the man who had laid it down had followed her instructions when he did so. It was to be like a floor which she had seen in Rome before she came to live here. And then a man was speaking to her. He was behind her and at the sound of his loved voice such joy ran through her as she had never felt before.

She turned to see him, standing in a doorway. He

was wearing a magnificent tunic of scarlet and gold. He had a fillet of gold on his black curls and his amber eyes shone with love as he held out his arms to her and spoke. This time she could understand what was said to her, although the language in which he spoke was strange. It sounded a little like Italian.

'Oh, my love, at last, at last we are together again, and shall be parted no more,' and she knew him. It was James, of course, but who was James?

Who he was did not matter, for she knew that he was her love and she flung herself into his arms, saying to him, 'Oh, you have come for me, my darling,' before the dream vanished into blackness and a man was shaking her and he was not loving, like the man in her dream, but angry.

Cressy awoke — and the dream vanished. She could not remember it, even though she tried to hold on to it, and from a distance she heard the goodwife's voice. 'Let go, child, let go. It will come again.'

So she laid her head on the breast of the man who seemed to be a part of her lost dream and tried to return to it.

James looked down at the sleeping girl, her face full of love and trust, and his anger seeped out of him. He held her close for a moment, and then shook her again, gently this time.

'Cressy, wake up.'

She stirred and murmured so softly that he could barely hear her, 'No, I am so comfortable like this. Let me sleep.'

The expression on James's face was rueful. He had intended to scold her, to berate her for frightening them all, for running into unknown danger, but he found that he could not wake her up to do so. She was so warm and soft in his arms — and her warmth and softness were temptation itself.

He settled himself against the wall, and tried to think of neutral things, of the plans he was making to reform the estate, of the necessity for him to go to London shortly to speak and vote in the House of Lords. Would he, dared he, take his wilful ward with him to launch her on to Society? No, forget that, try to think that what he was holding was a child, not a desirable young woman — whom he desired.

He should be thinking of returning, once the torrential downpour was over, but the storm still raged on and he could not subject her to it, lightly clad as she was in her boy's clothing.

She had stuffed her hair in a silk jockey cap, but while she slept the jockey cap had fallen off, and her mass of tumbled dark chestnut curls was resting against his chest.

The softness and scent of it was yet another potent distraction. He must put her down, but when he tried to move her, again as gently as possible, she made a small dissenting sound and put one arm up around his neck, to lie the closer to him.

St Anthony himself, the great resister of female temptation, could not have resisted this. To have the loved object in one's arms, even though sleeping, when in that sleep she persisted in caressing him, would have destroyed the dedicated celibacy of even that saint.

James's hand rose to stroke the tiny breasts visible through the damp silk of Cressy's shirt. He pulled it back at the last moment, stared at the treacherous limb — and became aware of the even more treacherous

stirrings of his long-deprived body. He made a small
sound of self-disgust and decided that, come what may,
he must be cruel to be kind. He must wake her up and
sit away from her, so far as the ruined house would let
him.

'Cressy,' he said sharply. 'Wake up, it is your guardian. I must speak to you.' He shook her when she tried
to resist him, so that she finally awoke, blinking at him
in surprise.

'Sir,' she muttered, yawning a little. 'How came you
here? I was dreaming, such a pleasant dream, but I
have forgotten it,' she finished inconsequentially. And
then, 'Is it still raining? There was thunder in my
dream.'

James moved away from her as she sat up and began
to try to pin up her errant hair. 'My dear ward,' he said
as coldly and impersonally as he could, to try to quench
the fires that raged within him. 'What in God's name
did you think that you were doing? To ride off into wild
country which you do not know, to try to take a coach
to a town which is equally unknown to you. You were
like to be the prey of every rogue and cut-throat who
haunts the highways and byways looking for easy pick-
ings. You must know that you have frightened us all to
death.'

Cressy stared at him, her eyes filling with tears. 'I
didn't think that you would be other than relieved to
see the back of me,' she faltered. 'I was so unhappy. I
had not meant to hurt you by behaving as I did over
the Roman Villa. I thought that perhaps I would be
better out of England and back where no one was
troubled by my behaviour. I never thought that you

would come to look for me. Have I been a great nuisance, sir? I am sorry if I was.'

James sighed. 'Not only have I been riding around Wiltshire like a demented Bow Street Runner chasing a criminal,' he said severely, 'but Frank, Captain Dumaine and half the grooms at Haven's End have been searching for you, instead of sleeping in their beds. At least now that I have found you I need not worry, but think how they must all feel, and will feel, until I return with you safe and sound.'

He saw, with remorse, that the tears were threatening to fall. Cressy gave a great sniff and wiped her eyes with the back of her hand. 'Oh, I do apologise, sir. To you now, and will do so to the others later. I see that you had the right of it when you told me that I did not think carefully enough before I spoke or acted. I shall remember that in future.'

She hung her head to avoid looking at him, then said under her breath, 'I have hurt you again, and I never meant to, truly. I thought that you would be pleased to see me gone, and so I wrote in my note. I thought that you no longer cared for me at all.'

'No,' said James, almost violently. 'Never that. I. . .' and all his common sense flew away. He caught her to him, to comfort her, to do something, no, anything, anything to wipe her misery away. 'Oh, God, Cressy, I care for you too much.' He kissed the top of her head, and, sense returning, tried to push her away.

Cressy resisted him. She was in his arms at last, and as she had entered them, her dream had returned. It was James she had been with in the villa in Farmer Mason's field, and if the goodwife was right, James was her true love and she would never let him go, never.

Her resistance, far from confirming James's belated resolution to push her from him, had the opposite effect. Her clinging to him destroyed his last reserves of propriety. Here, in the dark, the rain falling outside, away from civilisation, they were not Cressy and her guardian any more, but man and woman. He had the woman he wanted in his arms at last and everything could go hang.

His mouth came down on hers and Cressy responded as enthusiastically as she always did, kissing him back as though she had been kissing men for years, instead of this being only the second occasion on which she had done any such thing.

Such willing compliance excited James the more. His kisses now roved down her neck, towards the opening of her shirt. Cressy gave a little cry and put up her hand to stroke his head bent between her breasts, nuzzling the shirt away to find them. They had been sitting up after James had awoken her, and now he slowly bore her backwards to the ground.

The sensations running through Cressy's body were so sweet and powerful that they overwhelmed her quite. Each time that he touched her, or she him, produced such a feeling of delight that she was almost transported out of her body. Just before her questing mind shut itself off altogether and she became pure body, she thought, oh, I knew it would be like this, if only I could persuade him to love me.

Love her he did. Every part of her body became James's territory to explore, and for her part Cressy discovered his, an explorer in the erotic arts for the first time. She was as fearless in her discoveries as he was. Her own broken words, her sighs, matched by groans from James, taught Cressy that love was not a silent thing. She also learned that in the end, her body did not need to be taught; it understood only too well what it wanted.

'Please,' she gasped at last, 'please,' and pressed herself against him in her ecstasy. 'Oh, James, I love you so.'

These first coherent words from Cressy, particularly her loving use of his name, penetrated James's consciousness. He suddenly became aware that he was on the point of ravishing a girl who was not only a virgin, but had also been confided to his care for him to protect and to cherish, not to despoil.

In the very act of preparing to take her, his whole body ready for final consummation with a most willing partner whose passion matched his own, he drew back. His reviving conscience affected him as though a bucket of cold water had been thrown over him.

His body aching and throbbing, he rolled away from her to lie beside her, his arm thrown across his face, unable either to speak or to act, so consumed was he by the enormity of what he had so nearly done.

Cressy, who had been in paradise, found that paradise snatched away. For a moment she lay breathless, quiet, her body screaming its anger at James's sudden withdrawal. She turned towards him, to put out a hand to touch him. But when she did so he groaned and drew away from her as though he had been scalded.

'James, what's wrong? Oh, why did you stop?' Bereft, she moved towards him again, only for him to scramble away from her, so that now they were out of the shelter of the broken roof and the rain came pelting

pitilessly down on them. So absorbed were they both in
their private world that neither of them noticed.

'Are you ill? James, my love, are you ill? Speak to
me.' Her cries became so frantic that James, shudder-
ing, sat up to quieten her. In doing so he registered for
the first time that they were both becoming soaked in
the downpour and said angrily, 'For God's sake,
Cressy, get out of the rain.'

The tone of his voice was so unlike its recent loving
one that she stared at him, white-faced, and retreated
under the shelter of the roof again.

James made no move to join her. He rose, and
walked out of the rain to lean against the wall as far
away from her as possible. With his face turned to it,
he was a picture of such abandoned distress that Cressy
became alarmed, rose herself and walked towards him,
to touch him timidly on the shoulder. Again he moved
fiercely away from her, but this time he lifted his bent
head so that she saw his white tormented face for the
first time.

'James! What is it? Oh, you are ill!'

He turned his face away from her, and said to the
wall rather than to her, his voice hoarse and unrecognisable, 'Oh, Cressy, don't you understand what I so
nearly did to you? God forgive me, I was on the point
of seducing you, of ruining you with no thought of
anything but my own pleasure. A young girl. . .my
ward. . .a virgin. . .who trusted me and I behaved like
a beast of the field taking his mate. . .'

'Oh, is that all?' exclaimed Cressy, greatly relieved.
'But why are you reproaching yourself so? I wanted
you and did nothing to discourage you. On the contrary, I am only sorry that you stopped when you did.'

'Child, child,' he groaned. 'You don't know what you are saying .'

'Oh, but I do.' Cressy threw out her arms towards him, inviting him back. 'Robert explained to me what men and women do when they love one another. I wasn't a bit afraid, because I love you, you see, and I'm sure that you love me, so why are we arguing? We can be married just as soon as it can be arranged, so there is no need to worry that you might give me a baby. Oh, think, James, a baby. . .our baby. . .' And her face shone with such pleasure that James's resolution nearly withered at the sight.

'Dearest Cressy, if only everything were as simple as you make it sound. I am twice your age, I stand in the same relationship to you as a father. You have, from what you have told me, seen little of men and the world other than your father's immediate circle. I am almost the first man whom you have encountered under the age of sixty. Naturally you think that you love me— and I so nearly took advantage of that. You must meet many others before you decide whom you will finally marry.'

Cressy made a small dissenting noise. 'Oh, no. You're wrong. I don't love you because you are the first young man I have ever met, I love you because you're James. I don't love Frank or Captain Dumaine, even though they are younger than you are. I don't want to meet other men, I'm sure I shan't love them half as much as I love you.' The small face turned towards him was so artlessly trusting that James's heart turned over.

'It's not simply what the world would say,' he began, only to have Cressy eagerly interject,

'Oh, I don't care what the world would say. I never have, and I'm sure that you don't either. No, you can't reject me, you can't. You'll break my heart. . .' This brave speech ended in such a wail of grief that James nearly took her in his arms again to comfort her, but he knew where that would lead.

The downpour had begun to ease a little, and when it finally became lighter they must return to Haven's End. There was a miniature world awaiting them there, with a larger world outside, and both worlds would ask what James Chavasse, Earl of Lyndale, and his ward, the Lady Cressida Mortimer, had been doing together, alone in the night, away from everyone!

It might already be too late to save her reputation but, thank God, it had not been too late for him to stop committing the unforgivable at the last minute. He had certainly destroyed much of her innocence, even if he had left her virginity intact.

'Cressy,' he said gently, 'try to understand. You only think you love me. . .'

'And you,' she was like lightning in the speed of her response, 'and you, James, do you love me?'

'That is beside the point,' he replied firmly, but hopelessly, because he knew such an answer would tacitly admit that he did. 'The point is that I would have been taking advantage of you, and our situation, if I had made love to you just now. If you will only reflect for a moment, you will know that what I am saying is true. You must go into the world, meet others, find out what the life you will be living is truly like, and not judge it, or men, by a few weeks spent at Haven's End. I. . .we. . .must do the honourable thing. I am so much older than you are; you deserve a young man, not a battered creature like myself.'

Cressy put her face in her hands. She could tell that James meant what he said. He was rejecting her, and either he did not love her, which was like the end of the world to her, or he did, and that was worse, much worse. She could live with the first belief, but not the second, because the second meant that although he loved her, he would never marry her because of some mad male notion about honour.

She lifted her head, and exclaimed fiercely, 'Honour! Is that all men think about? Where is the honour in my broken heart?'

James could do no more than say gently, 'But I do not think that your heart is truly broken. You may think it is. Let me take you to London. Emily and Verena can go with us to chaperon you between them. There you will meet young men of your own age in a society in which you have never lived before. At the end of the season, I dare swear that you will not be talking to me of a broken heart.'

'You do not know me,' said Cressy sadly, at last turning away from him. 'I shall not change. That is the motto of the Mortimers,' she said defiantly, lifting her head again, but still keeping her back to him. '"*Changeless, not changing*".'

'And that of the Chavasses is "*In honour rooted*". Where would my honour have been, Cressy, if I had taken you outside marriage in a derelict hut? Could a man who truly loved you do that?'

She wanted to shout 'yes' at him, but she knew that he had recovered, and was now implacable. The James in whose arms she had lain had gone, perhaps never to return. That was the James she wanted to remember, not this stern man who was rejecting her. He could not know how deeply she had come to feel for him.

The rain had finally died down. Like the passion in the hut, it had surcease. The thunder and the lightning had moved on and everywhere was peace, except in the hearts of the man and the woman who stood apart, and were still apart as they mounted James's horse to ride back to the house now so inappropriately named Haven's End.

CHAPTER EIGHT

LONG after midnight Frank arrived back at Haven's End empty-handed. Verena and Emily, faces white, still fully dressed, met him in the entrance hall. Miss Sykes hovered in attendance.

'No news?' his mother said, her lips quivering at the sight of his face. Verena, more stoic, put an arm around his shoulders.

'Never mind, Frank, I know that you have done your best.'

'Not good enough,' said Frank briefly, not at all his usual cheerful self. He was exhausted. It was not every day that he chased through the night, first over bad roads, and then across difficult country. The storm had started in earnest when he had reached the inn on the Wells road. Riding home through it, he had trembled at the thought of Cressy on her own in such weather.

None of the party felt any better when Barrett Dumaine arrived a little later, his face grim. His story was the same as Frank's. Later still his groom arrived, and then Stephen came in, to tell of parting from his master some hours earlier. So it became a case of waiting for James.

The men prevailed upon Emily and Verena to go to bed. Miss Sykes refused to do so. She felt responsible for Cressy's flight; she should have been alert and prevented it, she said, and could not rest until she was safely home again.

171

Barrett Dumaine settled her in an armchair, and took Frank by the arm to lead him to the big sideboard to pour out a large glass of port for them both, saying wryly, 'If we must stay up, then we may as well get drunk, but only slightly. Wouldn't do to be overset if they both return safe and sound.'

Mid-way through their attack on the bottle, Verena came downstairs to say that she was unable to sleep and might as well join them. Cocking an eye at Frank, Dumaine poured her a glass of Madeira. It was no surprise to them when shortly afterwards Emily arrived saying, 'I cannot sleep for thinking of that poor child and James out in this terrible storm.'

While she was speaking and accepting a glass of Madeira with small cries of, 'Oh, no, I shouldn't — but if you are all drinking, then I might as well,' it became apparent that the storm had passed its height. The rain had ceased to beat upon the drawing-room windows, and the rolls of thunder were moving into the distance.

It was well into the small hours when Emily, over-come by worry, weariness and liberal draughts of Madeira, fell asleep in her armchair.

Frank, half cut, surveyed her owlishly, and said, 'Never knew Mama to drink like that before. Shows what it can do to you when you're not used to it.' So saying, he subsided into an armchair and promptly fell asleep himself, felled by nearly a bottle of port.

Barrett Dumaine, who had not drunk nearly as much as he had appeared to do, a favourite exercise of his, and Verena, who had merely taken one glass, looked at one another ruefully, Miss Sykes a silent ghost in the background.

'Best thing, I suppose,' ventured Dumaine, staring at

the snoring Frank. 'No use to man nor beast sitting here worrying. Even if Lyndale found her, he would hardly have brought her home in this storm. What was she wearing, d'you know?'

'Boy's clothes, Miss Sykes thinks,' answered Verena, unable to prevent herself from giving a small sad smile in the direction of the sleeping duenna. 'Miss Sykes said that she hadn't taken any of her new clothes. That she had some boy's wear in her trunks, worn when she was on the site with her father, one supposes, and that they had gone.'

'Still not enough to protect her on such a wild night as this. Four o' the clock and still drizzling. . .' commented Dumaine. He was interrupted by the sounds of activity outside. Barker and his cohorts had been keeping watch for the return of m'lord and his errant charge. Voices rang out, running footsteps were heard, and then the door was flung open by an excited footman, lost to all due forms and ceremonies, carried away by the drama of the night. 'They've been sighted, Lady Verena, Master Frank.' This to Frank, who was stirring, roused by the noise of the grooms shouting and horses on the move.

'Roger saw 'em coming in from the direction of Salisbury. He says m'lord was leading his horse, with Lady Cressida up.'

'Thank God,' said Verena gratefuly. 'Emily, Miss Sykes, wake up. James and Cressy are both safe and sound and nearly home.'

Frenzied activity followed a night's painful inaction. Miss Sykes was pulling the bell, calling on Cressy's maid, the housekeeper and James's valet to be in attendance. 'Hot water,' she announced frantically.

'And clean dry clothes — they must be soaked.' Warming pans had been ordered for the beds earlier, and had been several times renewed. Servants, kept from their beds until the master and his ward were safe, ran about.

Now the excited voices were immediately outside, James's among them, demanding and curt, and the whole party, including an eye-rubbing Emily, adjourned to the entrance hall as James entered, carrying an exhausted Cressy.

His whole demeanour was so stern and grim that even Frank quailed before it.

'What the devil. . .?' James stared balefully at them. 'This is no raree show. The child is beside herself with weariness. You were all best in bed.'

And as Emily broke out with, 'Thank God that you are both safe,' he dismissed her with the barest civility.

'Save your rejoicings until tomorrow, sister. At the moment they are inappropriate. She has been in the rain and may have taken a fever.'

He turned on his heel to half run up the great staircase to Cressy's room, leaving the whole party staring after him, expresions of mixed surprise, shock and relief on their faces. Miss Sykes followed them after a moment's hesitation.

'Now what the devil has got into *him*,' exclaimed Frank, his honest face scarlet. 'She's safe, ain't she? A touch of civility wouldn't have come amiss. We were all as worried as he was.'

'Oh, I think not,' murmured Barrett Dumaine under his breath, to be heard only by the shrewd Verena.

Barker had come into the entrance hall to speak to Verena and Emily. 'M'lord thought that you ought to know that Mercury fell lame early on in Lady Cressida's flight. That he and Lady Cressida shared a ride on Hector until he feared that Hector might be falling lame too, at which point he led him home on foot, which is why it took them so long to return.'

'Convenient,' muttered Dumaine, *sotto voce*, to be heard again only by Verena, but he merely echoed her own thoughts. A moment or two later, James came down to them, still wearing his sodden clothes, making a belated effort to preserve some of the decencies. He was more forbidding in his manner than ever. And this attempt to preserve the decencies was so perfunctory as to be non-existent.

He walked over to the sideboard to broach a new bottle of port, saying as he did so, 'I found Lady Cressida some considerable time after we discovered that she had not reached the inn on the Salisbury road. Stephen and I split up shortly after that to search the open country between Haven's End and the London road.

'She had lost her way, Mercury had fallen lame, and she had taken refuge in a ruined farmhouse in the hinterland between here and Salisbury. It was there that I found her. We waited until the storm had abated. She grew fevered on the way back and we had to stop again. After that I led Hector home with Lady Cressida up, because she was the lighter weight and he had already done too much for one evening. And now you may all go to bed for what is left of the night.' He turned on his heel and walked out of the room, still carrying his glass and the full bottle.

'The devil *is* in him,' announced Frank, 'but at least little Cressy's safe home.' He stretched and yawned inelegantly. 'Let's go to bed, Barrett. I never spent a worse or a longer night.' He looked at his mother and his aunt, silently gathering themselves together before returning to their rooms. 'I can only hope that the way he's carrying on don't mean he's going to ring several peals over the poor little thing in the morning. Ain't it enough that he drove her away once? Carry on as he is doing, and she's likely to cut line again.'

'Frank,' said his mother reprovingly. 'That's no way to talk.'

'And no way for him to behave, either,' returned Frank, living up to his name as usual. 'Well, you may all think as you like, but I think he ought to unbend a little before he becomes permanently frozen.' Without another word to anyone, he stumped indignantly up to bed. If the rest of the party agreed with Frank, they did not say so, even if they thought it. Good manners and discretion alike kept them quiet.

Cressy sat on her bed the next morning being fed gruel by Miss Sykes. 'Take it away, I don't want it,' she had exclaimed.

When Miss Sykes, a worried look on her kind face had advanced on her with it, saying, 'Lord Lyndale wished most particularly. . .'. Cressy had snorted rudely.

'I am not interested in Lord Lyndale's wishes,' she had uttered before diving under the bedclothes, only to emerge a moment later. Poor Sykes. It wasn't her fault that James, Lord Lyndale, was a monstrously priggish man of honour, who hadn't the decency to keep from breaking a poor girl's heart, but was determined to force gruel on her instead, as a poultice for it doubtless.

'I'm not ill,' she murmured plaintively. 'I had much worse fevers when I lived in Italy.'

'Most likely,' replied Miss Sykes, sharply for her. 'Who knows what illnesses one might contract in foreign parts.'

'Italy was not foreign parts to me,' Cressy managed, between spoonfuls. 'It was home, which is more than Haven's End is now.'

'A very naughty thing to say.' This morning Miss Sykes had developed a sudden habit of talking to her charge as though she were a badly behaved nine-year-old.

Cressy responded in kind. 'I don't care.'

'Don't care was made to care,' was her chaperon's only answer to that.'

'Please don't rebuke me as though I were a small child,' said Cressy, summoning up all the dignity she could while sitting up in bed having over-large quantities of gruel thrust into her face. But she received no change from her previously submissive companion, who sniffed, before saying in the manner of one offering an incontrovertible truth, 'Then don't behave like one.'

The rest of the day lived up to its beginning. She was not allowed up until the doctor arrived, to pronounce that her temperature was back to normal, and that she might rise from her bed, but only to stay in her own suite of rooms.

'The patient is not to be over-exerted,' he remarked solicitously to Miss Sykes. 'I understand that she has been overdoing things.'

'Underdoing them, more like,' remarked Cressy under her breath, lest Miss Sykes begin offering her more nursery platitudes about her behaviour.

After that, for James to arrive to speak to her as though he were addressing Parliament, so coolly impersonal was he, was only to be expected. Cressy felt a wan dowd, while James looked magnificent, dressed to kill in a formal black suit with knee breeches, even if his eyes were bloodshot and any over-loud noise made him wince. He was regretting his previous night's excessive drinking, but at least it made him less inclined to be over-indulgent to his ward.

It was 'Lady Cressida' and 'sir' all over again. Last night's frantic passion might never have happened.

'I am happy to hear, Lady Cressida, that the doctor considers your malaise to be only a passing one.'

'I never had a malaise at all. . .sir,' replied Cressy, as coldly as she could. 'Only you and Miss Sykes seemed determined to assure me that I had, and the doctor obliged you. Naturally, since you pay him.'

'Insolence in a young woman is not a pretty thing,' pronounced James as magisterially as he could, the sight of Cressy having its usual dreadful effect on him.

'Nor pomposity in a man who is not yet quite past his prime,' said Cressy nastily. If insults were to be exchanged, then she was only too willing to oblige him.

James sighed and wished his thundering head would go away. 'I have consulted with the Ladies Emily and Verena. They have agreed that it might be good for you to have your come-out and take part in the London season. It will give you something other to think about than your wrongs. Lady Verena and Mr Davenport will remain here before accompanying us to London. Lady Emily and Frank will join us there later.'

'And Captain Dumaine?' asked Cressy. She had not the slightest interest in anything Captain Dumaine might do, but thought that it would provoke her guardian if she mentioned his name. It did.

'Captain Dumaine's plans are unknown to me, which is fortunate, seeing that I have no interest in them. You will oblige me by consulting with Miss Sykes and Lady Verena at all points before we leave Haven's End.'

Cressy nodded, her heart too full to allow her to speak. How could he be so cold and formal with her? And twitting her about her wrongs, too, as though they were not wrongs at all. Robert would not have wanted her to be so confined and restrained.

Surely he might unbend if she smiled at him? But neither smiles nor tears nor impassioned words would move him, she could tell that, and besides, her own pride would not let her beg. Damn him! She would be as cool as he.

James continued. 'There is one more thing to say. We were alone last night, for most of the night. I understand from our companions here that their discretion will be absolute. This unfortunate occurrence, created by your own wilfulness, I must add, will remain private to us. Your reputation will be preserved intact.'

'Oh, what a pity.' Cressy's voice was vitriol itself. 'Otherwise you might have had to marry me to restore it, and that would never have done.'

James broke a little on that. 'You impertinent baggage. . .' he began, fire shooting from his tiger's eyes. He took a step towards her before restraining himself. 'No, by God, you will not work your arts on me, madam. We shall remain as distant as a guardian and his ward ought to be. Propriety will be maintained between us. Last night never happened. You understand me, *Lady Cressida*?'

'Perfectly.' Cressy was shaking between rage and frustration. She knew that she had nearly had him in her arms again but, alas, she had lost him. 'We are to lie, and lie again, m'lord. Tell me, does anyone in your fabled society ever speak the truth? Or is a minute gun fired on the rare occasions when they do?'

James decided to ignore this last piece of impudence. He stared down at her, using his height to intimidate. Every dart he fired at Cressy pierced his own heart, and for each wound he suffered, he knew that she had one to match it. But he had his duty to perform and perform it he would, even if his scarred heart broke in the doing.

Cressy sank into her chair when he had gone. If her fever had subsided before James had arrived, his words and his manner had served to raise it again. However was she to get through the remainder of her time at Haven's End? More to the point, how was she to live through the London season which, judging by everything which Miss Sykes, Emily and Verena had said to her, they considered to be such a great treat. Her greatest treat would be to stay here with James. Or go to London with him, not as an unwanted responsibility to be endured, but as someone he loved and cared for.

But, of course, life being what it was, Cressy's heart did not completely break, nor was she unable to enjoy herself a little when she was allowed in company again. She was even allowed to go to the villa and arrange with Farmer Mason and James for the excavation to go ahead slowly during her absence.

After that there was the excitement of packing for London and saying goodbye to Lady Emily, Frank and Captain Dumaine, when they left with promises to see her again when she entered Society. Emily and Frank were to stay with them at Lyndale House in Piccadilly after they had settled their country affairs. Captain Dumaine's destination was more imprecise.

Only James remained aloof, rarely meeting his guests, pleading pressure of business or anything which he could think of so that he might not be in the same room as Cressy. He had thought that at Haven's End he had at last found peace, but since his unexpected ward had arrived his peace had been shattered, for good, probably.

As for Cressy, despite her outward calm, no girl had ever prepared for her come-out with less enthusiasm. *He* meant to take her to London to pair her off with some young man for whom she would not care a fig, she knew he did. Well, she would beat him at his own game. She would refuse everyone, yes, everyone, until she was twenty-one, and her own mistress. If by then she had not succeeded in changing his mind, she would return to Italy and would become an antidote, past her last prayers. If she could not have James, she would have no one.

So when the great day came and James, Cressy, the Davenports, and all their servants and possessions, ceremoniously walked down the front steps of Haven's End to the train of coaches, curricles, mounted horses and attendant grooms, it could not be said that any single member of the party was happy.

James was unhappy because he had fallen in love with his ward to whom he stood *in loco parentis*, as her father, and therefore he felt that he could not in honour offer an inexperienced girl marriage, particularly since he was so much older than she was.

Cressy was unhappy because she had fallen in love with James, and knew in her bones that it was not calf-

love, or simple affection for the first clever and handsome man whom she had met. Verena was unhappy
because James was unhappy, and her husband Fred was
unhappy, because he did not care for London or the
season, and was only going there as a favour to his wife
and his brother-in-law.

The train of vehicles moved slowly down the drive
towards the Salisbury road, making for their first stage
the inn which Cressy had tried to reach a fortnight
earlier. She was travelling with Verena and Fred. James
was alone. His secretary and his valet were in another
coach, together with Dr Soames, who would be needed
to take charge of the large library at Lyndale House.

It was Cressy's first experience of travelling in state.
In Italy, her father had always dispensed with
ceremony, and she thought miserably that, as usual, the
Bible had the right of it. Great riches and formal
splendour did not usually bring happiness to their
owners. Until Robert had died, she had had no idea of
his wealth and the homes he had possessed back in
England. She had been content with her shabby clothes
and the equally shabby splendours of an ageing Italian
palazzo. She could not wish herself back there, because
that would have meant not knowing James, but she
would have given anything to see Pompeii and
Herculaneum again when she had possessed an undiv-
ided heart.

CHAPTER NINE

'PERFECT, quite perfect. You will take the evening by storm, I am sure,' exclaimed Verena Davenport, who was overseeing the preparations for Cressy's attendance at Lady Leominster's grand ball.

Mason had dressed her in a creation of cream-coloured silk, decorated with the most delicate embroidery above the high waist. It was carried out in gold, tiny roses appliquéd on the bodice, each rose with a small cluster of seed pearls at its heart. The same embroidery ran round the hem of her skirt, which cleared the ground slightly higher than fashion decreed, to reveal a pair of ankles clad in cream silk stockings, and shoes of white kid whose decoration was a rose identical with those on her skirt and bodice.

The lines of the dress were more severe and sculptured than had been prevalent for the last twenty years. The flowing Grecian robes of the early nineteenth century were at last disappearing. But the fashion might have been created for Cressy.

She carried a fan to match her gown, an exquisite thing with tiny gilt sticks, and Mason had just placed reverently on her carefully dressed hair a wreath of cream and old gold roses.

Miss Sykes nodded her agreement, before adding in her gentle voice, 'Yes, the child looks delightful, I agree. Who would have thought what a *succes fou* she would be; that she would carry all before her. Here is your shawl, my dear.' She draped the fine thing, also in cream and gold, around Cressy's shoulders.

Cressy smiled at her image in the mirror and rose as dutifully as she could, to take the arm which Lady Verena held out to her.

In the coach on the way to London, she had debated several strategies. In one she was as surly and uncooperative as she could be, her début such a disaster that no one, absolutely no one, would offer for such a churlish thing. In another, she was dutiful but dull, offering co-operation of a kind so that *he* could not reproach her, but she would not be successful.

And then, as they reached the outskirts of London itself, the spirit which she had possessed until James's refusal of her suddenly rose from the grave to which he had consigned it. She decided that if he did love her, the thing which would hurt him the most would be for her to be a roaring success, with every young, middle-aged and old man in Society on their knees before her, offering her coronets, titles and love, while he was compelled to watch. He would not be able to say a cross word to her, for had he not told her that that was what he wished for her, or so he had said?

What a splendid revenge it would be, even if her heart broke in the doing. Yes, that was the best answer to him, designed to break his heart and perhaps break his honour, too.

She had succeeded beyond her wildest hopes. The inborn gaiety and charm which she had brought with her from Italy was revived, tempered by the instruction and advice given to her first by James at Haven's End, and now by his sister, who was delighted to discover

that Cressy was so willing to be instructed, so ready to
guard her tongue.

Not that she lost all the spontaneity which was her
greatest charm; simply she reined it in, conformed a
little to the demands of the polite world, and the polite
world fell before her. Old Silchester's heiress might
have arrived late in the season, but once she had arrived
she became the season's greatest star.

Everywhere she went she was in demand. To win her
became the goal of everyone, from fortune-hunter to
the Marquis of Axforde himself, looking for a suitable
wife to found a new dynasty. Cressy possessed every
trait which a man of power required. If she could not
be called beautiful, she was something better: attractive
after a fashion which would survive youth, blessed with
a bountiful inheritance which, added to Axforde's own,
would make him the richest man in England.

To be with her was exciting and stimulating, for her
conversation was truly witty, and to compliment her on
it meant that a man need not strain truth in the doing,
which was a bonus. Of course, after marriage she would
need to damp down her fires, guard herself a little but,
until then, one might enjoy her wit unhindered, even if
it did rankle a little that she might share it and her
charms with others. The Marquis was one of the new
breed of men who deplored the looseness of morals of
the recent past.

Cressy knew that Axforde would be waiting for her
at Lady Leominster's ball, and that he and others had
embarked on a chase in which she was the fox, to be
caught, not to be torn to pieces, but to be swallowed all
the same, and be transformed into a matron married to
a man whom she might not love, but who was, to use

James's weasel word, 'suitable'. The notion did not attract.

Before taking Verena's arm, she turned herself about for Mason's final approval, smiling at Miss Sykes as she did so. Well, she would enjoy herself, she would flirt with every man in sight, so that no one might say she favoured anyone in particular, and hope that James would be watching her, agonised.

One thing puzzled her. He was so insistent that the difference in their ages meant that he could not marry her. But that difference appeared to have little significance for anyone else. Her youngest pursuer was a silly young boy of nineteen, but her oldest was nearly sixty, and there were several others nearer James's age, who hinted that she would be a desirable bride for them if she only cared to say yes.

So why was James so hipped by the disparity between them, so much less in his case? That was a puzzle worth thinking on, but not at Lady Leominster's, where the evening began with her being presented to a number of worthies whom she had not yet encountered.

She was standing between James and Verena when a rather dowdy woman in her early thirties with a plain, clever face advanced on them. Behind her, bent over her a little solicitously, was her tall husband, exquisitely dressed.

He was in his early forties and was quite the most handsome man whom Cressy had ever seen. His profile was perfectly Grecian and his eyes were long and blue and luminous. He smiled and bowed at James and Verena, as did the strange woman, who put out a hand to James and said frankly, as frankly as Cressy would have done, 'Now, Lyndale, you must introduce your ward to us. We hear that she is the talk of the season, and that to introduce her to the *ton* you have come out of your seclusion.' She raised her lorgnette to inspect Cressy.

But the smile she gave robbed her tone of hauteur, and gave her face a sudden distinction as James performed the introductions, saying that they were his old friends, the Viscount Granville and his lady.

'Very old friends,' said Lady Granville, and her husband gave a languid confirming nod after he had bowed over Cressy's hand, giving her the benefit of his beautiful eyes.

So this was the Lady Granville of whose wit James had spoken, and now she was rallying James. It appeared it was her habit to rally everybody, as Cressy later found that it was her husband's to charm people. The Granvilles, she had already been told, were famous for their civilised hospitality and did not normally visit London for long.

'We go back,' said Lord Granville gently to Cressy as his wife spoke to James, 'to the days when we were George Canning's young men, only Lyndale here chose to throw over a political career.'

'Yes,' said his wife. 'We thought that the Cavalier was going to be one of Parliament's great guns, but then he inherited and changed his mind.'

'The Cavalier?' wondered Cressy, staring at James. James, a Cavalier? He seemed more like a Puritan to her.

'Oh, we all had nicknames,' said Lord Granville who, despite his apparently idle charm, had noticed that the name had stumped Cressy a little. 'Canning was the Pope and James was the Cavalier. He was so wild, you see, in the House and out of it. A positive Prince Rupert of a fellow.'

'Oh, indeed,' added his wife, waving away James's protests. 'He was nothing like so grim as he is now. And Granville's nickname was Antinous.'

'And other names not quite so flattering,' Granville put in, giving his wife a knowing smile.

James, a Cavalier, thought Cressy. Well, here was a turn-up! What had happened to change him so? Lady Granville took her arm and said, 'Let us leave the men to talk shop, while you and I take a turn round the ballroom and try to dodge our hostess. Naughty of us, I know, but if she pins us down she will not rest until she has drawn everything from us, including our teeth. I used to know your Mama, and you are a little like her, but more like Silchester, whom I only knew by reputation.'

'Oh, everyone knew Robert only by reputation,' responded Cressy daringly. She liked Lady Granville's witty conversation and if Lady Granville could be straightforward then she, Cressy, could take a leaf out of her book. 'But was my guardian really called the Cavalier because he was so wild and gay? He seems very severe to me now.'

'Time changes us all,' said Lady Granville seriously, perhaps thinking of her husband, who was famous for his faithfulness to her, when before her marriage he had been society's most celebrated rake. 'Time has changed James more than most of us. He had a most unhappy love affair—but I must not gossip,' she added quickly. 'Gossip can hurt even if it does not mean to. Now tell me about Italy.'

Cressy obliged, but Lady Granville had successfully

shaken the kaleidoscope which was James, and when
they had rejoined the two men, and the Granvilles had
left to meet and mingle with others, Cressy could not
help shooting a glance or two at James and thinking of
the younger man who had been Canning and Lord
Granville's friend and noted for his wildness. And he
dared to read sermons to her!

Men said that women were mysterious, but so far as
Cressy was concerned, men were mysterious to her.
Perhaps each sex was a mystery to the other. The
thought stayed with her throughout another evening in
which she carried all before her.

Later, eating supper with Axforde, whom she had
not been able to hold off overmuch, he was so determined, she found to her surprise that the food was
ashes in her mouth.

She was so distracted by this discovery that she didn't
attend to her escort's conversation, and was compelled
to ask him to repeat his last sentence. 'You were saying,
my lord?'

'That I wish that you might accompany me to the
Park tomorrow afternoon. I have a new matched pair,
superb greys, and I would like to drive them in company
with this season's equally superb star.'

Cressy looked at him. He was twenty-five years old,
reasonably good-looking, turned out to the last inch, a
tribute to his valet and every servant who attended him,
but he was dull, dull, dull. He was a little cleverer than
Frank, but did not possess his good heart, yet not as
clever as Barrett Dumaine, whom she could see watching her in the distance. Nor was he as handsome as
Dumaine, either.

But his title, his acres, his standing in Society, his

age, everything about him made him, she supposed, in the eyes of the world, a fit suitor for the Lady Cressida Mortimer, Lord Silchester's only child and heiress, who deserved a husband as grand as herself.

She did not want to drive in the Park with Axforde. To do so would almost be a declaration, and there was one thing she was determined on. She would not fix herself on anyone, least of all a man whose conversation bored her even before marriage. The only thing which she would share with Axforde would be bed, and he would surely be dull there, too. She knew that James would not be dull in bed. She already had proof of that!

The thought made her giggle naughtily, so that Axforde wondered what it was about an invitation to ride in Hyde Park with him which should amuse her so.

'Madam?' he queried a little stiffly.

'Oh,' exclaimed Cressy belatedly. It would not do to offend him. 'Alas, my lord, I regret that I may not have the pleasure. I am already engaged. A dress fitting and a harp lesson,' she improvised wildly, 'will prevent, I fear. I have already postponed them both once, and must not do so again. One has one's duties towards one's dependents, after all.'

There, that should quieten him. He frequently droned on to her about duty, and although Cressy tried to do hers, she disliked people who talked about it overmuch.

'Oh, it does you credit, madam, to exhibit such consideration towards others. If I may say so, too few young ladies have a care for those around them. It is one of the qualities I most admire in you.' He thought once again what a Marchioness she would make for him.

Cressy thought that Axforde's pomposity, unlike her guardian's, was real, not assumed. She must disabuse him as soon as possible of the notion that she particularly favoured his suit. He had little understanding of the true Cressy behind the charmingly amiable mask which she had assumed for Society, and she knew instinctively that he would not approve at all of her intellectual interests, and would wish her to renounce them, should she marry him.

But he was now asking her if he might escort her on the following day and more fibs flowed from her lips in an effort to fend off his unwelcome attentions. The arrival of Captain Dumaine proved timely. He had been watching them for some time and the moment that she and Axford appeared to have finished eating he pounced on them.

After the polite rituals expected of a man greeting a young woman and her partner, he turned to the Marquis. 'Come, Axforde, you have monopolised the evening's brightest star long enough. I implore, nay, I demand that you surrender her to another, even if only for a short time. The dancing begins again, Lady Cressy. May I have the honour of your hand for the next waltz? We seemed to have mastered it most successfully at Haven's End.' He bowed again, his eyes promising her release from Axforde's boring bondage.

The Marquis disliked being called Axforde by such as Dumaine as much as James did, but was compelled to cede Cressy to this unpleasant pretender, only saying, 'Remember, you promised to stand up in the next cotillion with me, Lady Cressida. I shall hold you to that.'

'Of course.' Cressy was all charm now that she had

the opportunity to escape and even smiled a little when
Dumaine, leading her on to the dance floor, said softly,
'How can you endure such a dull fellow, Lady Cressy?
He might be the richest man in England, but that does
not make him other than a dead bore.'

'Come, Captain Dumaine,' smiled Cressy. 'We
cannot all be monsters of wit and charm. Lord Axforde
does possess great integrity and a fund of common
sense, after all.'

'Oh, quite,' sighed Dumaine, making a comical face.
'You bear out what I was saying, madam. A dead bore,
fit only to prose in the Lords, and collect his farmers'
rents. Now let me entertain you a little, for you
certainly deserve more than common sense to keep you
company in a ballroom.'

Cressy knew that she really ought not to encourage
him, for, while she liked to spark at him in conversation, she had no intention of ever marrying him. It
was not so much that he was poor, or even a loose fish,
but that for all his intelligence, he was what the late Dr
Johnson called a man without bottom. He was not
reliable, and whether that was caused by his nature or
by the fact that, penniless, he needed to marry money,
Cressy did not know.

Nor did it matter. He was not for her. She would
rather marry poor silly Frank, because he had a good
heart, while she was not sure that Captain Dumaine
possessed a heart at all.

They whirled and wheeled about the dance floor, and
more than one person watching them thought that
Axforde might be the better catch, but that Lady
Cressida Mortimer and the dashing adventurer sorted
well together. One of them was Frank, compelled to

watch his friend cutting him out with yet another pretty girl. But he comforted himself with the knowledge that his uncle would never allow Cressy to marry Dumaine, and at the dance's end he went over to claim her for himself.

Captain Dumaine released Cressy as the music stopped and, leaning towards her, murmured softly, 'We deal well together, you and I, Lady Cressida. Think on that when you remember this night. Never say that a dull fellow like Axforde can hope to please a woman of your discernment. Why, I dare swear he hardly knows a Greek from a Roman, and thinks that Aristotle is the name of a horse!'

Cressy began to laugh at such impudence, just as Frank arrived, fixing them both with a cold eye. 'You had better allow me to take your place for the next dance, Dumaine,' he said. 'You will occasion comment if you detain Lady Cressida overlong and entertain her so publicly.'

'Now, Frank, my boy,' drawled Dumaine, almost contemptuously, 'I never thought to find you a stickler for the proprieties. Lady Cressy and I were just discussing the true nature of Aristotle, an excellent subject for a ballroom, would you not say? I dare swear that any conversation you might offer her would not be half so learned.'

'No, indeed,' replied Frank, his face scarlet. 'But you must not be dog in the manger, you know. You have had your share of the evening's success and must surrender her to another. Lady Cressida,' and it was a signal of his earnestness that he was formal with her for once, 'you will allow me to partner you in the quadrille which is about to begin.' He bowed to her and held out his hand.

Dumaine shrugged his shoulders as Cressy, amused and a little flattered to be fought over by two such handsome young men, said, 'I know, Captain Dumaine, that you do not really mean to keep Frank from dancing with me.' She took Frank's hand as she finished her sentence.

'One dance,' she told him, 'and only one. To dance twice with either of you would cause comment, as well you both know.'

'You must not take too much note of Barrett, you know,' advised Frank, as he led Cressy on to the floor again. 'He is a good enough fellow, but right up the River Tick, and while he may like you, everyone likes you, his main aim in marrying you would be to secure your estates!'

Cressy thought, with some amusement, that only someone with a heart as simple as Frank's would tell the young woman whom he admired that another man only admired her because of her fortune.

Dancing in the quadrille she saw James enter the ballroom with the Davenports and Miss Sykes, saw him scan the dancers to discover her with Frank. Axforde, leaning against the wall, quizzing glass up, also watching the dancers, spoke confidentially to James. The pattern of the quadrille took her away from them and when she next looked towards the door, Axforde had gone and James was handing Miss Sykes to a seat, his eyes still on her.

Well, she would give him something worth watching! The dance ended and Frank murmured tenderly, 'Take a turn in the orangery with me, Cressy. There is something I wish to say to you.'

The look on his face was so doggishly adoring, contrasting with the hard suspicion of James's expression, that, without thinking what it was that Frank might wish to ask her, Cressy answered, 'Yes, of course. Of all things the most delightful.' The Leominster's orangery was famous.

Frank took her arm and led her towards it. James's eyes still followed them as they crossed the room. Just before Frank handed her through the glass doors, Cressy saw him speak to Miss Sykes before walking away from her.

The orangery was warm, brilliantly lit with the new gas lighting, and full of the most delightful scent from the plentiful blossoms on the trees. The floor was a mosaic one, vaguely reminiscent of that which they had found at Farmer Mason's villa. Seating was in the form of marble benches copied from those which Cressy had seen at Herculaneum, and Frank led her to one of them and reverently sat her down.

He then stood back and fixed her with his bright blue eyes. His whole face was glowing, his manner full of a suppressed excitement. Cressy swallowed. Too late she realised why he had brought her here, and her common sense told her that she should have avoided at all costs being alone with him.

'Cressy,' he began, and looked around him to check that they were alone before dropping on one knee before her. 'You must know how much I care for you. Oh, what a word—how much I love you. I'm sure that it won't surprise you if I ask you to allow me to ask my uncle for your hand in marriage.'

He was concentrating so hard on making his request for her hand conform to all the proprieties that he failed to notice the look of dismay on Cressy's face, and that she did not immediately answer him. Her distress was because she did not wish to hurt him by refusing him, as she must, and her delay was caused by her careful consideration as to the best way in which she could let him down gently.

Frank, however, took her hesitation for maidenly confusion, and because she did not immediately reject his request he hurried on, anxious to assure her that if she said yes to him, she would be his only consideration.

'And if you married me,' he went on eagerly, 'I wouldn't be a dog in the manger like my uncle, by no means. There are plenty of fields around Deniston, my home, and you can dig them all up if that is what you want to do. My father didn't care much for the library and let it go hang, but if you marry me, I'll hire someone like Dr Soames and you can talk to him about the Greeks and Romans all day long, if it pleases you. And, who knows? We might even find another floor with a dog on it, or perhaps a bird, or a horse. Oh, do say yes, I vow I'll make you happy!'

He ran down at last, his honest face rosy with pleasure at the idea of making his little love happy, and he grasped at Cressy's hand, which lay lax on her lap.

She hardly knew how to answer him, and perhaps it was fortunate, although it did not seem so at the time, that James came in, having been detained on his way to them by my Lord Axforde looking for Cressy to dance the promised cottillion with him.

Frank did not at first see his uncle and remained on one knee until James's cold voice brought him back from his dream of walking in Belsize Park, Cressy beside him, their dogs romping behind them, and perhaps a little fat Frank or two trotting along in the distance, their hands in Miss Sykes's, or someone very like her.

'So there you are, my ward. I understand from Axforde that you were to dance the cotillion with him, but he has failed to discover you in time for him to stand up with you. I said that I would try to find you, but I fear that the music began while I was doing so.'

Frank rose slowly, and said to his uncle in an aggrieved voice, 'I might have trusted you to arrive quite *malapropos*, and ready to rebuke poor Cressy. Living with you must be like being under the thumb of a cross governess. I was about the business of asking her to marry me, and I will thank you to stand off until she gives me her answer.'

'I guessed as much,' replied his uncle grimly. 'It did not occur to you to speak to me first, I suppose.'

'Yes, it did,' said Frank sturdily, 'but knowing how matters stand with you these days, I thought to ask Cressy first, and save myself a sermon from you, which I seem to have received anyway.'

Both men glared at one another. Before Cressy's arrival, James had been only too willing to marry her off to Frank, but now that Frank had actually proposed, he was full of the most agonising fear that she might have accepted him.

Cressy rose to her feet. Frank had called Barrett Dumaine a dog in the manger. He had more accurately also given his uncle the title. She knew perfectly well what was eating James up, even if his nephew didn't.

'You will, perhaps, allow me to speak,' she said. 'I was about to give Frank his answer before you arrived, sir. It would be good of you to retire so that I might give him his answer in private. As for Lord Axforde, I shall apologise to him myself for my lack of courtesy in failing to keep my promise to him. But I owe Frank his answer first.'

James had never heard her speak in so coldly measured a voice. It was as unlike her usual bubbling spontaneity as speech could be. He looked at her and saw that frustrated love and an introduction to the world's most sophisticated society had changed her. She had grown up. He had wanted her to grow up, but now that he had got his wish he wanted her to be artlessly naïve Cressy again, not this commanding woman.

But he must respect her, if only because part of the reason for her changing so dramatically was, he knew, to please him. He bowed.

'It was remiss of me,' he admitted, 'to interrupt you, even if I thought that I had good cause. You are right, Lady Cressida. I will retire. You will accept my apologies, Frank. I had not meant to cause you distress.'

Frank bowed back and said stiffly, for he too was growing up, 'As you have offered them so kindly, sir, of course.' The pair of them watched James walk from the orangery.

Cressy, who seemed to have taken command of the little scene, said to him, 'I must give you your answer, dear Frank, and oh, I know that I am about to disappoint you, which was why I could not answer you immediately.' She saw his face change, saw him swallow.

He hung his head and muttered, 'I knew it. You

cannot accept me. It was too much to hope, but hope I did.' He stopped, and then added hesitantly, 'Is there really no hope for me? You would not, perhaps, on reflection, change your mind?'

Cressy shook her head. 'Oh, Frank, it would not be proper for me to do any such thing. I like you very much. You are my dearest friend, but I could not marry you, and it would be wrong for me to encourage you to think that I might say yes one day.'

'No, of course not,' he said sadly. 'That is one reason why I love you. You know your own mind, and would have helped me to make up mine. You are such a clever girl. Why should you care for such a dullard as I am?'

Cressy suddenly became once again the impulsive girl she had been in Italy. She took Frank's hand and kissed it.

'Oh, no, Frank,' she said earnestly. 'Do not say that. You are so good and kind, and I am sure that if and when I do marry, it will be to someone not half so good as you.'

'Oh, you'll marry,' he said sadly. 'I only hope that it will be to someone who will look after you as well as I would have done. And now let us go back to the ballroom. I trust that Axforde will not be too unkind to you for missing the dance. If so, I shall tell him it was my fault, not yours.'

But when they arrived back in the ballroom and Axforde came towards them, he accepted Cressy's apologies gracefully, and waved a Marquisly hand at Frank, for above all he wanted to remain in the Lady Cressida Mortimer's good graces. If she was a little wilful before marriage, no matter; that could be remedied after it.

Going home in the carriage, with Miss Sykes seated beside her half asleep, and James opposite, James said stiffly, 'I hope that you made your peace with Lord Axforde, Lady Cressida.'

Cressy was as formal as he. 'He was most gracious, sir,' but spoiled the effect a little by adding, 'but I do not think that he was best pleased by my defection, even though I apologised as prettily as I could.'

James was suddenly surprisingly contrary. 'Oh, you could not have known that Frank was about to propose to you, and once he had started, you could not abandon him.'

Miss Sykes awoke with a start. 'Mr Belsize proposed? What did you say to him?'

'No, of course,' said Cressy coolly. 'I like Frank very much, but I could not marry him. I would be bad for him, you see. He needs a nice girl who loves Frank, horses and dogs in that order, not a wild bibliomaniac.'

If James was a little surprised by this self-knowledge and by the shrewdness which accompanied it, he did not betray himself, contenting himself with remarking, 'I agree with you, my ward, and if once I thought that it might be a good thing for you to marry Frank, seeing you together convinces me that I was wrong. I hope that you let him down gently.'

'Oh, sir,' said Cressy wickedly. 'You, of all people, should know that in such a situation there is no way in which one is able to let a person down gently, if one is compelled to refuse them.'

They stared at one another. Yes, the dart had pierced his heart, no doubt of it, which proves that he does possess a heart, thought Creasy sadly. Is there no way in which I can compel him to offer it to me?

CHAPTER TEN

ONLY James's strength of will kept him faithful to his resolution not to declare his love for Cressy. Living near to her, seeing her change from the wild girl she had been when she had arrived in England a few short months ago to a composed and poised young woman, only made him want her the more.

To watch her success, to see a procession of men worshipping at the feet of Society's latest goddess, was agony. But he could not take advantage of the fact that he was the first man to whom she had been attracted, or that he was her guardian. Besides, there was one other reason for his holding off, and a strong one.

The morning after the Leominsters' ball he arrived early in the breakfast-room. To his astonishment, Cressy was there, looking as fresh as the proverbial daisy. Miss Sykes was yawning and mooning by her side, proclaiming that she was growing too old for late nights. There was no sign of any of the other members of his family. All busy sleeping off the night's excesses, he supposed.

Cressy was wearing a simple muslin dress, rather like the ones she had worn when she had first come from Italy. Her hair was tied back loosely, and the whole effect was one of such youthful charm that he wanted to throw himself at her feet.

The more so because once breakfast was over, she took from her embroidery bag a copy of the *Gentleman's Magazine* and held it towards him.

'Sir,' she said gravely. 'I have to thank you for your great kindness in forwarding to this magazine an account of the discovery of the Roman floor at Haven's End. You have given me all the credit, I see, and that makes my conduct in trying to run away from you all the more reprehensible.'

This noble apology touched James's heart. He said hoarsely, the tiger's eyes gentle for once, Cressy noted, 'I thought it only fair that you should receive the credit before someone else stumbled over your work and claimed it for his own.'

'Seeing that you disapproved of what I did ——' began Cressy, only to be interrupted by James, who thought afterwards with a little wry amusement that both of them seemed to be bent on apologising to the other.

'Not at all,' he replied. 'I have never disapproved of your work, only of the manner in which you behaved over it. I thought afterwards, even before you tried to run away, that my conduct towards you had been churlish in the extreme. The least that I could do was to see that you received the credit due to you for such a magnificent discovery, as well as the careful way in which you had carried it out.'

Cressy was quite overwhelmed. 'That is truly magnanimous of you, sir. . .' She paused. By now they had both moved towards one another. James had taken the magazine from her hand, but it was not the magazine in which he was interested. The world and Miss Sykes had disappeared. They were alone together, rapt, lost in one another.

Cressy began again. 'I ought to tell you, sir, that my most stimulating memories of Wiltshire are the happy evenings when we dined together before Frank and the rest arrived. Particularly the good conversation about matters in which I am interested. It was quite like being with Robert and his friends again. Not that I objected to Frank and the others coming, you understand. But I missed our *conversaziones*.'

James was about to take her hand, to assure her that he, too, had enjoyed those evenings and the informed enthusiasm which she had brought to them. As he was about to do so, he suddenly saw that Miss Sykes was staring at them both, at the loverlike attitudes which they had begun to assume.

He drew back. 'Which reminds me,' he said, as formally as he could, 'that I have just received the volumes of Pliny's *Natural History* of which I told you yesterday. I think that you would like to see them. They are nearly two hundred years old and the wood-cuts in them are most interesting. If you would like to come to my study at, say, eleven of the clock, when I have finished with Gimson, I will show some of the volumes to you.'

'Oh, indeed,' breathed Cressy, who had decided to spend the morning shopping, to buy some new ball-gowns, the ones which she possessed having been seen too often already. Although clothes had begun to assume for her an importance which they had never possessed before, what were they compared with look-ing at an interesting book with James? Were her strategies working? Could it be that James, seeing her with others, was regretting that he had refused to have her for himself?

As though he had read her mind, he said in a careless voice, 'Oh, by the by, I see that Axforde has been monopolising you lately. Is he serious, do you think? I

should not like to believe that he is toying with you.
Such marked attentions would be misread if they had
no serious meaning behind them.'

James spoke casually, but he could hardly bear to
hear her reply, lest Cressy tell him that Axforde's
intentions *were* serious, and that she was responding to
him in kind. The thought of her marrying such a
pompous young ass, so full of himself and his importance was gall and wormwood to him. But on her reply
he breathed again.

'Oh, I think he is serious. No, I am sure of it, for his
pride would not allow him to toy with me,' she
announced, 'I think that if I encouraged him I could
become Lady Axforde, but I am not sure that that is
what I want.'

'You do not love him then?' James ground out
painfully.

'Love?' said Cressy, raising her beautiful eyebrows.
'What has love to do with most marriages in the *ton*?'
Which only went to show, he thought, even more
painfully, how much she had learned during her short
time in England. 'No, I do not love him. The question
I suppose, is, could I live with him? I don't think I
could. After a time he would be sure to make impossible demands of me. He does not really approve of my
interests, I think. *He* would not write to the
Gentleman's Magazine of my exploits! No, indeed.'

This forthright declaration brought a smile to James's
lips. It was so like Cressy's early manner when she had
arrived in England, particularly when she went on to
say, 'I suppose I should have learned by now not to
speak in such a frank manner, but I find it difficult to
think such things and not say them aloud!'

'And *I* think,' said James, trying to be grave and failing, 'that we ought to continue this conversation later. We are beginning to worry Miss Sykes, and that would never do.'

'No,' Cressy replied, adding, 'and there is something which I wish to ask you which she would be sure to disapprove of, so I shall not raise it now, but will save it for my interview with you.'

James could not resist the playful way in which she came out with this, and bent to take her hand to kiss it. Better to do that, than give way to his unruly heart altogether — the desire to embrace her being so strong — and at nine of the clock in the morning, too!

'After such a declaration, I shall be all agog until you arrive. I cannot imagine what it is which you may not say here, seeing that such a consideration has never prevented you from being frank — whatever the company — before.'

When James was like this, Cressy found him more irresistible than ever. He might claim to be old, to be more like a father than a lover ought to be, but none of the men whom she had met in London could match him when he unbent in this fashion. She would have put out a hand to reclaim his, were it not that she could almost feel Miss Sykes's eyes on them.

She bowed. 'Until later, then, sir. And now I must behave myself, and contain my impatience until we meet again.' Her eyes, nay, her whole body, flirted with him. She was trying out her new-found powers to attract on him, and attract they did. Like Cressy, he could hardly wait until they met again.

* * *

Cressy arrived promptly in James's study at eleven o'clock. She was carrying a three-volume novel with her. She had, to Miss Sykes's surprise, changed her clothes again. She was usually quite content to wear the gown which she had assumed for breakfast all day, unless reminded that the afternoon would require a fresh toilette. Yet here she was putting on her new amber muslin with the fine cream stripe at half-past ten in the morning, and demanding that Mason dress her hair for her in the new style, with drooping ringlets at the back, which she had previously refused in favour of a simple knot.

She made, in short, such a fuss, that Miss Sykes thought that she might be sickening for something. She said so, only to meet her charge's amused stare. 'Yes,' replied Cressy, thoughtfully. 'I do think that I might be. I wonder what it can be.' Then, seeing her companion's worried expression, she impulsively threw her arms around her neck. 'No, there is nothing wrong with me. I almost wish there were. Illness is sometimes described as "interesting". Would I be more so if I were ill?'

She really meant more interesting to her guardian, but could not say so to poor Sykes, who put her head on one side and said in an agitated voice, 'I shall never fathom you, my dear. Why cannot you talk and behave like other young ladies of your age? Life would be so much simpler.'

'But dull,' carolled Cressy, picking up her book, preparatory to running downstairs, her fashionable clothes not having the power to make her behave correctly. Would she — dared she say to James what was in her mind, and perhaps provoke him to the declaration which she wished him to make?

She was still asking herself these questions when she arrived in his study. He was standing at his splendid desk, for he had not yet accepted the new fashion of seating himself when working, with his quarto copy of Pliny open before him.

'I cannot fault you for unpunctuality, my ward,' were his opening words as he looked at the big clock opposite to his desk to see that it pointed exactly to eleven.

'No,' agreed Cressy, putting down her books on a side table. 'Rob. . .my father, was a stickler for punctuality. He abhorrred time-wasting.'

'A trait I share with him,' agreed James. 'Now, come and have a look at these superb woodcuts,' and he indicated that she should join him behind his desk.

Cressy was not loath to agree, and they spent some happy minutes leafing through the book together. James stood back for a moment to enjoy the sight of her. When she was interested in what she was reading she became as quiet and still as she was normally ebullient. She felt his eyes on her and looked up at him.

'You have secured a treasure, sir,' she remarked, indicating the book.

'And one for which Dr Soames has been searching for some time,' said James. 'It fills a gap in my library. I believe that my grandfather owned a copy once, but it disappeared, as books sometimes do.'

Cressy nodded, and then, looking across at the books she had brought with her, he asked, 'And have you a treasure of your own for me to see?'

'Not exactly, sir.' Cressy was being formal with him. 'It is a novel, and it is one which has made me think. It has also been responsible for the question which I shall shortly ask you.'

'Not a Minerva Press romance, then?' James was naughty.

'No, indeed. Lady Verena lent several of those to me, and while I find them most entertaining, many of them are set in Italy, and it is an Italy which I do not recognise! This novel is set in England and is written by "a Lady". It is called *Emma* after its heroine, and is all about quite ordinary people, like *Pride and Prejudice*, which this unnamed Lady also wrote. No one is kidnapped by bandits. There are, after all, few in the English countryside. And Emma is very wilful. . .a little like me,' she finished, almost shyly.

'And does everything end happily for her, this wiful heroine? Oh, yes, I see by your expression that it does.'

'Very much so, for she marries the hero. Only, at first, one does not see him as the hero.'

James thought that his ward's expression had become a mixture of guile and innocence, although where one ended and the other began was a little difficult to tell. 'Now, I see that you are longing for me to make some comment along the lines of, Oh, and why is that? or, I take it that you have some deep meaning behind that apparently simple remark?'

'Well, sir, the hero — his name is Mr Knightley — is quite a number of years older than Emma, but that does not prevent her from suddenly realising that she loves him, even though he does correct her for her naughtinesses — as you do me — or him from loving her and asking her to marry him. The authoress, who is very proper, as in her previous novel, quite plainly approves of their marriage despite the disparity of their years, and that does puzzle me. It puzzles me, because you are so adamant that a similar disparity between the pair of us prevents you, in honour, from making to me the declaration which would not only make you happy, but me also. And since several gentlemen older than yourself have also seen fit to indicate that they would be willing to marry me, your holding back leaves me even more puzzled. For if you were to behave towards me as Mr Knightley did towards Emma, I would, of course, accept you.'

The face she turned towards him on finishing this speech, and handing the novel to him, was so artless that at first James did not register that she had virtually proposed to him.

He could not do other than take the three volumes from her, to place them on the desk beside the Pliny.

'It is not usual,' he said desperately, 'for the lady to propose to the gentleman.'

'Oh, did I do that, sir?' replied Cressy, all innocence. 'Oh, pray forgive me if I did, but if I did, you could perhaps overlook the unwitting offence and forgive me — and consider the offer!'

'You baggage!' began James. She had not moved since she had handed him the book and stood, quite composed, her hands folded before her, as though a young lady proposing marriage to a gentleman was quite the most commonplace thing in the world. 'You know quite well what you are saying and doing. I learned long ago that your apparent artlessness conceals the most sophisticated guile. Milton's tempter Belial was not more subtle than you. In fact, I think that he must have been a she.'

'Never say so, sir,' responded Cressy, eyes dancing. 'But you have not yet given me an answer.'

'But you know what the answer must be. There are reasons, which I cannot tell you, why I must resist you. I collect from what you have said, and some memory of Verena's discussing this novel with me, that Mr Knightley was somewhat nearer in age to Emma than I am to you, and she was not his ward.'

'Oh, but,' said Cressy, all eagerness, 'he really stood *in loco parentis* to her, her own father being so ineffectual, you understand, so our cases are very similar. And if there are difficulties in our way, you could explain them to me, and I might be able to dismiss them. I am quite capable of discussing the most abstruse topics, as you well know, and Robert instructed me in the art of intellectual argument. . .'

'And every other sort of argument,' interrupted James, 'from the simple to the complex. I said once that you ought to be a lawyer. I was wrong. You should be a politician.'

Cressy bowed to him in response. 'I thank you, sir. But *you* have sidetracked *me* now. Perhaps we could return to the main subject of our discussion again. . .'

James closed his eyes so that he might not see her ardent seducing face. In vain. 'The main subject,' he said thickly, advancing on her, his eyes open now, his whole body roused, 'is this,' and he moved to take her in his arms.

She had won! She had broken down his resistance. And if she could make him compromise her completely, his blessed honour, of which he was forever prating, would compel him to offer for her if only she could seduce him successfully. Her own eyes closed, Cressy began to raise her arms to embrace him, as he plainly meant to embrace her.

But she had rejoiced too soon. Lost though they were in their private world, the world outside went on, and the distant noises of the house grew nearer, became urgent. One of the voices was a strange male one, and even as James bent his head to claim her lips, the voice became identifiable. He sprang back to put distance between them, to turn away so that he should not betray how roused he was, either to her, or to another.

What the young man was saying became audible. 'No, March, don't trouble to announce me, I'll announce myself. No, there's nothing wrong. I thought I'd call to see my guardian before travelling onwards to Haven's End.'

James swung towards the door, his face blanching. It opened, pushed by a vigorous hand, and a handsome young man burst into the room. 'Oh, there you are, sir. I hope you'll forgive me this informal visit, but I had to see you.'

His eager eyes, tiger's eyes, were trained on Cressy standing immobile, shocked, by the desk. 'Oh,' he said ingenuously. 'Forgive me, sir, you have someone with you. My pardon, madam, but you must be his other ward, the Lady Cressida Mortimer?'

Cressida could not help but stare at him. This must be Luke Harcourt, James's ward, of whom both Lady Verena and Frank had spoken. He had moved towards James, so that they stood side by side. He was almost exactly Cressy's age, tall, handsome, completely in charge of himself. He was carefully dressed in charcoal grey breeches, beautifully polished boots, a black frockcoat, and a gay waistcoat with tulips embroidered on it. His stock was tied in a waterfall of which James might have been proud, and his black curls were brushed in a fashionably windswept style.

But what was really remarkable about him, apart from his poise, was his likeness to James. He resembled him at every point — or, rather, resembled what James must have been at his age. The proud, slightly haughty face, the tiger's eyes, the long mouth curled into a slight smile were all James's. But, as befitted his youth, his face was softer, age had not yet firmed and thinned it. Even his erect carriage and manner of speech resembled his guardian's.

James, keeping his eyes averted from Cressy, said, 'Before I introduce you to Lady Cressida, Luke, pray reassure me that you have not been sent down from Cambridge.'

'Oh, nothing to that, sir,' announced Luke cheerfully. 'Term ended a little early and I left immediately. Can't wait to be back in Wiltshire. Oh, I did famously in my exams, too, you'll be happy to learn. But enough of that; pray introduce me, sir, to your other ward. At once, I insist. We must know one another as soon as possible, if only to conspire against you,' and he made Cressy another elegant bow. His self-possession and his assurance were those of a man beyond his years, but his manner was so winning, so charming, that it did not offend.

James introduced him to Cressy, said, quite shortly, 'Lady Cressida, allow me to present to you my scamp of a ward, Mr Lucius Harcourt, always known as Luke.'

'Lucius I may be, but no Roman,' announced Luke. 'Although Frank Belsize writes me that you are familiar with them, and the Greeks, too.' He took a startled

Cressy's hand and bowed over it. 'A pleasure to meet you, madam. You are as charming as Frank said you were.'

'And now be off with you,' ordered James, a trifle grimly. 'Since you are here, here you will stay for a little. Wiltshire may wait.'

'Charmed to remain, sir, with such a beauty to keep me here. And the aunts as well to entertain me, to say nothing of Frank. Does Captain Dumaine still haunt him? I trust that I will see you later, Lady Cressy.'

He was gone, and it was as though a whirlwind had passed through the room. The passion which had briefly raged between Cressy and James had subsided, even though they faced one another again. James's expression was unreadable. Cressy wondered whether her own was as opaque. Perhaps not, for James began to speak, his voice sharp and cool, quite changed from the hoarse passion with which he had advanced on her a few moments ago.

'So, now you know, Lady Cressida. My one and only guilty secret and the reason which lies behind my refusal to marry you.'

Cressy hardly knew how to answer him. Every line of him betrayed that he was suffering. In her usual forthright way, but keeping her voice strongly neutral, she said, 'He is your son, of course. One sees that. But why should his existence keep us apart?'

James said, violently for him, 'Think, child, think. He is older than you are. He is the product of my youthful folly and a living proof of the years which lie between us.'

Luke was not legitimate. Cressy knew that without being told. But he had not been left to moulder in the country, farmed out to live a restricted life. His father had adopted him, cared for him, sent him to University, even if he had not openly acknowledged him.

'You must have been very young when he was born,' she ventured.

'Younger than you are now. His parentage is officially known only to my immediate family, but, given his looks, everyone must know who his father is like to be. I was seventeen and the youngest son, unlikely to inherit, when I fell in love with a rich farmer's daughter, Margaret Morgan. I thought, being so far off the title, that we might marry. In that belief we became lovers. Until I met you, I never felt such a passion again. Even the woman who left me at the altar — I am sure that Verena told you *that* story — never moved me as much.'

He was speaking levelly and coolly, as though of someone else. Only his right hand, clenched, betrayed him.

'When they heard that we wished to marry, my father and hers parted us. The match was not suitable, they agreed. She was sent away to relatives. I never saw her again. I did not know that she was carrying Luke nor that she had died having him. Her mother, who had opposed her husband's and my father's separation of us, came secretly to tell me of her death and his birth. I claimed him. He was mine, when all was said and done, and I would have married his mother if they had let me. I paid for him to be brought up as a gentleman, which was hard enough to sustain until I inherited, and could care for him properly. By then, as you know, I hoped to marry, but was cruelly rejected.

'Partly because of the years between us, and your

being younger than my son, and partly because of the
disasters which follow whenever I allow myself to love
a woman, I dare not allow myself to love you.'

'That, sir,' replied Cressy severely, 'is not a rational
statement. No logical reason can exist for such a belief.
And what you have told me does you no discredit.
Robert would say. . .'

'Oh, Robert!' James was dismissive. 'You are more
suited to marry Luke, who is my son, so far as age is
concerned, than myself.' He walked to the window to
stare out of it at nothing.

Cressy could see that he was adamant. They had
been so near to achieving the rapport which she desired,
when Luke's arrival had driven them apart again. She
stretched out a hand to him, then withdrew it. To speak
carelessly, to argue with him would be useless, and
could only damage her, perhaps betray her youth,
might only serve to confirm him in his present attitude.

The new maturity which she had achieved since she
came to England guided her tongue, and told her that
she must go carefully. She followed him to the window,
and said to his averted back, 'Oh, my dear, what a
terrible story. I am so sorry. What a dreadful thing to
do to you both.'

'I think that, afterwards, her father and mine regretted what they had done, but it was too late. When I
fetched Luke away, the woman who had nursed my
Margaret through her difficult confinement told me that
she thought that she had died of grief. She took one
look at Luke, she said, when he was born, then turned
away from him and died.'

His voice was stifled, as though the old grief was on
him again. For a moment, the years had rolled back

and he was with the girl's mother, refusing to believe
that he had lost his love forever, then demanding to be
told where his son was, so that he might have something
of her. Luke was all that was left to him, the one thing
which told him that James Chavasse had once been
young and had loved with all the carefree passion of
youth.

And now a new passion was on him. Cressy was not
like his lost love, who had been gentle and submissive,
but he felt for her the same fierce and protective love.
He could not love her and lose her. It would be true to
say that he dared not love her.

She must say no more. The old Cressy would have
assailed him with her love, but the new Cressy instinctively knew that, for the moment, she must leave him
to his bitter memories.

But if he had given way once, why then, he might
give way again, and with that hope to sustain her she
left him. She knew that before Luke's arrival, he had
been on the point of acknowledging his love for her,
ready to accept it and her. All might need to be done
again, but Robert had always said that perseverance
was the thing, that nothing could be done without it,
and she would hold that maxim to her.

CHAPTER ELEVEN

'I SUPPOSE,' remarked Luke, turning all his charm on Cressy, some afternoons later, 'that it was tactless of me to arrive without warning. But I never see enough of my guardian. We usually get on famously together, but I could tell at once that I had presumed too much.' He paused, then went on with his eyes turned firmly away from Cressy's. 'He seems very high in the boughs with everyone. I thought that he was going to bite Frank's head off at dinner last night. He's usually very kind to Frank.'

'I don't think that Ja. . .Lord Lyndale feels very kind towards anyone at the moment,' said Cressy slowly. 'After all, he had me decanted on him without warning, and now he has the responsibility of my estates, of seeing me settled, or so he thinks. Robert, my father, never thought about settling me. He probably thought that I was perfectly capable of settling myself.'

Luke gave a crack of laughter, throwing his head back, which made him look more like his father than ever.

'Oh, yes, indeed. Forgive me, I have never met a young lady more capable of settling herself than you are. That is a compliment, you understand. I never need to consider overmuch what I say to you, and what a relief that is. Females who fall into the vapours at the slightest wrong word are never my favourite thing, I do

217

assure you. Tell me, what could I say that would give you the vapours?' His eyes challenged her merrily.

Oh, yes, she could see now why James had been nicknamed the Cavalier when he was younger, if he had been at all like his son. Luke's arrival had brightened the whole house, cheering up Frank, who had been mooning about looking miserable ever since she had refused him. He was obviously a favourite with his two unacknowledged aunts and had quite put Barrett Dumaine's nose out of joint.

But, for all his gaiety, it was plain that he was as hard-headed as his father, with a shrewdness astonishing for his years. Did he know that James was his father, and, that being so, James felt himself barred from Cressy? Surely not, but with Luke you could not tell.

He sat himself on the floor at Cressy's feet, and she informed him, quite correctly, that life with an eccentric father meant that little anyone could say or do would surprise her, let alone give her the vapours. When she added that he was not to take that as a challenge, he looked up at her and laughed again. His expression was so like James's when he was happy that it gave her the strangest pang.

It was, perhaps, unfortunate that James should arrive in the drawing room at that very moment. He stared at Luke's lazy posture with a jaundiced eye. It was bad enough that he had to contend with Frank and Dumaine's worship of his ward, but that Luke should join the gallery of her admirers was the biggest blow of all.

It should have pleased him, he knew, that Luke and Cressy should get on so well. It reinforced his statement to her that she needed a younger man, not a disillusioned older one like himself. But jealousy and reason are unknown bedfellows, and as he had detested seeing her with Frank and with Lord Axforde, both of whose suits he ought to have encouraged, so the sight of Luke and Cressy being happy together was yet another arrow in his heart.

'A little decorum would not come amiss, sir,' he said stiffly to Luke.

'Oh, forgive me, sir.' Luke was all contrition. He sprang to his feet, and seated himself in an armchair where he might see Cressy's charming face. Cressy addressed herself to her canvas work so that she might not smile at Luke's insouciance, for she was certain that it would annoy James if she did, and she did not want to do that. He was suffering, she was sure, and she tenderly damned him for his idiocy. Oh, why would he not give way and make them both happy? Surely he could see that she was amusing herself with Luke so as not to betray her broken heart?

The door opened. Captain Dumaine was announced. 'We are not at home,' said James glacially. At the same time Frank started up, saying, 'Oh, famous, he is sure to brighten up a dull day.' Verena and Emily announced their pleasure at the news.

'Oh, very well.' James was ungracious, he knew, but he felt that he could not bear the gallant captain on top of his attractive brute of a son paying court to his ward.

Barrett Dumaine entered, to be welcomed by everyone. Luke, who did not particularly care for him, allowed good manners to take him over, while James offered the newcomer a cool nod.

'I came,' announced Captain Dumaine, 'to say that I

have acquired a new curricle, and I had the notion of showing it off in the Park. If, sir,' and he bowed to James, 'I might have the pleasure of escorting Lady Cressida — ' on seeing James's scowling face at this proposal, he added hastily to appease him ' — and being accompanied by as many of your party as care to take the air, it would make me extremely happy.' The last part of his offer had not been his original intention, but half a loaf was always better than none at all.

James, Cressy saw with sad amusement, had no alternative but to agree. The only ploy left to him was to make sure that his whole family would accompany the Captain and Cressy on various different mounts and in various different conveyances. Fred and Verena, together with Frank and Emily, would be in curricles, Frank and Fred driving. James and Luke would be up on two of James's best hunters, all so that Cressy's drive with Captain Dumaine would be seen as having no real meaning.

If Dumaine felt that James had checkmated him by accepting his belated offer of a family party, he gave no sign of it. He had, in any case, gained his objective. Cressy would be in his carriage, so he was content to take sherry and biscuits in the drawing-room of Lyndale House, while the whole party dressed themselves for their jaunt, and various grooms and servants readied the horses and carriages for them.

Cressy dressed herself carefully in a deep blue riding habit, and a top hat with ribbons of pale blue silk wound round the crown and streaming down behind. Her half-boots were modelled on those of a gentleman rider and she carried a little jewelled whip to finish off her turn-out. She was particularly concerned that she would give no outward signs of the distress which she was beginning to feel since Luke's arrival. James had not hidden himself away, but he had been so icy, both with her and everyone else, that she had been unable to penetrate his armour.

For the first time since her early days at Haven's End he had retreated from her completely. He was offering her no opportunity to win him over with her bright looks or her clever tongue.

So determined was she to deceive the world that when she walked into the mews at the back of Lyndale House, just off Piccadilly, almost at Hyde Park itself, Frank gave a low whistle and said reverently, 'I say, Cress, you do look a stunner. Pity that you're riding with Barrett and not with me.'

Cressy said nothing, merely nodded regally. She could hardly tell Frank, or Barrett Dumaine for that matter, that she would much have preferred to be mounted on Hector or Paris and riding with James, and Luke, of course.

Luke, indeed, walking to his horse, muttered to her as he passed her, 'Much better if you were riding with me instead of the military popinjay. Or, perhaps, with my guardian.' And the eyes with which he regarded her were speculative.

James was the last to arrive and he looked, in his maturity, Cressy thought, the most impressive of an impressive group of men. All of them, even Fred Davenport, were in their different ways not only handsome, but impeccably turned out. There was little to choose between them.

But James, with his splendid green coat, his white breeches, his boots in which you could see your face, resplendent with gold tassels, his new-fashioned wide-crowned top hat and his majestic bearing, enhanced by the width of his shoulders and the narrowness of his waist, was a nonpareil. Yet it was not only for his body that she loved him, remarkable though that was. It was for his mind as well. The mental rapport between them was as strong as the physical one and for a fleeting moment she dropped her guard, naked desire written on every line of her body.

It was Luke, standing by her, who saw the impassioned look which Cressy turned on his guardian, before she hooded her face. And, as though he had felt the look, for he could not have seen it, James turned towards where Cressy stood with Captain Dumaine before being assisted into his curricle by Stephen and gave her a fleeting glance in kind, such yearning in it that Luke blinked at the sight.

He was not the only person present to see James and Cressy's moment of betrayal. Barrett Dumaine saw it, too, and his mouth tightened a little.

And then he was all charm as the train of horses and carriages, led by James and Luke, Luke mounted on his guardian's best black, Hector, James up on Paris, at last turned down the drive and made the short journey into the Park to see, and be seen by, the *ton*.

Cressy, seated high above the crowds on this, her first excursion into the Park, was too engrossed in looking about her to wish to say much to her companion. Once in the Park, James abandoned his role as leader and fell back to ride beside Captain Dumaine's curricle to speak to her for a moment.

'Dumaine.' He nodded briefly at the Captain to grudgingly acknowledge him, before saying to Cressy his first real words for her since Luke's coming had parted them. 'You are enjoying yourself, my ward?'

'Oh, indeed,' replied Cressy eagerly. 'And Captain Dumaine's horses and his carriage are as splendid as he said that they were, and I am grateful to him for allowing me to share in their first outing.'

If he had not been hating Dumaine so hard for having Cressy with him, and Cressy for being with him, James would have been proud and pleased at the cool and composed way in which she was being so gracious towards her escort, quite unlike the wild excitement which she would have shown on such an occasion when she had first arrived in England.

She had responded so nobly to his wishes, had listened to Miss Sykes and his sisters so earnestly, that here in London she was a credit to him and not an embarrassment. But he must ride on. He must not allow Dumaine to guess what lay between him and his ward.

He doffed his splendid hat to Cressy and Dumaine and rode forward to join Luke. Barrett Dumaine's eyes followed him and he watched Luke with knowing eyes as he leaned forward to speak to his guardian.

Many others, including the Marquis of Axforde, came up and spoke to them, looking at Cressy and her escort with eyes as speculative as Luke's had been, and probably, thought Cressy, drawing all the wrong conclusions. Finally, Captain Dumaine drew up his curricle, his tiger dismounted and held the horses steady for him, and they stood in the shadow of the great Achilles statue.

He laid down the reins and turned towards her. 'Now my lady Cressy, you have been singularly silent ——'

'And you, too,' put in Cressy irrepressibly.

'And I, too,' he agreed, with his charming smile. 'Now I shall be silent no longer. May I say that you look absolutely enchanting, madam? I thought that you were a nonpareil at Haven's End, but here you have excelled yourself. Axforde is at your feet, they say.'

'Oh, they say many things.' Cressy was almost prim.

'And what do you say, Lady Cressida Mortimer?'

His blue eyes were soft, and really, thought Cressy, he is a most handsome man, better-looking even than James, because more conventionally handsome, if one is honest, and, I think, nearly as clever. So why does he not attract me? He is a pleasant companion, more pleasant than most, but nothing more than that.

'Oh, I think that I am a new face, and new faces please. When I am better known, then I shall compel less attention.'

The look which he gave her was respectful. 'Modesty,' he said slowly, 'but modesty tinged with an understanding of the way in which the world works. To win you, madam, would be to win a treasure.'

Cressy held on to her composure. They were quite alone, even though they were in a Park full of people. James was introducing Luke to Lord Granville, who had brought his wife in another curricle drawn by a pair of white horses even more beautiful than Captain Dumaine's. The rest of their party had scattered.

'You must not say such things to me, Captain Dumaine.'

'Indeed I must, and pray call me Barrett. I think that we deal well together, Lady Cressida. We share the same interests and I would certainly allow you to continue with yours, were you to become mine. I must ask you to allow me to speak to your guardian, to offer for your hand. My fortune is not large, I know, but my feelings for you are true ones.'

Cressy did not disbelieve him. She thought that he would not have offered for her if she were penniless, he could not have afforded to, but he would still have liked her, and enjoyed talking to her. No, she was wrong, she thought, as he turned his blue gaze on her. A certain fire in his eyes, which she recognised immediately—she had seen it in James's—told her that he desired her.

She took so long to speak that he spoke again, and this time his voice was a little hoarse, another telling sign. 'You have not answered me. Does that mean there is no hope for me? I know that you refused Frank, which does not surprise me; you have little in common. Now, you and I——'

She interrupted him. 'We have much in common, but one thing is lacking.' She tried to be calm as she spoke. 'I like you, I would wish you to continue my friend, but I do not love you, Captain Dumaine, and I would not wish to marry without it——'

'Friendship would be a fine start,' he said eagerly. 'I am sure I could teach you to love me. I would be proud and honoured to have you for a wife. As much as a man may love a woman, I love you, and have done so since I first saw you at Haven's End. You are what I would wish for in a wife. Come, you cannot want such a creature as Axforde.'

Perhaps if she had not met James—but no. She liked him, yes, but that was no basis for marriage, and she did not entirely trust him, but could not say so.

'You should not have proposed to me here, in Hyde

Park,' Cressy came out with at last. And yes, that was another count against him. He did not ring true. He was like a handsome pot which you struck, and the sound it gave off was subtly wrong. Not wrong enough to make him a villain, but wrong enough for her not to trust him, even if James had not existed.

'Why not? We may never be truly alone. In a ballroom your protectors and your duenna hover about you. Lyndale glowers at anyone who comes near you. He may not do that now. He is occupied with his old friends and, even if he sees us alone, in the distance, politeness tethers him to their side. No, if I want a truly private place where I may speak to you, unchecked, it is paradoxically here in the most public of rendezvous.'

He was clever, she must not forget that, subtle even, but he was not for her.

'I would rather that you did not speak to Lord Lyndale,' she said when he had finished. 'I would keep you for a friend and I would protect you, if I could, from his refusing to allow you to speak to me, for I do not think that you figure in his plans for me.'

Disappointment made Dumaine drop his guard for a moment. He had hoped, knowing that he and Cressy sorted well together, that she might agree to become his wife. Common sense might have told him otherwise, but had he let common sense rule him he would still have been sitting lonely on his barren acres, instead of being a valued member of the polite world. He loved Cressy well enough, but it was her ability to enrich him, to end his precarious status, both social and financial, once and for all, which he valued the most.

'And who does figure in Lyndale's plans for you?' The true man spoke at last, his tone hard and cynical.

'He *says*, I understand, that he wishes to settle you, to see you well married, but everything he *does* is calculated to drive away your suitors. Now, why is that? They say that you have already refused several splendid offers. Rumour has it that you are holding out for Axforde. I do not believe that, I believe that you are holding out for someone quite different. I wonder who that someone is, Lady Cressida? Did a night spent alone under the stars with your oh, so strict guardian teach you a lesson which you do not wish to unlearn?'

There was something so barely restrained, so savage about his quietly spoken questions which frightened Cressy more than if he had ranted at her. He was right to say that they were private, so that they might speak as they pleased, but they were in public, too. She could not leave him, she must stay and try to hold him off.

'Oh, shameful!' she exclaimed, at the same time that the memory of herself in James's arms, ready to surrender her maidenhood, and he ready to take it, was shamingly revived by what had just been said.

Captain Dumaine had spoken nothing but the truth, and it was a truth which she must deny, for the sake of both James and herself.

'You forget yourself, sir; you demean both of us. You had the right to propose to me, and I had the right to refuse you, without you reproaching me after such a fashion. I must ask you to drive me home at once and I shall try to forget what you have said.'

Barrett Dumaine knew that he had lost Cressy for good. Worst of all, he had not only lost the right to propose to her again at some future time, but he had lost her friendship as well. He did not want her friendship, he wanted her love, and the wealth and position which she could give him and which he so dearly needed. One moment of pique had ended that possibility, and all others.

Frustrated desire as well as frustrated ambition drove him on. He looked across the Park at James talking to the Granvilles and to Luke, looked again at Cressy, seated by him, head averted from him, as though the sight of him was too much for her. It was too much for him.

'They say that the truth hurts, madam. Does it hurt you? I think so, and *him*, the man of honour there, with his bastard son. How does he justify his conduct?'

Cressy's head swung round, and she said as fiercely as she could, 'He has nothing to reproach himself for. I can assure you of that. I have asked you to drive me back to Lyndale House. If you do not do so within the moment, I shall leave your curricle, whatever the cost to the reputations of both of us. Obey me and I shall try to forget what has passed between us. The choice is yours.'

Barrett Dumaine's head swam as reason returned. He had spent his entire career coolly working the odds to bring him a life which he could not otherwise have hoped for. Later, alone, he was to understand that he had behaved as he did because, for the first time in that long career, his emotions had been engaged. Had he not been in love with Cressy, had she been prey, merely, he could have taken her refusal coolly. It was his baffled feelings for her which had betrayed him. He tried, too late, to master himself.

'Very well,' he said, and ordered his tiger to resume his position behind them. Nothing could be gained at this point by trying to retrieve anything from the débâcle of his hopes. He also knew that Cressy's threat to leave him publicly stranded was no idle one.

'I will drive you over to him, and you may give him what excuse you will for our early departure. You will accept my apology for what I said to you. It may be the truth, but I should not have confronted you with it.'

Cressy made no answer to that. She was too busy trying to master herself, while wondering how many others had fathomed a secret which she had thought hers and James's alone. Of all her failed suitors, she would have thought Barrett Dumaine the least likely to behave as he had just done. She was sufficiently mature to recognise the complexity of feelings which had provoked him to attack her so cruelly, but that did not excuse him.

What she did understand was that, as baffled desire had made her miserable, so too must it be making him. In that she could pity him, if nothing else. Meantime there was James to see, for he would be sure to ask her why she and Dumaine had returned so early from the Park, and she would be able to make him a little happy by telling him of yet another suitor refused!

Happiness, however, eluded her. She reinforced her lie that her retiral from the Park was caused partly by a malaise by retiring to her room. Miss Sykes, worried over her, saw her into bed and drew the curtains, but not before Cressy had made her way to the library to find some serious reading matter.

Robert had always said that if one was troubled or suffering from deranged nerves, then not light but the most demanding reading should be undertaken to take the mind off one's own foolish obsessions.

She looked through the volumes of French literature.

She had neglected the language lately, although in Italy she, Robert and the Countess had spoken French and read the language as much as they did English and Italian. She remembered that Robert had once recommended Pascal's thoughts as embedded in his *Pensées* as a useful correction to the megrims — and there it was.

Dr Soames, who had been hovering behind her as she made her choice, nodded his approval. There were those who said that Lady Cressida Mortimer was flighty, but he had never found her so, and her choice of reading matter confirmed the solidity of her intellect. He would have thought even more highly of her if he had seen her, after Miss Sykes had gone, draw back the curtains, pick up Pascal and begin to read.

If Cressy had thought that reading Pascal would take her mind off her troubles, she was mistaken. What he did was clarify them in some strange way. Robert had said that the best way to read him was to flip through the text, after Dr Johnson's notion of tasting a book.

The book fell open easily at two separate places. The first extract she read made her smile. 'If Cleopatra's nose,' he wrote, 'had been shorter, the whole face of the world would have been changed.' Translated, that meant that if Lady Cressida Mortimer's father had not made his mistake over the identity of James Chavasse in his will, James would not have become her guardian, she might never have met him, and would consequently never have fallen in love with him!

Had Pascal really been so clever, after all? Was it not a simple truth, so artistically stated that it appeared more remarkable than it was? She turned to the second easily opened page where someone — James? — had underlined one of the thoughts in pencil: 'The heart has its reasons which reason does not know of.'

Now that sentiment made her tremble indeed. It confirmed something which she had already discovered about love, for when Pascal spoke of the heart it was love which he meant. Love defied reason, made its own reasons. She and James had defied reason by falling in love, and James was trying to reinstate reason in his life, by rejecting the reasons of the heart and re-embracing those of the intellect.

Captain Dumaine, on the other hand, was trying to combine the two sorts of reasons, and both men were failing as a consequence. Cressy thought that she understood what she must do. It was to accept the reasons of the heart and defy the intellect, which had no place in the life of passion. It did have a place, of course, but not in the affairs of men and women in love. Love transcended everything, in the old Latin phrase '*Amor vincit omnia*'. Oh, if only James would understand that, admit that, then all might yet be well.

She had meant to read on, but her lie became the truth, for early though it was, she slept. The book, still open at the quotation, lay unheeded on the counterpane.

Unknown to her, as she roved in dreams through the country of love, meeting James yet once more on the pavement in the field at Haven's End — for that dream had become a recurring one since the night of the storm — the door opened.

James had prevailed on Miss Sykes to admit him to Cressy's room. He had told her that it was urgent that he speak to her and would do so only in her presence, for Miss Sykes had shown him her shock at his insistence on entering a young lady's bedroom. But when he entered to see Cressy sleeping, a smile on her lips, one hand on the volume before her, he had not the heart to ask Miss Sykes to wake her.

Gently he slipped the book from under her hand, which quested a little as he did so, before falling still again. He lifted the book to look at what she had been reading, and read the thought underlined by an unknown hand.

Like Cressy, he was struck as though by a bolt from the God Jupiter himself, who lies in wait to confound unwary mortals, and had now confounded James. Unlike Cressy, he was not able to read it with the simplicity which her untutored but intuitive heart had brought to it.

He equivocated with it, asked himself what Pascal really meant, for, again unlike Cressy, he was fearful of accepting its full meaning. He had no doubt that she had read it and wondered what she made of it. He forgot Miss Sykes, forgot the world, knew only the sleeping face before him, her innocence as white as the sheets on which she lay.

He would have liked to fall on his knees beside the bed and worship at her shrine. Instead, recalled by the world, by reason, he closed the book, laid it gently on the night stand beside the bed, and equally gently took Cressy's hand and pulled the sheet over it.

She stirred again and said his name. Mindful of Miss Sykes, he controlled himself, took the duenna by her arm and led her from the room, to say to her as the door closed behind them, 'I could not disturb her, she looked so at peace. I will speak to her tomorrow.'

CHAPTER TWELVE

'REFUSED? She has refused Axforde? One knew that she had refused young Belsize, the dubious Captain and a dozen more beside. But Axforde! The *on dits* must be wrong. It was Axforde the little Mortimer was holding out for, surely.'

Lady Cowper, that arbiter of fashion, was speaking to her distant relative, Harriet Granville, Lyndale's friend, who was sure to know the truth of the matter. Harriet Granville was that rare person who liked gossip, but never gossiped. Her letters to her sister, who was rarely in town, told of all the *on dits* running about the capital, but how she knew them was a mystery.

Now Lady Granville merely nodded and resumed her stitchery. She was always busy; a childhood being spent instructed by the severe Selina Trimmer, her evangelical governess, was responsible for that, Emily Cowper knew.

'I don't think,' said Harriet Granville, her voice mild, 'that she was ever serious about Axforde. He is not at all her type, you understand. He would never have let her express herself, or follow her inclinations. A dull dog, Axforde.'

Emily Cowper shrugged her beautiful shoulders. 'But a useful husband, do admit. And what are husbands for, but to indulge their wives' fancies?'

'I doubt that he would indulge any wife's fancies,'

remarked Harriet. 'He would expect his wife to indulge his, not her own.'

'Then she could go her own way,' yawned Emily, who always went hers. 'We are not all as lucky as you, Haryo, to have a lover and a husband combined,' and she gave Harriet the benefit of her shoulder to punish her for her luck. Emily's husband and her lover were most definitely not the same person.

This conversation was similar to many taking place all over London when the news that Lady Cressida Mortimer had refused her most distinguished suitor broke on an astonished world. Disbelief, amusement, malice, relief on the part of mamas who hoped that one of their own daughters would now be able to claim this matrimonial prize, were the most common sentiments expressed.

'Means to refuse 'em all, does she?' was all that masculine opinion could offer, compared to the torrent of comment which flowed from feminine lips. Barrett Dumaine said nothing, grimly amused that he was not the only one to be given his congé, but aware — as was no one else but Luke Harcourt — of the true reason for Cressy's refusal of the brightest and best among the British aristocracy and gentry.

His hatred of James Lyndale became a festering sore, an aching tooth which his tongue continually found. He watched the guilty pair, as he wished to think of them, constantly, but neither gave any sign that could be construed as compromising.

As for Axforde, in approaching Cressy he had done everything with the utmost correctitude. He had spoken to James first, rather than to Cressy, unlike Barrett Dumaine, and had gained permission to propose to her and had done so one afternoon at half-past two of the clock, both of them dressed to kill.

He had dropped on one knee, offered to make her his marchioness, spoke of the dukedom which he hoped one day to gain, which would make her a duchess, told her, belatedly, of his undying love — and all to no avail.

Afterwards, Cressy could hardly remember what had passed. She was so little involved with him that she felt nothing so strong as the sorrow which she had experienced after refusing Frank, or the distress which Barrett Dumaine's angry response had caused her.

Axforde had been so sure that she would accept him that after her refusal he had been quite nonplussed. He had obviously come prepared to make a graceful speech to her after receiving her grateful consent to his invitation to become his Marchioness. The notion that he might have to make a graceful speech of quite another kind had been beyond him.

Worst of all, he treated her as though it were shyness or coyness which caused her refusal. He assured Cressy that he quite understood her maidenly diffidence, it did her credit, in fact, and later, when he proposed again, he was certain that she would accept him.

'Oh, no,' said Cressy desperately. She was growing tired of refusing suitors and the thought of having to fend Axforde off once more made her feel quite faint. 'Oh, no. I am certain, my lord, that I shall never accept you. We can be friends, yes, but I am not suited to be your marchioness.'

'Oh, I agree,' he said complacently. 'If that is what is holding you off, then there can be nothing to bar your ultimate acceptance of me. Your guardian, his sisters and your estimable companion, Miss Sykes, will between them smooth off the rough edges which living an unsuitable life in Italy has left you with. Six months of such careful tuition will, I think, be sufficient to transform you into a biddable bride.'

A biddable bride! Cressy wanted to giggle. It was the only phrase he uttered which she distinctly remembered afterwards. When at last he departed, after saying that he would watch her progress and would propose to her when she was ready for him, she didn't know whether to have the hysterics for the first time in her life, or dance the fandango over the fact that, far from upsetting him, she had simply confirmed him in his matchless egoism.

After that there was her guardian to see. He had brought Axforde to her, saying that he had something important to say to her, and she could tell at once that he was in two minds about the whole thing.

Well, she had refused the pompous Marquis, which ought to make James happy, but so contrary was he these days that he would probably gloom at her when she told him her news.

She was just about to go to his study when the door opened and he entered. It was one of his days for being informally dressed, and much though she admired him when he was in all the glories of his fashionable clothes, there were times when she thought simplicity became him the most.

'So you refused him.'

'Yes, he told you?'

'Oh, indeed. He also told me that, as was common with most young women, he did not think that your yea was your yea or your nay your nay, and that he had the distinct impression that if he asked again in the near future, he would receive your happy agreement. Tell me, Lady Cressida, did you really give him an ambiguous answer? Most unlike you if you did.'

Cressy could not tell whether James was rallying her or not. His tone was aloof, impersonal. They might have been discussing the accounts which had arrived that morning from his coal mines in north Nottinghamshire.

'Of course I did not!' Her voice was indignation itself. 'I was most firm in my refusal. But he could not believe in the answer I gave him and chose to think instead that it was my maidenly modesty speaking. He said. . .he said. . .' and, dreadfully, she began to laugh. She had risen on James's entrance to speak to him formally, but as mirth overcame her she sank on to the sofa, tears running down her face and, whether it was joy or grief which caused them, she did not know.

She pulled out her pocket handkerchief and wiped her streaming eyes, before looking up at James whose expression was, to say the least, enigmatic.

'I might have expected anything from you, madam, except this unseemly laughter.' Oh, dear, he was at his most pompous worst. Which meant, of course, that he was greatly disturbed. She controlled herself with difficulty, and, stifling further laughter, spoke as seriously as she could.

'He said that he was prepared to wait for a biddable bride and hoped that between you all — although I don't think he included Frank and Luke in the number — you might turn me into a presentable well-behaved Marchioness, and was prepared to wait as much as six months for the miracle. I don't think that he really grasped that I had refused him. A biddable bride! That is what I am meant to be.'

Despite himself, James's lips twitched. He had a vision of that pompous stick Axforde unable to believe that any girl to whom he deigned to propose could possibly refuse him. His rational mind said that he ought to be sorry that Cressy had turned down such a grand settlement in life, his heart told him quite the opposite.

He began to laugh. 'A biddable bride, Cressy, my darling. How far from the mark could a man get!' His laughter mingled with hers, and before either of them knew it, they were almost in one another's arms again, joined once more not only by mutual passion but by the quirkish sense of humour which they both shared.

They were side by side on the sofa. Cressy's pocket handkerchief was wet, so James solemnly offered her his large dry one, or rather, he took it from his pocket and tenderly began to dry her face.

'I should not admit it,' he murmured, 'but I am relieved that you refused him. What a life you would have had with such a stick. A most suitable match, the world would say, but I am glad that you were not condemned to it. Hold still, my love, there is a tear, there, running down that damask cheek.'

Boldly, Cressy twisted round to kiss the hand which held the handkerchief — and ignited the fire which lay between them. . .

But they lived in a world where privacy was rare. As once before, it was Luke who interrupted them. He came bursting in, full of indignation.

'Lady Verena,' he exclaimed, 'told me that ass Axforde called this afternoon to propose to you, Cress.

Never say that you accepted him——' Some hint of what was passing between Cressy and his guardian hung in the air. James had sprung to his feet, his face turned away from his son. He swung round when he had removed himself as far from Cressy as he could, and said in great exasperation, 'Luke! How many times have I told you not to burst into rooms unannounced. One day. . .' James paused, appalled at the tactlessness of what he had been about to say, having regard for the circumstances in which Luke had surprised him and Cressy.

To inform Luke that one day he might arrive at a scene which he would much rather not have interrupted or discovered. . . He hesitated, saved by Luke who said, apparently a little bewildered, 'One day what, sir?'

'Oh, never mind. And for your information, Lady Cressida has refused Lord Axforde, but we had both much rather that you did not run about London gossiping about it. He seems to think that her refusal is not final.'

This delighted Luke. 'Light in the attic as well as a stick. Couldn't believe anyone would refuse him! Well done, Cress. I'd never have spoken to you again if you'd become Lady Axforde. Save yourself for me. Think of the fun we could have together.'

Cress indeed, fumed James inwardly, before the full import of what Luke had said struck him. No, it could not be, that Cressy and Luke of all people should become enamoured of one another. Was that why she had refused Axforde? Luke was her age, after all, and even a stern father had to admit what a sterling fellow he was turning out to be. Was he now to be jealous of his own son? To have him for a rival?

'I say, sir,' enquired Luke anxiously. 'Are you quite well? Not been overdoing things lately?'

'Damnation, sir,' exclaimed James. 'I am not yet ninety. Yes, I am quite well. No, I have not been overdoing things, although to keep you and Lady Cressida in order would be to tax the patience of a saint.'

'If you say so,' murmured Luke, and Cressy, watching them, was certain that Luke was baiting James. She rose to her feet.

'If you would excuse me, I think that I would like to go to my room for a short rest. It has been a difficult afternoon.'

James and Luke had quite forgotten her in staring at one another, James belligerently, Luke solicitously, after a fashion which made James feel older than ever. Her voice reminded them of her presence.

'Oh, yes, indeed, very proper,' came from James, while,

'Oh, Cress, I thought we were to ride in the Park this afternoon. . .' came from Luke.

'That will be quite enough, Luke,' snapped James. 'Have you no studying to do? Is your life all play? If Cressy wants a ride in the Park once she has refreshed herself, *I* will escort her, and no one else.'

Luke gazed from his guardian to Cressy, who now stood at the door, opened his mouth, closed it, and finally said, his voice quiet and serious, 'Oh, yes, sir. I quite see. Frank will be coming later. I can ride with him. Cress deserves a rest after such an eventful time.'

'Good.' James lowered his voice and his eyebrows.

'Now, Lady Cressida, if you should wish for a ride, I shall be in the hall at five of the clock prepared to escort you.'

It was almost a royal command, Cressy thought, amused. Her new maturity told her that James and Luke had been sparring with one another like two dogs disputing a bone, only the bone was Lady Cressida Mortimer. It was time that she left them.

She couldn't, however, leave Society, nor the gossip of Society, behind. Everywhere she went, eyes followed her, as did the buzz of conversation. Was it true she had refused Axforde unconditionally, or was she holding him off, promising him an answer later, as he had suggested? Or was Axforde simply saving face? And why was she refusing everyone, rich and poor, young and old? It was plain that Lyndale wished to fix her — or did he? And if not, why not?

Barrett Dumaine heard the news several nights later at Watiers, the gaming house which he, among others in Society, frequented. The delight he felt that another man had failed was mitigated by the reason for the failure. It was Lyndale, he was sure of it. Lyndale, who had taken advantage of her on the night of her flight, and who was besotted with her as she was with him. And dog in the manger that he was, he was making sure that no one else succeeded with her while holding off himself! It was the outside of enough, particularly from a man who, however wild he had been in the past, was reputed to be a man of honour.

Lack of success at the gaming table made Dumaine's temper worse. He loved Cressy, no doubt of that, but her fortune called to him as well as herself. Married to her, his troubles would have been over. The night that the news of Axforde's failure became generally known, he had drunk heavily after the cards had gone against him.

One of his cronies, young Worcester, whose own life was so wild that his father, the Duke of Beaufort, and his uncle, Lord Granville, had been compelled to rescue him from the clutches of the notorious courtesan, Harriette Wilson, to whom he had foolishly proposed marriage, said with the confidence of the newly saved, 'By God, Dumaine, now she's refused Axforde, your own chances might look up again,' for gossip had linked Dumaine's name with Cressy's, too.

Dumaine looked savagely up from the bottle which he had taken from the sideboard and was trying to open, difficult in his half cut condition, and said, his voice raw, drink making him indiscreet, 'Good God, Worcester, no one has a chance with her, no one, now that her guardian has placed his brand on her!'

It was, theoretically, against all the rules to gossip publicly about women, to attack the virtue of an unmarried girl, but in drink anything might be said and often was. Worcester's face was bright with curiosity, his own sobriety doubtful. 'And good God to you, Dumaine. What's that you're saying?'

Dumaine leered at him over the glass he was raising unsteadily to his lips, winked and said, 'Why, this, my friend. When a man spends most of the night rescuing his ward, who has run away from him, when he could have brought her home in a quarter of the time, no need to wonder what they were at!'

The next day, his head thundering, Dumaine was to regret what he had subsequently said in explanation, torn between drink and distress at losing a possible prize. He had wanted to hurt Lyndale more than Cressy, but in the doing he had damaged Cressy's reputation, too, and regret the next morning was no substitute for indiscretion the night before.

He saw Worcester's face change, and knew that this was a splendid piece of gossip which would be going the rounds, and he spent the rest of the night in heavy drinking to try to erase what he had done. To no avail. Memory told him only too well what he had started on its way, and he had no means of retracting it.

This simply added to the furore over the little Mortimer. Her father's eccentricity was revived; even the memory of a great-aunt, long dead, reputed to be the mistress of Frederick, Prince of Wales, was dragged from its grave to support the notion that all the Mortimer men were mad and all the women lacked virtue. Small wonder, then, that this one had been running wild. One wondered what she had been up to in Italy. Everyone knew what Italians were like. Axforde had probably had a lucky escape.

Everyone might know, but no one said anything aloud. Gossip was usually subterranean. Only when the scandal was too ripe, as was the case when it was revealed that Lord Byron's wife had deserted him because she had discovered that he and his half-sister, Augusta Leigh, had been lovers, were the subjects of it driven from public and private life.

Cressy might wonder a little at some of the unpleasantly frank stares she received when she attended Lady Cowper's grand ball several days after Barrett Dumaine's indiscretions had started to go the rounds, but she put that down to jealousy over Axforde's proposal. Even James, usually well aware of what was what in polite life, remained unaware of what was being said about them. No one, knowing him and the reputation he had borne when younger, dared twit him about his relationship with his ward.

Lady Verena spoke to Cressy and Miss Sykes of the strange atmosphere at the ball as they went into supper with only Frank and Fred Davenport attending them, James for once being absent. Lord Granville had called for him to accompany him to Watiers and James had agreed to go with him. Anything was better than having to endure the sight of Cressy receiving so much homage from young men. Luke was not yet allowed out in Society to such events as the Cowpers' ball but, as a great favour, James had consented to his attending him to Watiers, although he had told him that he would only be allowed to watch, and must understand that gambling could ruin a man very rapidly, whether his fortune was large or small.

Miss Sykes, experienced in the ways of the world, nodded her head. 'I am wondering,' she said diffidently, 'if some scandal has broken of which we do not know. Everyone seems all of a quiver. Perhaps, dear Cressy being so young, means that no one likes to inform us of it.' She was quite unaware that Cressy, whom she had come to love, was the focus and the heart of the scandal.

She and Verena would dearly have liked to know what the scandal was. Cressy, a little put out by James's absence, for she had grown used to him accompanying them, usually at a small distance, was not interested in Society gossip. Robert had brought her up to despise people, usually women, who could only talk about such small beer as who was whose lover, or who had changed partners and who hadn't. 'Society's meaningless country dance,' he had dubbed it, and had told her to think of higher things. Higher things being the interesting past and a present occupied by philosophers and *savants*, whose theories he had encouraged her to discuss.

If she had become more frivolous since arriving in England, her frivolity had not, and would never, reach the point where she could enjoy the petty ripping to pieces of the reputations of others.

She did think it a trifle curious that one young miss, who had made a point of cultivating her, cut her dead on the stairs up to the supper room, but she put that down to jealousy over Axforde's proposal. More curious was the fact that Axforde, who had been haunting her every time she had been at the same function since her refusal of him, never came near her; indeed, seemed to be avoiding her. But on the whole she was grateful for that and counted it her good, not her bad, luck. Eating her supper, and later dancing the quadrille with Frank as a partner—he was another to whom nobody dared speak of the Lyndale/Mortimer scandal—she wondered wistfully what James was doing at Watiers.

She hoped that he would not be losing much money there, particularly since he was accompanied by Lord Granville, who, Verena had told her, was a great plunger at the card tables. 'Quite unlike his usual style,' Verena had added, 'seeing that in politics and diplomacy he is so cautious, but as a gamester no such thing.'

What Cressy did not know, although all society was to hear of it soon enough, was that James *was* plunging at Watiers—although not at the card tables. . .

* * *

'I promised Lady Granville that I would not play for high stakes tonight,' said Lord Granville mournfully to James, 'and when I told her that, I believed what I was saying. But. . .' and he heaved a great sigh. 'How do you do it, old fellow? Resist the temptation to stake your fortune on the turn of the cards, I mean?'

Later James was to tell Cressy that the gambling mania which occasionally overcame his friend was his one great failing. However often Lord Granville tried to renounce the tables, when the fit was on him, he could not. James never felt any such temptation. Invariably, after quite a short time, he became bored. He liked Watiers as much for it being a meeting place where one met one's own kind as for the cards. He was fortunate, he thought, in not being the victim of an obsession which Lord Granville shared with many others.

That night was no exception. He sat down at a table playing whist for low stakes and was amused at his own reticence. He was a skilful player and knew how to work the odds, but, whist being as much a game of chance as of skill, that did not always answer. Granville was a skilful player, but his luck was always bad and he was always hoping for it to turn.

The rubber came to an end and James rose to go over to the tables at the end of the room which were spread with food and wine. Gaming hells like Watiers always supplied excellent food to draw in the gamblers. The wine was good, too, and James began to pour himself a glass of burgundy. He was irritated by the fact that his presence seemed to be causing amusement, if not to say derision, at a table near to him where a

group of men, most of them half cut, were talking
together, their eyes on him.

Luke, who had been reading *The Times*, one of the
papers laid out for those who were either not gambling,
or were taking a break from it, lifted his head sharply
when Cressy's name came floating through the hubbub.

Barrett Dumaine formed one of the group. The
gossip he had started on its way several nights ago had
now become an uncontrollable roar and he had resigned
himself to that fact. A loser again, and drunk again, he
had even hallooed the gossip on its way. He knew that
he would again regret it in the morning, but for some
reason he could not stop himself. Frustration fuelled
his every action.

James, too, heard Cressy's name. He rose from the
armchair to which he had taken his food and drink, and
stared at the direction from which it had come. He
recognised Barrett Dumaine and Granville's dissolute
nephew, young Worcester, but the rest were unknown
to him.

One of them, drunker than the rest, recognising
James and unaware of his reputation as a master with a
sword or pistol, staggered towards him, a leer on his
face.

'Ah, Lyndale, there you are. Tell me, is it true, what
Dumaine here says, that you spent a happy night in the
hay with that pretty ward of yours earlier this summer?'

Everyone, including Luke, who jumped to his feet
on seeing the expression on his guardian's face, heard
the insult. For a moment James stood paralysed — and
then the tiger sprang. First the contents of his glass
were flung straight into the face of the debauchee
baiting him, and then he seized the man by the collar

and threw him bodily straight on to the sideboard laden with food and drink. He followed that up by grabbing the spluttering man by the hair and grinding his face into a dish of vegetables.

The ferocity of his attack was rendered the worse by his silence. His first enemy demolished, he flung off Luke who had seized him by the arm, and turned towards Barrett Dumaine. Several of the group advanced on him to restrain him. Some of the waiters and footmen standing about to prevent such violence also ran towards the scene. Crockford, the notorious gamester, and one of the joint owners of the club, was called for by the more timorous.

'Stand back,' said James, his voice deathly quiet. 'I have no quarrel here with any but that man.' And he pointed at Dumaine. 'By God, sir, I understand that you have been putting lies about, traducing my name and that of someone whom I will not mention here. I will have satisfaction, I say, and by God I mean to have it now.'

The tiger sprang again. This time Dumaine was his target and he reached him before anyone could stop him, seized him by the throat and began to maul him, pulling him to the ground. As one of the watchers said afterwards, the Cavalier was back with a vengeance.

By now Watiers was in a state of uproar. In drink men were known to express themselves violently, but rarely as violently as this. The table at which Lord Granville was seated stopped its play, and he joined those who surrounded James and his victim. The bruisers whom Watiers employed to keep order had now arrived and pulled the struggling men apart.

Breathing heavily, James, who had kept his temper

under restraint for as long as he could remember, stared at his enemy, who, blue in the face, was now slowly recovering.

'Damn it, Lyndale,' said Lord Leominster, one of the older men present. 'This is no way to go on. Remember who you are. If you want satisfaction, demand it like a gentleman, not brawl like a pothouse bruiser.'

'Satisfaction?' said James, pulling his arm away from the ex-pugilist who was holding it. 'Pothouse satisfaction from a man who is no gentleman will do for me. Let him retract, or by God, one way or another, I'll kill him here and now.'

'No, damn you, Lyndale,' ground out Dumaine fiercely, as he recovered his breath and his wits. 'I am as good a man as you are, and I want satisfaction for an unprovoked attack on a man who was only telling the truth.'

James bared his teeth and snarled at him. His frustrated love for Cressy, the pain he had felt on sacrificing it for her good as he saw it, had combined with Barrett Dumaine's light destruction of her reputation to smash his self-control.

Granville, ever the diplomat, put his long, beautiful hand on his friend's arm. 'For God's sake, James. You do yourself and the lady no good by forgetting yourself completely. First of all, both you and Captain Dumaine must try to conduct yourselves in a civilised fashion. Next, I beg of you to attempt to resolve your differences without resorting to violence. Dumaine was wrong to speak lightly of your ward, you were wrong to attack him so savagely. But if you are unable to conclude matters peacefully and a meeting becomes inevitable, then you must attempt to agree on the choice of weapons. As to who has challenged whom, that is a little difficult to tell in this case, but your seconds may find a way out of that impasse. . .'

'I don't mind what I kill him with, so long as I do — pistols or swords, anything.' James was still as deadly as a tiger, poised to spring.

Granville ignored this outburst and shook James's arm slightly, adding, 'And above all the lady's name must not be mentioned again. You quarrelled over a difference at cards, or for nothing at all, drink speaking merely. You understand me, Lyndale?'

His beautiful voice was so soothing that it almost moved James. He nodded his head, and said indifferently, 'Yes, of course. But only let me at him.'

Granville sighed. 'Eventually, in proper form, Lyndale. You are not assassins, having at one another without warning.'

Barrett Dumaine said, his eyes on James's face, 'You may send your seconds to me, Lyndale, or I will send mine to you. It makes no odds to me.'

'Oh,' said James, showing his teeth again. 'There is really no need for either of us to wait. I am willing to meet you at dawn tomorrow. My seconds are here, Granville and Byng will act for me, I am sure. And you, you are surrounded by friends. Surely two of them will act for you?'

The man whose face James had pounded into the vegetables and had been wiping himself clean ever since, grated, 'Jervis Graham at your service, I shall be delighted to be Barrett's second. Nothing would please me more than to see him cut you down.'

Lord Granville sighed. Nothing about this hugger mugger business pleased him. The last of the *grands*

seigneurs, as he had once been dubbed, he liked everything to be done in proper form, and this whole fracas
had been most improper.

'Very well,' he said reluctantly. 'Although I am
bound to say that I deplore such a havy cavy way of
going on. It does not reflect much credit on any of us.
Mr Graham, sir, you will find another man to support
you so that we may begin to arrange the venue for the
meeting and the weapons you will use.'

James shook himself as if to clear his head, and said,
again indifferently, 'Putney Heath will do for me at six
of the clock. I am at Captain Dumaine's disposal so far
as weaponry is concerned.'

'Pistols, then,' called Dumaine, dispensing once more
with the niceties, to Lord Granville's open and pained
regret. 'I'd fight you here, only I don't suppose
Crockford would be best pleased if we did, would you,
Crocky?'

Crockford, who had been standing a silent witness to
the nobility and gentry at their murderous play, shook
his head and said nothing. He wished to displease no
one, neither Granville who was an old gambling
opponent of his, nor the others present, nor the
authorities.

The watching crowd returned to the tables again.
Luke, who had been holding his breath, sat down.
Granville and the other seconds moved away to arrange
matters. Dumaine, with one last burning glance at
James, walked to the sideboard and began to pour
himself a much needed drink.

Luke touched his guardian's shoulder. 'Is there
nothing that I can do, sir?'

James, who was slowly turning into his usual calm

self, said painfully, 'No, Luke. I will order a cab for you to go home. I shall not return to Lyndale House. Granville will give me a bed for the night, I know. He will wish me to be with him until the duel is over.'

'I wish, sir. . .' Luke began.

'What do you wish? That this had never occurred? So do I, but Luke, you must understand I could not allow him to speak so of a lady in my care. I don't regret challenging him. I do regret that I lost my composure and my temper both. I hope to keep them tomorrow. It will give me the greatest pleasure to kill him and silence his wicked tongue for ever.'

'Oh, sir.' There was desperation in Luke's voice. 'Do but think. The times have changed where duelling is concerned. Should you kill him, they will charge you with murder.'

'Should I kill him, I shall make for the Continent. Not the best way to end my career in England, but. . .' He shrugged his shoulders. 'At least you have not pointed out that *he* may kill *me*!'

'That, too,' Luke said. 'I did not like to say so.' And then he burst out with, 'Oh, what shall I say to them all if anything happens to you? I could not bear it. And Cressy, poor Cressy. . .'

'Not here,' replied James swiftly. 'Don't mention her name here.'

'But what will she think? How will she feel? If anything happens to you, it will destroy her, you know it will. You would not want that. You, of all people, must be aware. . .'

'I am aware of nothing.' James's voice was iron. His control was back again. 'Oblige me by ending this line of conversation, sir. You know nothing. Nothing, I tell you. The Lady Cressida is my ward and no more than that. I am about to fight Dumaine for suggesting otherwise. I don't want to fight you as well,' and he turned his hard eyes on to Luke with such a stare that Luke quailed before it.

'If you say so, sir,' he came out with at last.

'I do say so, and now I will see you are sent home. Granville and the others have made their arrangements and you must leave at once. I will ask one of the footmen to summon a cab for you.'

There was nothing more to be said, Luke thought. Not at Watiers, at any rate. By the morning the town would be abuzz, and whatever James did or did not do to Barrett Dumaine, his and Cressy's reputations had been thoroughly blown upon.

Cressy had not particularly enjoyed her evening at Lady Cowper's ball. The Lyndales' party did not arrive home until the small hours and on reaching her room she sent a yawning and protesting Mason to her bed. The protesting occurred when Cressy announced that Mason was not needed and that she would prepare herself for the night.

Miss Sykes came in after she had slipped on her night rail. Cressy had washed her face perfunctorily, and said to Miss Sykes who, with a reproachful air, had begun to hang up her discarded clothes, 'Oh, do leave all of that until morning. I am quite out of humour with everything, and wish only to sleep.'

Miss Sykes was about to come out with some nursery platitude on the lines of 'A place for everything and everything in its place,' when she saw that Cressy, for some reason, was at the end of her tether.

She sighed and watched Cressy climb painfully into bed, before putting her dress away. She hesitated, then murmured 'Very well,' and made for the door, just as a tremendous knocking began. Before she could reach it, the door was thrown open to reveal a breathless Luke standing there. He entered the room without so much as a by your leave, and even in her weariness Cressy thought that so far her meetings with Luke had been punctuated by doors being thrown open without much ceremony.

'Sir!' exclaimed Miss Sykes, scandalised. 'Pray leave at once. You have no business attempting to enter a young lady's bedroom.'

'No,' cried Luke, all youthful impetuosity, quite unlike his usual calmly insouciant self. 'I must speak to her, and alone, if you please. To save the proprieties, you may remain in the dressing-room with the door open, but I insist that my conversation with Lady Cressida must remain private.'

Miss Sykes responded to him as severely as she could. 'Not at all, by no means. I cannot allow this, sir. Whatever would your guardian say if I allowed his wards to behave in such a compromising fashion?'

Cressy took one look at Luke's ashen face, and knew that something dreadful had occurred. She slipped from the bed, pulling on her dressing robe as she did so.

'Miss Sykes,' she said sharply, in a voice which those who knew her in Italy would have recognised, it was so coolly commanding. 'You will do as Mr Harcourt asks, and immediately. It is surely plain to you that he has come here with no low motives in mind. You may stand where you can see us and you will not enter again until I call for you. You understand me, madam?'

Even Luke stared at her a little. Miss Sykes coloured, bridled a little and, muttering ungraciously, 'Oh, very well,' beat as dignified a retreat as she could.

'Sit down, Luke. No, I insist.' Cressy began to shiver. She felt quite sick. It was James, of course. He had taken Luke to Watiers and something awful had happened to make Luke look as he did.

Luke sank into the big armchair by the fire, and Cressy sat on the edge of the big bed, something she had always been forbidden to do.

'Now, tell me what has happened to James. Something *has* happened, has it not?'

His task made easier for him by her percipience, Luke began his tale of the night's events. He laundered it a little, but watching Cressy's face grow as white as he feared his own was, he knew that he was not deceiving her. 'And the upshot of it all is that my father and Captain Dumaine are to fight at six of the clock tomorrow morning——' he corrected himself '—*this* morning at Putney Heath, and by their behaviour the duel will be a fatal one. . .'

'Your father!' Cressy could not help interrupting him. 'You know that James is your father?'

Luke noted the 'James' before he answered her, looking away. 'Of course I know that he is my father. I am not a blind fool, neither am I hen-witted. I asked Aunt Verena to tell me the truth when I was taunted at Harrow about it when I was fourteen. She told me at once, but I never said anything to *him*. The affair did him no discredit, you know, even though he obviously does not think so. He could hardly have done better by me. Aunt Verena said that before he inherited he lived in penury in order to ensure that I was looked after properly. Oh, I minded being a bastard, and sometimes I mind that Haven's End will never be mine, but when I think of how most great men treat their bastards, then I can forgive him anything. And he is so kind behind that stern exterior that I could not reproach him either for fathering me, or for not wanting me to know that I was his son. I think that he was trying to spare me by inventing this distant cousin whose son I was.'

Apart from the one conversation with Verena he had never before spoken so frankly to anyone about his sad condition. But Cressy was different from everyone else. He could tell at once that she understood how he felt.

'Oh, poor Luke and poor James. He told me, you know, because I taxed him with it. And now he is to fight Barrett Dumaine because he spread lies about us.'

She had been looking Luke firmly in the eye until she reached this point in the conversation. She now looked away from him, and said in a stifled voice, 'I wanted him to make love to me that night, Luke, the night when I ran away and we were alone together, and that is the truth. He held off to spare me and my honour. Besides, I don't think that he truly loves me. It was just our being together, you know, and I think, from something he once said, that I. . .that I. . .remind him a little of your mother.'

Luke slipped out of his chair to kneel at Cressy's feet, to take her hand into his and kiss it.

Miss Sykes bridled at the sight, but when he did nothing more, she subsided again.

'Oh, Cressy,' he said, and his voice was a caress, and so like James's that tears sprang into her eyes at the sound. 'I love you, you know, and if things were different I would offer for you. But you must know that you are wrong about my father. Of course he loves you. He looks at you with his soul in his eyes, as you look at him. I suppose he has some clever-silly notion that he is too old for you, but what has age to do with love? Look at old Coke of Norfolk marrying a girl young enough to be his granddaughter, and they both madly in love with one another. James is not half Coke's age and you are older than his bride. But this is all beside the point. He is so in love with you that he is prepared to risk his life to kill Dumaine for slandering you. Oh, Cressy, what can we do? Are there no means of stopping this?'

Cressy's eyes were full of tears. James did love her, after all, so dearly that clever Luke, if no one else, could see it. What a terrible way in which to find out! Immediately before he might be killed while defending her good name.

She looked down at Luke and stroked his head. 'Where is he, dear Luke? Did he come home with you? No, I suppose not,' as Luke shook his head.

'No. He went off with Lord Granville, who is his second, to spend the night with him. In the morning they will drive to Putney Heath — and then. . .'

'And he's doing this for me, Luke? For me? He's risking his life for me?'

Luke almost glared at her. Women! he thought disgustedly, they were all the same. This was not at all what he had expected from Cressy. He had thought that she would be bursting with plans and ideas for stopping the duel and all she could do was moon about James loving her.

'Yes,' he said, almost sullen with disappointment. 'He is.'

He wronged her. Cressy knew at once what she must do. But she could not tell Luke. She was sure that he would not approve at all, and would think of ways of trying to stop her. He would raise all kinds of objections, and would want the duel cancelled in such a way that no one taking part in it would lose any of their honour — the whole ridiculous business was called an affair of honour, forsooth! No, she must keep quiet about her intentions. Let him think that she was afflicted with maidenly megrims.

On the other hand, she could also make some suggestions, although she was sure that Luke would not think them useful. The only useful thing was what she proposed to do.

'Is there no one we can consult? No one who would stop it?'

'Who?' exclaimed Luke despairingly. 'We could tell the Bow Street Runners, I suppose. But can you imagine what Lord Granville, James and the rest would think of me if I did any such thing? To bring them into an affair of honour. . .no, I should be done for forever.'

'Then suppose that I. . .?'

'No, no, the same thing applies. The authorities must not be brought into it. It's an affair of honour, you understand.'

'An affair of honour! And if either kills the other, or they both die. . .what then? Where is the honour in that!'

'The survivor would have to fly to the Continent. It would be murder, you see. Most duels are not fought *à l'outrance*, to the death, but this one will be, I fear. My father was beyond himself.'

'I shall never understand men and their talk of

honour.' Cressy almost declaimed this last sentence. She rose from the bed and began wringing her hands. Through the open dressing-room door she saw that she had agitated her companion.

'Oh, Sykes, do be still,' she exclaimed. 'The last thing which Luke and I are thinking of is what is passing through your mind! Find an improving book, read it, say a prayer, but stop glowering at us, please!'

Luke also rose to his feet. 'No, I can think of nothing. If I went to Fred Davenport, he would say that, deplorable though it all is, we cannot interfere. Cabinet ministers engage in such activities and no one thinks any the worst of them. When Barrett Dumaine publicly took your name in vain, it was inevitable that a duel would follow.'

He let his head drop on his chest. 'I shouldn't have told you. It was wrong of me to do so, but you are so resourceful, I thought that you might think of something, anything.'

Cressy put her arms around him to comfort him. 'You were right to tell me. I shan't sleep, but the shock of what might happen in the morning will be the less when it comes.' She wasn't at all sure that this was true, but she had to say something to comfort him.

Of course, it didn't, nothing could. Cressy walked to the dressing-room door, and said to Miss Sykes in her commanding voice, the one she rarely used to servants, short and discourteous, 'Sykes! Pray fetch a bottle of wine and three glasses—no, make it two bottles, and take them into my drawing-room.'

Miss Sykes began to demur at leaving Cressy alone, but Cressy's stare was so baleful that she stopped in mid-sentence. 'I shall stay in my bedroom while Mr

Harcourt goes to the drawing-room. I give you my word on that. Really, Sykes, what a time to burble about the proprieties. By tomorrow I shall have no reputation left!' For she was sure that the scandal would be all over London even before James and Captain Dumaine fought their duel over her.

To hear the scrupulously polite Cressy call her Sykes without preamble had Miss Sykes scampering away to ring for the butler and the bottles, which arrived at the double. Luke was sitting, dazed and hopeless, in Cressy's little private room, and Cressy herself came through to send the butler away, to pour the wine and to press glasses of it on Luke and Miss Sykes to the degree that they were both rapidly overset.

She drank sparingly herself, and when Luke, eyes glazed, finally sank back, half asleep in his chair, she rang for the butler again, and both he, supported by the butler, and Miss Sykes, aided by an awakened Mason, were taken to their beds to sleep the sleep of the dead.

Cressy, wide awake, sat on her bed and waited for the hour before the dawn.

CHAPTER THIRTEEN

JAMES had thought when he was shown into the pretty little room at Bruton Street where the Granvilles lived that he would not sleep, but exhaustion claimed him immediately.

He did dream, though. He dreamed of Cressy, A strange dream in which the dog in the hall at Haven's End, and the one on the floor in the unearthed villa, were strangely mixed up. Cressy was standing on the mosaic floor, looking at him with beseeching eyes. Luke was present, too, and once, fleetingly, he saw Luke's mother, whose face in his waking life he had forgotten, but here in his dream it was as plain to him as though he had last seen her yesterday.

He spoke in his dream, as did those whom he loved, but as so often in dreams what any of them said he could not later remember. Finally, just before he awoke, he saw Cressy and his first love, Luke's mother, together. Luke was standing between them, his arms around them both. He sat up in bed and knew that he had summoned in his dream the three people whom he loved most in the world. Strangest of all, through Cressy he had found his lost love again. For the first time in nearly twenty years, he could think of her without the bitter resentment at her loss, which had always previously come over him when he had tried to summon her ghost.

He could let her rest in peace at last. She had given

him Luke, and he must be grateful for that, for Luke was all that and more than a man could ask for in a son. Better than that, he now knew that despite the disparity in their years, all the barriers which he had erected between himself and his last, his truest love, had fallen away. If he survived the morning, he would ask Cressy to marry him.

He thought wryly of something which Dr Johnson had once said. 'Depend upon it, sir, when a man knows he is to be hanged in a fortnight, it concentrates his mind wonderfully.' Well, he might be dead by the morrow and the knowledge of that seemed to have done the trick for him. All his rational excuses for not acknowledging and acting on his love seemed suddenly quite hollow.

He slept again for a short time until Granville sent his valet in to him to help him to dress. Granville had lent him a clean shirt, and although he was shorter than his friend, Granville being one of Society's tallest man, it answered very well.

He had never questioned the belief that a duel between gentlemen was an affair of honour before, but now, unknowingly like Cressy, he asked himself how much honour there was in it. What did it prove if either or neither of them fell, or did not fall? In one sense, he had been wrong to attack Dumaine and cause the affair, because he had, after all, wished to make love to his ward on that fatal night and had nearly done so.

Machiavelli had once written of the lie in the mouth — that which was spoken or done — and the lie in the heart — that which was merely thought, but not expressed aloud — and had tried to differentiate between them. He had undoubtedly wished to make love to his ward, even if he had not done so, and did not that give Dumaine some justification for his slander? At this point, he gave up and tried to concentrate on what was to come. He felt as he had always done before battle, expectancy and fear so closely mingled that he could hardly distinguish one from the other.

He laughed soundlessly to himself at the thought that Captain Dumaine, who report had said had been a good soldier, might be feeling the same.

Granville was his usual calm self. He was perfectly dressed as always. His man was carrying a case of pistols which he showed to James. They were Mantons, even better than his own, for Granville was noted for the beauty of all his possessions.

'I remember,' he said, as cool as ever, as though driving a friend to a duel was an everyday occurrence, 'George Canning telling me about the duel which he engaged in with Castlereagh. He had never fired a pistol before, and had to be shown how and what to do. There will be no such difficulty for you, I am sure. This is your first engagement?'

He was seated by Granville in his curricle, Byng behind them, driving a phaeton, when this came out in Granville's lazy drawl.

James laughed. 'No, but to be truthful I remember little of the only one which I ever engaged in before. It was in Spain after a night's heavy drinking. I am not even sure what it was about, I was so drunk at the time. My opponent was drunker. Neither of us saw the handkerchief fall, and we both had to be called to order by the Colonel of the Regiment who, although he was in nearly as bad a way as we were, was determined to see the proprieties enforced. Just as the handkerchief fell for the second time, my opponent, his arm out-stretched, ready to fire, fell flat on his face, unconscious.

'I fired as he did so and was told afterwards that had he been on his feet I would have shot him dead. Fortunately for both of us the drink felled him before I did. We became firm friends afterwards. Neither of us could ever remember what we were fighting about. It probably seemed important at the time.'

Granville smiled; he never did anything so undignified as laugh out loud. 'I fear that the reason for this engagement is somewhat more serious. I am astonished that Dumaine, who seems to be a reasonable fellow, should allow himself to smirch a lady's name in a gaming house.'

'Jealousy fuelled by drink, I fear,' explained James. 'The lady refused him.'

Granville nodded. It was an explanation which he understood.

'You must know,' he said, a few moments later, negotiating a difficult corner, 'that I shall ask you both if you are prepared to be reconciled before I allow the engagement to begin. That is only proper.'

'Indeed,' replied James cheerfully. 'That is to be expected. But I think that you know what my answer will be. Tell me, is it true that when Canning's opponent, Lord Castlereagh, was driven to the encounter by his friend Yarmouth, they both sang opera songs on the way there?'

'So Castlereagh afterwards said. I must beg of you that you do not ask me to do the same. I am not sure that either my knowledge of the opera or my voice is sufficiently up to snuff to do myself justice.'

Granville looked sideways at his friend and admired his *sang froid*. He had never engaged in a duel himself. He had once wished to be a soldier, but his father had forbidden it, and it was something which he had always regretted.

And suddenly they were at Putney Heath itself, and there in the distance were the carriages of the other party, out even earlier than themselves, although James, glancing at his half-hunter, saw that they were both well before the arranged time.

Everyone behaved as though preparing to fight to the death was a commonplace event. Dumaine was as well turned out as James, and the seconds were, of course, equally well dressed. Any event with which Lord Granville was connected was always carried out with extreme correctitude, and this one was no exception.

The principals were asked if they wished to be reconciled. Both refused emphatically, James saying that if Captain Dumaine would withdraw his statement about Lady Cressida Mortimer, with a due apology for having made it, he would agree to the affair being brought to an end. Dumaine hesitated for a moment, before saying, 'No,' in a firm voice. 'I stand by what I said.' At this James shook his head and said, equally firmly, that in that case he was determined that the duel should go on.

The seconds conferred, settling the order in which the whole business was to be carried out. Granville had arranged for a doctor to be summoned to treat either James or Dumaine, should they be wounded. A post-chaise had been hired to take either James or Dumaine immediately out of England, if one of them were killed.

Their seconds would see that their affairs were arranged so that servants and support would follow them.

Since both James and Dumaine had been soldiers, and both had duelled before, they needed little instruction on how to conduct themselves.

Nothing, however, was neglected. A few working men, walking across the Heath at this early hour, stared incuriously at them. The day was overcast and gloomy. It was not, thought James, a day to die on, but was there ever a suitable day? He wondered if Barrett Dumaine was having the same thoughts as he was. His principal one was simple enough. For God's sake, let's get this over with.

The final moment arrived. The seconds stood to the side. The handkerchief was ready to be dropped. Nothing remained but for James and Dumaine to stand back to back to measure out the agreed paces, to turn and then to fire as the handkerchief fell. James, his pistol in his hand, faced the road which had brought him here. He could see a horse in the near distance, a horse being ridden at speed towards the Heath.

There was another horseman behind the first and they were both being ridden *ventre à terre*. He shrugged. By the appearance of the riders, they were boys entertaining themselves. Perhaps their untoward arrival might hold up the duel. The seconds had seen the horses, which were now almost upon them, and had ceased their preparations, calling to their principals to wait. Both James and Dumaine lowered their pistols to their sides. . . .

Cressy dozed a little uneasily before dawn. She awoke, checked the time, threw herself out of bed and ran to her dressing-room to rifle through her trunks for the first time since she had run away at Haven's End.

She found her boy's clothing, and began to pull it on. Her knee breeches were of a fine black cloth, her white shirt was the silk one she had worn on the night of the storm. Her top coat was also black, with silver buttons, short at the waist in the front, long in the two tails at the back.

Her boots which she pulled on, huffing and puffing were of the finest black leather. Finally she dragged back her glossy hair and secured it with a large silk bow after the fashion of the late eighteenth century. Dressed as she was, she made a handsome boy; the coat disguised her bosom and her hips, which had grown since she had come to England. Her breeches were a little tight, but not too tight to wear.

But she was beyond admiring herself. All that mattered now was that she reached Putney Heath and stopped the duel by one means or another. She checked the time again with Robert's half-hunter, which she had inherited when he had died, and ran lightly downstairs, through the empty ground floor, along the passage to the side entrance which opened on to the mews to hammer on the door of the room where she knew Stephen slept.

He came to the door in his long nightshirt, rubbing his eyes, and yawning. 'Lady Cressida?' he said doubtfully, staring at her in her boy's clothing, and half shutting the door so that all that she could see of him was his face around it.

'Yes, yes,' she said impatiently. 'I want Paris saddled immediately, Stephen. Throw something on as quickly as you can, I have no time to waste.'

Stephen began to argue. 'At this hour. . .'

Cressy drew herself up, and said in her best fine lady's voice, 'Do not argue with me, Stephen, I have given you an order. Jump to it.'

Stephen knew when he was beaten, but he made one last try to deter her reckless ladyship from whatever dubious enterprise she was embarking on.

'Paris, Lady Cressida. I can't let you have Paris, Lord Lyndale would not approve of you riding Paris.'

Cressy began to jump up and down in exasperation. 'I must have Paris. He is the fastest horse in the stable, none other will do. You know perfectly well that I can ride him. I order you, Stephen, if you value your position. . .'

'Very well,' he said reluctantly. 'But I ought to check with m'lord first.'

'M'lord is not here. Do as you are bid, immediately,' and she stamped her booted foot.

This seemed to convince Stephen. The head disappeared, and the rest of him emerged a few moments later, hastily dressed, even his shirt buttons unfastened.

'Quick,' she urged frantically. 'Do hurry, Stephen, a man's life may depend on it.'

'In that case,' Stephen's voice was firm, 'I shall saddle Hector and come with you.'

'That you will not. I order you to stay here. You are not to follow me or try to stop me. Nor are you to tell the head groom that I have taken Paris. Now, give me a leg up. I have no time to lose.'

He watched her ride out of the yard. He ought by rights to inform Barker, his superior, of what her wilful ladyship had done, but something in her manner made him hold off.

Shaking his head, he made for the block where the groom's lodgings were, only to meet Master Luke, also with a wild expression on his face, running towards him. What in the world was going on? Had all his masters run mad together?

Luke's bedroom was at the side of the house which overlooked the stable-yard, and dozing uneasily, after his first drink-sodden slumbers had ended, he had been awoken by the sound of voices below his window.

One of the voices was Cressy's, high and angry, the other was Stephen's. Stephen was an old friend; they had bird's nested together as children. He slipped out of bed, ran to the window to see two boys arguing together in the yard. It took him a moment to realise that one of the boys was Cressy. He had caught them at the end of the argument, a moment later he saw Stephen lead out Paris — Paris! James's best piece of cattle — and mount Cressy on it.

Now what the devil was she doing? But, of course, he should have known. He should also have known that she would deceive him. She was going to Putney Heath to try to stop the duel. Oh, why had she not trusted him?

He threw on his clothes, picked up his boots and, like Cressy, ran to the stables, to question Stephen, to learn that she had told him that a man's life depended on her action.

'Hector,' he shouted, pulling on his boots. 'Saddle Hector for me, at once.'

'Hector!' repeated Stephen. 'Good God, Master Luke, whatever will m'lord say when he hears that Lady Cresssy took Paris and you took Hector?'

'Get on with it,' shouted Luke. 'He won't say anything ever again if you haven't the sense to do as you're told.'

'It's not your position at risk, it's mine,' muttered Stephen sullenly, under his breath, but Master Luke would not be brooked and he had the dubious pleasure of seeing the second-best piece of horseflesh in the Lyndale stables tear out of the stable yard in pursuit of the first.

Cressy, unaware that Luke was pursuing her, rode in the direction of Putney Heath. She was not so stupidly worried that she rode Paris at his limits to begin with. Robert had always taught her to be careful with his cattle, and she neither wanted to attract too much attention, nor to destroy James's beautiful horse. On the other hand, she did not want to reach the Heath before the duellists arrived, and her light weight would not tire Paris as James riding him would have done.

She had no clear idea of what she was going to do when she reached the combatants. There were times when it was useful to have everything planned beforehand, but she had no notion of what kind of situation she was riding into. Would they have started their ridiculous business by the time she reached the Heath? Oh, she did hope not. What would she say? It was not a time to be missish.

Even in her desperation, the thought of arriving before Lord Granville, dressed as she was and shouting something like, 'Ho, there, desist at once!'—she remembered an actor saying that in a play Lady Verena had taken her to—made her laugh to herself. Well, at least she would have the pleasure of seeing whether his famous composure would crack before the spectacle of

Lady Cressy Mortimer, dressed in her boy's clothes, trying to stop a duel.

Whatever would it do to her reputation? Oh, pooh to her reputation. She had lost it in Watiers, last night, or when Barrett Dumaine had first gossiped about her. She must stop this, she must think of what she was doing and where she was going. It would not do to lose her way. At least, riding through the early morning, there were few people about either to hinder her, or stare at her.

The Heath was suddenly before her. She could see the various carriages drawn up on it and the small group of men before them. Oh, was she in time? For she could also see that James and Barrett Dumaine were standing together, pistols in their hands, ready to start their deadly business.

She clapped her legs to Paris's sides, urged him on, and then as she drew near, with all the party on the Heath staring at her, she rose in the stirrups, to shout, 'Stop! Stop it at once!'

James had barely time to register that the horse on which the mad boy was mounted was his precious Paris, before Cressy brought him to a sliding stop, dismounted and began to run towards them all, still shouting, 'Stop'.

Dumaine, now beside him, staring at the sight, realised that the boy was Cressy at almost the same moment that James did.

Cressy reached them, just as Luke, who had pushed Hector harder than Cressy had pushed Paris, appeared in the distance, riding rapidly on to the Heath. She came to a dead stop before James. He was so surprised to see her that he all he could come out with, ineptly for him, was, 'Good God, Cressy, what are you doing here in boy's clothes and on Paris, too? Who gave you permission to ride Paris?'

'Permission!' she shrieked at him, anger succeeding fear at the sight of him still alive, and reproaching her, as usual. 'What permission do I need to come and stop you from killing yourself over some mad notion that you were saving my honour? Oh, James, have you no idea what it would have done to me, had you been killed—over me? How could you, oh, how could you?'

James, distracted by the sight of her, his tiger's eyes soft, muttered so that none but she might hear, 'Oh, Cressy, do you care so much for me?'

'Care for you? Damn you, James, I love you, you know I do. I came to save you, and all you can say is, Who gave you permission to ride Paris! I might as well ask who gave you permission to risk your life for me?' The unheeding tears began to cascade down her face. 'I thought I would find you dead already. The pair of you are being quite disgraceful; Captain Dumaine for slandering us both and you for being so stupid as to attack and challenge him. Oh, James, I could not bear it if you were killed. . .' and she threw herself at him, for him to hand his pistol to the startled Dumaine and place his arms around her to comfort her.

Lord Granville and the other seconds, the whole party thoroughly surprised by this untoward occurrence, were upon them.

Dumaine's second, his face scarlet, who had not heard what was being said, thought that Cressy was attacking James. He caught her by the shoulders just as James was on the point of reassuring her that now the duel could not go on, and began to drag her away, shouting, 'Damn you, boy! What do you think you're at?'

His reward was that Cressy bit the hand he was holding her with. He released her with a roar, went to strike at her, but was then held off by James, who started to try to explain what was happening and who Cressy was. He never managed to finish, because the whole party was distracted by Luke, who had panted up, dismounted, and ran between them shouting, 'I would have stopped her if I could, but she never told anyone of what she proposed to do.'

'Her?' exclaimed the man, sucking at his bleeding hand and staring at Cressy, who was snarling at him like a cornered wildcat. 'She?' said Lord Granville, who looking more closely at her, added coolly, 'Of course. It is Lady Cressida Mortimer, is it not? You should not be here, madam.'

'Not be here?' cried Cressy fiercely, pulling herself away from James's protecting arms. 'What do you mean, I should not be here? You are only fighting your damn'd duel because of me and I should not be here! Whatever can you mean? And how do you think I would feel if my darling James were killed because of an idle word uttered by an idle man.' She stared proudly at Captain Dumaine, daring him to contradict her.

James thought that she had never looked more wildly desirable than she did in her boy's clothes, standing there, defying them all, destroying the orderly, if murderous, world in which they had been living until her arrival.

'Cressy,' he said hoarsely. 'You should not have done this, but. . .'

'But, James, but. What do you mean by your buts?

Do you mean that I should have left you both to kill one another like the pair of Kilkenny cats in the fairy-tale?'

They glared at each other for a moment, Cressy shaking, torn between love and fear, still fearful that at any moment the duel might be resumed. She flung herself at James again, her arms around him, trying to stand between him and Dumaine.

Overcome, James, caring nothing for what those present thought, began to stroke her hair and comfort her, saying, 'There, there, my love, my darling little love,' as though to a child and not a passionate young woman who had just told the whole world that she loved him.

Barrett Dumaine, whose bearing and expression had lightened since her arrival and her first impassioned words to James, broke into laughter. He staggered away, still laughing, to sit on a tree-stump, handing his pistol and James's to his second, who was morosely nursing his wounded hand.

Lord Granville, his composure unshaken, even Cressy's wild behaviour unable to shake it, said coldly, 'This is not seemly, sir. You forget yourself.'

'Not seemly. No, indeed.' He looked over to where James was comforting Cressy, still lost to the world. 'To think that I was about to risk death over a girl who had already made her mind up which man she wanted and would not rest until she had lassoed him, even if it took stopping a duel to do so. We none of us had the slightest chance once she had seen Lyndale. I honour the wench. I take back what I said of her, it was unworthy. I would marry her tomorrow if she would have me.'

Lord Granville's beautiful eyebrows rose. 'Sits the wind in that corner?' He turned to look at James and Cressy, lost to the world. 'Oh, yes, I see it does. The Cavalier has found a worthy partner. Although what Society will make of what has happened this morning has yet to be known. May I tell Lord Lyndale, Captain Dumaine, that you withdraw your words of last night to him and to others?'

'I think,' said Dumaine slowly, 'that, in honour, I ought to withdraw and apologise myself, don't you?'

Luke, who was watching his father and Cressy with sad eyes, said to Dumaine, his voice fierce, 'You should never have said what you did in the first place.'

Dumaine laughed again. 'If we are speaking of what should be said and done, who told Lady Cressy of what happened last night? For sure she could not have known what passed at Watiers, and who better than yourself who was there?'

'I thought she ought to know and, besides, I also thought that she might think of a means of stopping the duel. . .but I never thought that she would do this.'

'Did you not? You know the lady and say that? Oh, no, Master Luke, I think that you knew what you were doing, but doubtless when you had succeeded in your purpose you had second thoughts. I hope you did not ruin Hector.' All London knew of James's two prime horses and how he treasured them. 'And now I must speak to your father.'

Luke coloured, and muttered in a low voice, 'Does everybody know?' to have Dumaine laugh again and go over to James, Lord Granville with him, his second trailing behind, to make his apologies.

'One moment,' said James. 'Before you speak I ask

you to allow the Lady Cressida to return to her home
with my other ward, Mr Luke Harcourt. It is not proper
that she remains here. They may use the waiting chaise.
There can be no duel now, nor do I wish an apology
from you, sir. That you are prepared to apologise, as
Lord Granville has informed me, is enough for me. I
should not have attacked you publicly, although I think
you may understand why I did.'

'If I may not apologise to you, sir, then I wish to do
so to the lady,' said Dumaine smoothly. 'I take back
what I said of her. I wish her, I wish both of you, well.
Look after her, Lyndale, or you will answer to me!'

James's smile was wry. Cressy clutched at his arm,
and said, 'Oh, do not send me away! I don't trust you,
any of you, how can I? You will not start again once I
am gone?'

Lord Granville took her hand and bowed over it.
'You may have my assurance on that, madam. I will see
your guardian safely home, after you have agreed to
leave in the chaise with Mr Harcourt. It is not proper
for you to remain here. It was not proper for you to
come here, but that is another matter.'

'It was not proper for me to come,' returned Cressy
spiritedly. 'But had I not done so, blood would have
been shed. You give me your word?'

'I give you my word,' returned Lord Granville
gravely. 'Now, do as your guardian asks.'

Cressy nodded mute agreement. And, as she did so,
for the first time it struck her what she had done, what
the watching men must think of her dressed as she was
in her boy's clothes. She remembered that Verena had
told her that one of Lady Caroline Lamb's offences
against Society had been to assume the costume of a

boy page in public. And she, what had she done? She had broken into an all-male gathering, wearing not a page's uniform, but a full-blooded boy's suit, such as Luke might have worn.

Oh, what was James thinking? Was he ashamed of her? She turned to him as she left, face anxious, for him to take her hand and say gently, his tiger's eyes on her, 'Go with Luke, my darling. Wait for me. I will be with you later.'

My darling! He had called her his darling and said that she was to wait for him, and the shiver of ecstatic delight which had run through her when he took her hand was the strongest she had felt yet.

'You promise?' she almost whispered.

'I promise. Now go.'

Luke escorted her to the waiting carriage, and as they drove away the last thing Cressy saw was James and Captain Dumaine shaking hands. Men!

She returned to a house in uproar. Stephen had reported what had passed. Fred Davenport, sent for, had questioned him and learned that Luke had returned the previous evening without his guardian. He also learned, some half-hour later, that it was all round London that Lyndale and Captain Dumaine were meeting on Putney Heath. There was no doubt where Cressy and Luke had gone on Paris and Hector. The only doubt was what had happened when they reached their destination.

The arrival of the chaise with Cressy dressed in her boy's clothes created even more excitement. Once home Cressy ran to her room to bathe and change herself. Reaction had set in. She was sure that James would hate her forever for behaving like a hoyden after all that he had said to her since she had arrived in England. And Lord Granville, what would he think of her? Could she even be certain that the whole nasty business would not begin again once her back was turned?

Luke, in the intervals of lecturing her all the way home on what she had done, had said no. The duel was ended, he said. She could only hope that it was.

Mason dried her, helped her to dress. She put on her freshest and newest toilette, a chaste white cotton with a pale blue sash. Her hair was dressed in its simplest fashion, the black curls lifted above the nape of her neck with a matching blue ribbon. Now she could only wait for him. He had said, 'Wait for me', had he not?

Did that mean that he wanted to see her to reprimand her once more? She twisted her hands together, then looked up to see herself reflected in her long dressing mirror. She hardly recognised herself. It was as though the events of the morning had finally turned her into a woman, for no girl stood in the mirror.

The shining eyes, the polished cheeks, the parted lips, the lines of the body which had developed since she had arrived in England, her whole stance, all told their tale. Robert would hardly know her. Only in her boy's clothes, so recently discarded, had she resembled the wild girl who had so recently arrived in England.

Except, of course, that the wild girl had taken over this morning. She sat down, picked up Pascal and tried to read him to soothe her nerves. Thank goodness Verena, Lady Emily and Miss Sykes had not turned up to reproach her for what she had done. She had expected them to arrive one by one to reproach her.

She was not to know that James had sent word by Luke that no one, absolutely no one, apart from her maid, was to speak to her until after he had arrived back at Lyndale House and spoken to her himself.

There was a knocking at the door. Cressy started up, put Pascal down and called, 'Come in.' It was Sam, her personal footman.

'M'lord has asked that you attend him in the Chinese drawing-room, Lady Cressida. At once, if it pleases you.'

'It does please me.'

All the way downstairs, following Sam's broad back, she worried over what James might be about to say to her.

Sam threw the door open and announced her. The moment of truth was upon her.

He was standing in the window. He had, like her, bathed and changed. Like her he was absolutely *à point*. He had seldom looked so handsome — or so remote. Even his cravat was a valet's dream of heaven. That daunted her. She forgot that she looked like a lady's maid's dream. They were as unlike the informal pair on Putney Heath as they could be.

James bowed. 'Lady Cressida,' he said, as though they were at some formal court function. 'Pray take a seat.' He motioned her to a great armchair which stood in the lee of the hearth. Above the empty fireplace hung a portrait of a man in the clothes of sixty years ago who looked exactly like James, even down to the tiger's eyes.

Cressy obeyed him. She clasped her hands together in her lap, and crossed her legs at the ankles as Miss Sykes had taught her. She looked up at him, her face so anxious that James nearly gave way and swept her into his arms on the instant. But she deserved to wait a little for that.

'Lady Cressida. You must know that what you did this morning was quite wrong. It was not at all the thing for a young lady of the highest stare to do. To dress as a boy, to take my best horse — who is back in his stall and perfectly fit, no thanks to you — to arrive on Putney Heath to stop a duel, was not on the programme which Lady Verena and myself laid out for you.'

Creasy nodded, face blanching. Oh, he was cross with her after all! She shouldn't have done it. No, no. But had she not gone to Putney Heath he might not be standing here reprimanding her, he might be lying dead on the field of dishonour — for that was what Cressy thought it was, whatever men called it.

'But,' he began, and waited. When she did not answer, he looked down at her, his face haughty, the amber eyes hooded. 'Well, Lady Cressida, you were free with your comments on "buts" at dawn this morning. Have you no answer for me now?'

'Now is not this morning,' replied Cressy faintly. He was rallying her, she knew. Why? Was there hope for her after all?

'Very well, then, I will continue. *But* I am very glad that you did. Yes, on reflection I am well pleased that you prevented me from killing Captain Dumaine. He may have deserved it, but I did not deserve to spend the rest of my life on the Continent. No, indeed. And I don't think you would have liked it, either. You are strangely quiet, Lady Cressida. You were noisy enough this morning.'

He *was* rallying her. She told him so.

'Yes, indeed. I will resume. And wearing boy's breeches before Lord Granville, of all people, never mind Dumaine's low friends. Were you a boy. . .' He stopped, and smiled loftily at her.

'Were I a boy?' Cressy leaned forward, lips parted.

'Were you a boy I should not be addressing you here, nor would I be saying what I am about to say.' Then his whole manner changed. 'Oh, my darling love, I cannot tease you any longer, however much you deserve a little roasting,' and he dropped on to his knees before her, never mind his splendid clothes, the tiger's eyes ablaze with love.

'Oh, Cressy, it may be wrong of me, you may be young enough to be my daughter, but this morning, before I drove to Putney to fight Dumaine, I thought what a fool I was to let the years between us prevent me from asking you to be my wife. And when you arrived on the Heath, such a splendid boy you made, but what a waste of a splendid girl, I could hardly keep my hands off you.'

For her part Cressy could hardly believe what he was saying to her. He had taken her hands and was kissing them.

'Oh, my dearest heart, say that I have not driven you away by my folly in rejecting you; say that you will be my wife. Do not keep me in agony. You must care for me, or you would not have done what you did.'

She leaned forward to kiss him on the lips, and then to bend her head to kiss the hands which held hers.

'Oh, James, yes. You know that you have my heart, my dearest love. Ever and always. I shall not change, I know that now. But are you sure that you want such a flighty thing as I am? Have the reasons of the heart overcome reason itself? You are sure that you will not regret this?' For, now that he had actually offered for her, she was assailed by doubts about her own worthiness, her fitness to be his wife.

He took her head in his strong hands, the hands which had struck Dumaine for her, and kissed her gently on the lips, before saying, 'Not really flighty at all, my dearest love. What flighty young lady would quote Pascal at me as you have just done? When I read those words, that day I saw you sleeping after Dumaine had ridden with us to the Park, I was so struck by them that I questioned all my previous beliefs. That was when I began to change my mind and ask myself whether I was being a fool to sacrifice my chance of happiness with you when I loved you so much.'

'It *is* your heart which is speaking, then,' sighed Cressy, and she kissed him back vigorously before adding, 'Because Society will not want to know me after my adventure at Putney Heath this morning.'

'A fig for Society! I have never cared much for it and I do not wish to live in it or London any longer than my duties demand. You were happy at Haven's End, were you not? Could you be happy there with me for the rest of your life?'

'With you, my love, anywhere.' And their lips met again. James took her hand and held it against his broad chest.

'Feel how my heart beats for you, my darling. Let that speak for me, if nothing else.'

Yes, she could feel it, fast and true. James's heart, which had finally surrendered to hers, and now she was in his arms again, as she had been on the night of the storm, which unleashed a new storm in Lyndale House's polite drawing-room.

It was perhaps as well, for propriety's sake, that the door burst open. Yet again it was Luke, saying breathlessly before he took in the tableau before him, 'Oh, there you are. . .' and then, 'I suppose this means that you have come to your senses at last, sir. May I be the first to congratulate you.'

'You may indeed,' replied James pleasantly from his position on his knees before Cressy, his arms round her, 'and pray shut the door carefully when you leave. Lady Cressy and I are discussing some urgent and long-delayed business which cannot wait. I am about to satisfy her on some essential points of conduct. The final lesson will come later, after our wedding,' he called, as Luke tactfully shot out of the room to tell the rest of the family the good news.

It was a few short weeks later. They had been married that day, at Haven's End, a private wedding with only their immediate family present, and they had all left after an early nuncheon, Luke going with Verena, his favourite aunt. Cressy had stayed with her until the wedding day.

Once they were alone, James had turned to Cressy, a smile on his face. 'Would you care to ride with me this afternoon, my ward, who is now my wife?' he asked. He had kissed her at the end of the wedding, held her hand throughout the nuncheon and he was being strangely formal with her, she thought.

When she had nodded a shy yes, for the enormity of the fact that she had really, truly, married him had just struck home, he said, 'Then I shall ride Hector and you shall have Paris. He is your horse now, my love. He has been your horse since the morning of the duel.'

It was the first time since he had proposed to her that he had referred to the duel, and Cressy blushed and hid her face from him before running upstairs to change for the ride.

She wondered where he meant to take her, but when they set out in the direction of the Masons' farm, she knew that they were headed for the Roman villa. And so it proved. James stopped, tethered the horses and they walked down to the pavement. Since Cressy had last stood there more work had been done on it.

She sank to her knees to stroke the mosaic of the dog, brilliant in the early August sunlight. She looked questioningly up at him.

'Yes,' he said to her unspoken query. 'They continued your work for you while we were in London. Lenthall supervised it.'

Cressy straightened up, stood on tiptoe and kissed his hard cheek. 'Oh, thank you, James, thank you. The dog looks more beautiful than ever.'

'Lenthall says that there are more treasures kept for you to classify.' He looked down at the dog, and said, half to himself, 'And that's a strange thing, my dear.'

Cressy had taken his hand, held it to her lips, and said, 'What is, my love?'

He put an arm around her. 'That floor has haunted my dreams lately. And you were there with me at times. I visited it and you on the morning of the duel.'

'Oh,' said Cressy slowly. 'That is even more strange than you can know. For I have been meeting you here in my dreams ever since I accidentally slept with the wise woman's charm in my pocket on the night I ran away. She said that if I slept with it on me, I should see my true love's face in my dreams. And I saw you.'

James stared at her for a moment, then quoted *Hamlet* to her. '"There are more things in heaven and earth, Horatio, than are dreamed of in your philosophy." Against all my rational beliefs we have met in our dreams. And now, my love, at last we are together again, and shall be parted no more.'

Cressy's face was white. 'Oh, James, you said that to me in my first dream. . .' She clung to him for a moment. 'Do you think, is it possible, that once, long ago, we lived here, that the dog mosaic was mine, made for me, and now we share another at Haven's End? Robert believed that our souls transmigrated, that we have lived often before in different times. If so, then we were meant to love and marry and nothing could keep us apart.'

She stopped. She thought for a moment and then said, 'Robert! He never did anything which he did not mean to do. Although many people thought him vague, he was not really so. Do you think — is it possible that he did not make a mistake? That he meant to leave me to you, and not to your father? That he knew that your father was dead? That he sent me to you deliberately, in the hope that we might marry? That past and present conspired to bring us together?'

'It is possible. Yes, I should like to believe that.' James was grave, and for a moment they were silent.

'Come,' he said suddenly, his voice changed and lighter. 'We must not linger here, Lady Lyndale. Married in the past we may have been, but here in the present we have been handfasted only today.' He turned, swung her off her feet and threw her into the saddle, to stand, looking up at her, his whole face filled with love.

'The day I proposed to you, I told Luke there was a final lesson I wished to discuss with you. It is time that we returned to prepare for it. And, when you have learned it, we may celebrate it for the rest of our life together.'

And so they did.

LEGACY of LOVE

Coming next month

HOUSE OF SECRETS
Sally Blake
Penzance 1858

Bethany Leighton's situation was not happy. Left destitute by her parents' deaths, she had no choice about becoming a companion to widowed Mrs Evelyn Harcourt of Truro, a difficult employer.

It was not surprising that she should listen to Justin Carlyon's proposition, outrageous though it seemed, that she impersonate his cousin Georgina. But what seemed straightforward soon became complicated. Bethany knew she ought to extract herself from the consequences of that fleeting moment of recklessness—but could she leave Justin?

ELEANOR
Sylvia Andrew
Regency

Briefly in London for a family wedding, Miss Eleanor Southeran was intrigued to meet Mr Jonas Guthrie. He was more forthright than the polished gentlemen she had been meeting, which she enjoyed. But then she discovered he was being ostracised by the ladies of the *ton*, and, finding out why, she was confused. This interesting man surely couldn't be guilty of such accusations!

Still, once she was home in Somerset, she wasn't likely to meet him again…

LEGACY *of* LOVE

Coming next month

BRADEN'S BRIDES
Caryn Cameron
Australia 1835

Before Abigail Rosemont even arrived in New South Wales, her life of adventure had begun—with Duke Braden's searing kiss at sea.

But this was a land divided—by rich and poor, injustice and strife. Abigail lived in the opulent world of her cousins, but she dared to join courageous station owner Duke—only to become trapped in a raging feud. Could Abby's courage meet the passionate challenge of this proud land and gain Duke's love?

THE GENTLEMAN
Kristin James
Montana 1888

Stephen Ferguson had arrived in Montana to search for his father and brother...not for a bride. Until Jessie removed her hat, and he saw her long braids, he'd had no idea she was a woman, but somehow this tomboy touched him.

Jessie hadn't cared what men thought of her—until Stephen came. Now she wanted to be a lady, but how—and would it make a difference to Stephen?